"WEB OF DECEPTION"

-Novel by-

LaJoyce Brookshire

MORE PRAISE FOR Web of Deception...

"When I read, I feel like I'm eavesdropping on someone else's life, not in Web of Deception, I've never read a book where I became the character. I couldn't believe it."

Victoria Christopher Murray, Author, Temptation

"I read this book so fast, that when I got down to the last 20 pages, I dreaded that it was almost over, But I needed to read to the end to find out who dunnit."

Pat Clements, An avid reader,

Acknowledgments

First, I give honor to God who is the head of my life. The one whom I KNOW is necessary to seek first. By seeking Him first and His righteousness, I know that all things, not some, but *all* things will be added unto me.

I'd like to thank the following people sincerely from the bottom of my heart:

- My husband, Gus William Brookshire Jr. the Third, who is my childhood sweetheart, my soul mate in Christ, and my best friend. Thank you for declaring Christ head of our household. As our earthly head, you've served Tony and I well, and have definitely earned the title of "Bishop". Your encouragement is endless, your love limitless, and your guidance Godly. Who loves you bay-ba????

- My parents: Mommie Jo and Daddy Bo (Joana & Randolph Baker, Sr.), and my in-laws Ma and Dad (Zadine & Gus Brookshire, Sr.) thanks for being my biggest fans, for selling books from anywhere anybody would let you, and bragging about my being your baby girl. Mommie, here's to the hootin' good time we had on the road during the *Soul Food* book tour and to all of the tours to come. There is NO better road warrior than you. (And all the Circle City Classic's to come Ma Brookshire!) Mainly, it is my prayer that I will continue to make you all proud.

- My literary agent "Miss Marie" Brown who believed in this book when it had another title and only five chapters. Thank you for being my Fairy Godmama, creating magic, and making dreams come true.

- My attorney, Pamela Crockett, the baddest deal maker in the land!! I'm looking forward to our life-long friendship, deals done and deals to come, and weekends (or weeks) Indira will spend with me.

- Janine Coveny, my sister from waaaay back, for the brilliant editing and pointing me in the direction of someone who literally held my hand through the necessary research when I was too scared, to do in real life, some of the evils I had created on paper. The world is waiting on you know what...Ja-nine.

- Blessings to my researchers, this story would be nothing without you:

  • Brian Jacobs and Marcinda Ry, thanks for putting up with my endless questions, on our late night excursions of a world previously unknown to me.

  • Ossie Thompson, I love you for allowing me a peek into police procedure and answering my pages of stupid questions. Now, you owe me lunch!

  • Tanya Hill thanks for your legal insight on RICO laws. I'd hate to meet you in court.

  • Mona Lynn Wallace, couz your patience will never be forgotten for sifting through the Louisiana phone books to find Celeste's perfect Creole last name.

- Wylene Carter my bestest Pocono pal, thanks one million for going ahead with our plan to take the writing course and then putting that knowledge to use on the first edit this piece had ever seen. Wylie, you know how much I love you and your turkey meatballs. Now get to writing so that I can return the favor!

— My very, very first readers who lended comments and criticisms: Ruthie, Tyger, Michelle Joyce, Rhonda Sutton, Kasey, and Tracey Moore Marable (who insists she wants to be Celeste), I appreciate you dearly.

— Blanche Richardson, I cherish your editorial comments, and wisdom you've shared with me about the business. You are a jewel I will always treasure.

— My prayer warriors...I would never say you don't know, because you're my praying partners so you do. Thanks for sharing all of my trials and triumphs: Mayla Billips, Nina Lynn Billips, Claudette Dyches, Terria Taylor, Lencola Sullivan, Henzy Green, Bishop Sam Williams, Rev. Kenneth Pearman, Arlene McGruder, Theara Ward, Susan Ellis, Dawn Keith, Olga Turner, Dewanda Howard, Pamela Avery Pierre, Miss Lucille, Gordette "Sloopa" Lemons, Zee, David & Carol Sparkman, Walter & Cynthia Briggs, Stacey Dyches and Debra Fraser. Because of your support, I will forever be convinced prayer changes things.

— My brothers, sisters, 27 nieces and nephews, 2 grand nieces, and 5 Godchirren... just the thought of any of you, lifts me.

— For all of my Mama's on my block in Chicago...thanks for helping to raise me.

— My fellow author friends: E. Lynn Harris, Lolita Files (my loving Libra Twin!), Eric Jerome Dickey, Omar Tyree,

LaJoyce Brookshire

Victoria Christopher Murray and Suzette Webb. Thanks for sharing laughs, book signings, literary world wisdom, and hotel rooms with me. Look out world ... *Gifted, Published & Black* is here to stay.

- African-American booksellers everywhere...Thanks for allowing me in, let's get another best-seller. I'm in the house...just call.

- Blazon Entertainment and Films: I love, love, love you Blake Roberts, Zon Dumas and Cassandra Jackson...C'mon guys let's give the world movies...Roll 'em!

In Dedication To:

My Auntie, Celeste Hunter the only diva (Celeste Toussaint is my Auntie reincarnated) - Creating this story was another way of immortalizing you than just in my heart. I will always be indebted to you for buying my first electric typewriter when I was 10 years old. I'm sure you were tired of me shoving dozens of handwritten pages at you exclaiming "read this!" You too, were first to know that someday I'd be a writer. I have become a lady because of you.

My Grannie, Fannie Moore Hunter - You taught me how to type 100 words per minute, keep my nails polished in red, and use cash instead of credit. Your drive has helped me to live.

My Friend, Randolph Leland Johnson - You taught me how to enjoy "The City", take my craft more seriously, and get this story organized in a manner presentable for public consumption. I dream of you often.

The Best Male friend I have ever had, George Howard - As relatives from way back, I accepted the role as your "little sis". The world misses your music, but I miss hearing it over the phone first. Your music, still, in your absence, makes my heart sing.

ONE

That place is full of dirty streets and crazy people in them
Trash
    Stench
        Rodents
            Everywhere.
Even amongst the finest;
                no escape.

****

November 1988

*I*t was Thursday, and Celeste Toussaint was late for the taping
of her television show. Though she was being extra careful
not to let anything bother her today, everything went wrong.
    *She knew she should not have gone to that showroom sample
sale, but who could resist those bargains? Celeste flopped into
the high chair to have her make-up applied after arriving at the
studio exasperated, sweaty, and with less than half an hour to air
time.*
    *Not feeling the attitude of the make-up artist and all of his
flippant eccentricities, she pierced him with a look that demanded
immediate silence. She detested the heavy make-up anyhow, but it
was necessary for her overall appearance on TV--so they said.*
    Suddenly there was an urgent knock on the door, and an argu-

ment with the producer and a delivery man escalated. The persistent young man made his way past the over-protective super producer to present Celeste with a huge gift box. The producer reluctantly tipped the messenger while she tore into its wrapping, finding two dozen roses; one yellow, one white, her favorites.

Her heart silently soared as she opened the envelope instantly recognizing the handwriting on the card:

"Have a sensational show. Meet me after at the usual spot."
Immediately his gentle presence surrounded her and the troubles of the day fled as she effortlessly prepared her questions for the guest and slipped into her new outfit.

The show was not over soon enough. Celeste always spoke exceptionally fast, but today it were as though she were racing the Indy 500. The producer was waving wildly from the booth for her to slow down, but, oblivious to anything else, her only focus was on the camera and what would happen after the show.

"This is the longest half hour of my life," she thought almost aloud as the guest dragged out an explanation of a childhood illness. She knew her eyes revealed her every thought, they always did.

When the show was finally over, she said her goodbyes fast but cordially, signed for her check, and peeped out of the window. The car was there on schedule. Celeste and the driver exchanged nods dutifully as she glided onto the seat of the navy blue Mercedes limousine. There was a scented candle lit in the glass holder, a tape of Earl Klugh playing, and a full bottle of Moet in the cooler for the drive into the country.

"He is always so thoughtful," Celeste said aloud. She took one sip of champagne and took full advantage of the ride to the mountains to sleep off her grogginess. She wanted to be fresh as a daisy for him. It had been far too long since their last encounter.

Celeste was awakened by the sound of the slamming trunk.

She saw the driver carry the bag of groceries into the house. Being too impatient to wait, she got out of the car herself, gave the driver a nod of thanks and watched him drive off.

The house was dark and warm, lit only by the fireplace. She slowly climbed the stairs to the bedroom in order to slip into something more comfortable. Expecting to find him, instead she found a note on the bathroom mirror. "I went to get more wood. You just relax." Her decision was made: She'd never let this much time pass between them again.

After getting undressed, she thoroughly cleansed her face. He loved to see Celeste the natural, not at all the woman who was loved by her public. She pulled her thick sandy hair away from her face into a ponytail and secured it with an ornamented banana clip. He always marveled at how her eyes and hair matched in color and that her lips were the perfect pink, even without lipstick.

She lightly applied White Linen perfume to her pulse points and remembered how she still was not too sure if it was the White Linen or her winning personality that was the initial attraction when they met. Now she really did not care which it was, she was just glad that they had connected.

After putting on her favorite peach silk lounging pajamas, Celeste went downstairs and sat at the chess table. She allowed herself that rare pleasure of completely unwinding, and she lowered herself down onto the bearskin rug in front of the colorful, quiet fire. Staring into the brilliant flames, she held her hands up toward the heavens and vowed, "I promise, no work, no thoughts of work, no conversation of work." All she wanted was to be consumed with the beautiful thoughts of their brief time together.

She went to the kitchen to put away the groceries and make a salad for dinner. As she went to the sink to wash the vegetables, she looked out of the window. There, hung from a tree on his own property, was the man that Celeste was going to tell she would be honored to marry. And this was not a Justice Clarence

Thomas' version of a "high tech lynching". No, this here was a lynchin' done Louisiana style. The only thing missing was a burning cross.

After all she had seen in the last few months, her emotions had totally run dry. She could only stand there, staring. Her eyes were brimming with tears and a cry of grief stirred deep in her belly. As his body swayed gently with the breeze, Celeste wondered what could a man so wonderful have done to deserve to die like this.

Celeste stumbled into the foyer to phone the police, while she couldn't help but thinking that maybe he'd lived too dangerously. But, then again, so had she...

TWO

Chicago...August, 1988

The front page of the *Chicago Daily Courier* roared:

"Board of Education Scandal Breaks All Rules: 12 Jailed"
by
Celeste Toussaint

Yes, she was pleased with her investigative journalism. This was her best work yet. It had taken four years to get to the bottom of the wrong-doings that she always had a hunch existed. The wrong-doings her peers at *The Courier* thought were created in her mind.

Until Celeste came aboard, the daily business of the Board of Education was buried somewhere around page 25. Being assigned to cover this news beat was boring, even her editors knew that, but her stories often made the front page. She brought excitement forth from the halls of education, usually by reporting what didn't make the grade. From day one covering the board, Celeste knew there were stories to be told other than the news of the yearly school strikes and union contract renewals.

When she entered the newsroom, everyone stood and applauded. Even though it was a daily ritual for the byline that made front page, her colleagues knew how long she was trying to break the "big one." Her blood boiled when it came to controversy, deceit, those who thought they could get away with the unspeakable.

Twelve were going to jail as a result of her star reporting and her nose for news. Celeste received the accolades well, as she slapped high fives and exchanged hugs with the staff; catching the bad guys was no surprise to her. What surprised her was the note she found on her desk from the publisher himself, inviting her to lunch in The Executive Tower.

"Aw man!" she whispered to herself, "I'm fired."

She ran to the elevator, heart racing to go to her editor's office. All she could think was, *What did I do? What did I say? and to whom did I say it?* This would not be the first time that her mouth had gotten her into trouble. However, she had an ability that not many possessed: Celeste could talk her way into and out of anything--doing it one of three ways, with honey, butter or hot sauce.

The elevator was taking too long, so she ran up three flights, taking two steps at a time, ignoring the constraints of her high heels, stockings, and work dress-a little something her Mommie would find uncouth.

Wayne Stephens was her professional savior, confidant, and senior editor. He would know why their publisher wanted to see her. She burst into his office waving the message from Taylor Reed, written by him on his stationery. Wayne motioned for Celeste to sit down while he finished his telephone call.

"How can I sit?" she motioned with her lips, "This is important."

Wayne put his hand over the receiver and warned, "Chill out girl. Sit." Celeste sat with her head bowed in her hands. She was worried.

"Yes, Mr. Reed," said Wayne. Celeste jumped up and moved closer to the receiver to hear the conversation. "I'll be glad to join you and Miss Toussaint for lunch today in your office. Yes sir, noon will be fine. Thank you." Wayne hung up the receiver laughing.

Celeste was getting irritated now. "What is so funny?"

"You my dearest Celeste," Wayne replied as she balled up a piece of paper and threw it at his head.

"Frankly, my dear, since I know you care, give me the scoop, ice cream. Why does Mr. Soave Bolla want to see me today of all days?"

"Remember when you requested another beat?" he asked.

"Oh no! He's going to fire me because there's nobody left down at the board and it's all my fault," she wailed.

"No, Miss Know-It-All, he's granting your request," Wayne smiled.

"But I thought that was your job. Don't you assign or re-assign reporters and editors? Or are you fired now, too?" she sassed.

"Celeste, neither of us will be fired, OK? Taylor is simply going to comply with your request," he stated and leaned back in his leather chair.

"Oh, ho ho, so it's Taylor now," she said and narrowed her eyes. "And what, pray tell, will be my new beat?"

"I'm not so sure, but I know it will be within the guidelines you requested," he said matter-of-factly without looking directly into her eyes as he always did.

"Wayne, what's up with you? Look me in the face when you say that."

"Say what," Wayne asked avoiding her gaze.

"That little part about 'you're not so sure,'" she said, mocking him.

This little sucker had sold her out just as she thought. "Well it's mighty funny he's complying with a two-year-old request the day after every Tom, Dick, and Sue got busted down at the board," she huffed reaching for the door. "I guess I'll see you in the tower at noon."

"Meet me here and we'll go up together, OK?" he pleaded.

"Can't do it. I've got two follow-up interviews with the new regime at the board. Just meet me at Taylor's," she said sarcastically. Now Celeste looked him directly in the eye with the feelings she knew rang loud and clear: This crap stank to high heaven. And if he didn't hear that, she made sure he heard his office door slam.

Whatever was coming her way at noon today, she would take it like a champ. The phrase "Ask for what you want, you just might get it," kept rolling over and over in her head. Celeste knew that she must prepare herself for whatever the "it" may be. "Que sera, sera," she sighed. There was no time to ponder on "it" now. She had people to see, questions to ask, and stories to write. Her spirits lifted as she realized today's piece may very well be her last to come from the halls of edu-ma-cation.

The very thought of such a possibility made her smile as she ran back to her desk for her purse and tape recorder. She literally skipped out of the door and shouted, "Hallelujah!"

THREE

At ten minutes before 12, Celeste was browsing through the Marshall Field's reduced racks oblivious to the fact she could be late for her lunch date in The Tower. She threw two items over the counter for her favorite sales lady, Alana, to catch. Of course, the suits she'd selected were not from the reduced racks, but Alana would hold them for her until they had been marked down drastically and then make the purchase for Celeste with her employee discount. In return, Alana received complimentary subscriptions to the newspaper and unlimited books from the book review department of *The Courier*. Reading was Alana's passion, and Celeste's was shopping. The perfect relationship.

Alana simply winked and carried the items to their safe haven. Celeste ran onto Michigan Avenue wondering how she could think of shopping at a time like this. She knew she looked good today and that helped her attitude. Ivory was definitely her color. The Tahari coat dress adorned with gold buttons on the cuffs, with a single button holding the dress together, was exactly the ammunition she needed when facing Mr. Armani himself.

"Good afternoon Mrs. Schwartz," smiled Celeste. The elderly assistant and dedicated servant of the publisher, always had more than her share of blue dye to enhance her gray hairs and far too

many wrinkles as a result of sunning without protection in her day.
"Mr. Reed is expecting me."

"Indeed he is, Ms. Toussaint," she replied looking over her
half- moon reading glasses knowingly. "Right this way."

Celeste hated to be called "Ms." She was a "Miss" and liked
announcing to the world that she was single and proud. That "Ms."
thing was a cover-up for being married, divorced, or both. Celeste
felt she was not trapped anywhere in between, so why lie?

Mrs. Schwartz opened the golden handles of the double solid-
oak doors to the office and announced her like some pageant con-
testant taking her walk on the runway. Certainly the office was
just as long. Upon entering, Celeste took her time, slowly stroll-
ing in to shake the outstretched hand of Taylor Reed.

"Ms. Toussaint, so glad you could join me for lunch today," he
said, pumping her hand firmly.

Celeste smiled sweetly, looked him in the eyes, and covered
his hand with her left, "It's Miss, Mr. Reed. Miss Toussaint, but I
really do prefer Celeste. And thank you for the invitation," she
said, thinking, *"What was I supposed to do decline to meet my
publisher for lunch?"*

"Well then, Celeste it is, " he said bowing and kissed her hand,
"muy bella."

"Muchas gracias," she said with a mock curtsey, playing his
little game which was beginning to get on her nerves.

"Please sit," he said, holding out a high back leather chair at
the head of the mahogony table. She nodded her thanks.

"You have excellent taste, Celeste. I love women who carry
Chanel bags, and that Estee Lauder perfume! Mmmm. Let's see,"
he sniffed, "you're wearing White Linen. Very nice", he observed.

"Thank you, Mr. Taylor." The "Mr. Armani" reputation he had
received from his staff had not been off track in the least. His fully
tailored olive Armani suit looked as though it were sewn onto his
very attractive frame. Its color perfectly complimented his deep
green eyes. Mr. Reed's perpetual tan glistened against his heavy

starched white shirt with rounded collar. He wore almost too much of the designer's Armani cologne. With all of the compliments he was showering upon her, she now knew why they called him "Mr. Soave Bolla."

Mrs. Schwartz opened the oak doors announcing Wayne Stephens, who ran in apologizing, out of breath, and five minutes late. Celeste took the opportunity to ignore him and look out of the ceiling-to-floor windows at the dynamite view of the Magnificent Mile and Lake Michigan. *My sweet home Chicago*, she mused to herself. *How beautiful you are*.

"Lunch is served!" announced the bellman, and out of nowhere appeared silver carts, serving trays, and waiters to serve them.

It wasn't until the coffee was poured that Mr. Reed got down to the business at hand. "You know, Celeste, I'm quite pleased with the work you have done at the Board, and this morning our paper sold in record numbers. Congratulations to you," he said, raising his coffee cup.

"Thank you," she said.

"How long have you been with us now?"

Wayne jumped in, "Celeste came to *The Courier* in ..." Celeste kicked him under the table, and her eyes told him not to answer for her.

Quickly she stated, "Four years, sir. I was an intern here and came on board full-time right after graduation."

"Wayne told me some time ago you requested another beat."

"That's correct," she said, smiling, and kicked Wayne again to prompt him to say something now.

Wayne shoots her an "I just can't win with you look". "You're right Taylor, it was two years ago when I came to you with the request."

Mr. Reed looked at Celeste intently. "What was it that you had in mind?" he asked.

She took one second to respond, "Something that will never

be boring. A beat which will always provide excitement for me as well as my readers. I want it to give the appearance of never sleeping."

Taylor laughed loudly, "This is unbelievable. We are on the same page exactly. How do you feel about New York?"

Now it was Celeste's turn to laugh, "New York?! Are you crazy?"

Ssshh, she thought, *Watch your mouth, girlfriend, and rephrase the question.*

"I mean, New York? How, sir? We don't have a paper there." Then she realized what she'd said. They had no paper in New York. Oh goodness, she was definitely fired.

"You are right, we don't have a paper in New York, however what I have is a best friend with the number one paper there, The *New York Daily Courier*. Ed Townsend and I were roommates at Northwestern and Wharton School of Business. Our papers have the same name. Not a day goes by that we don't talk."

Wayne was sitting there with his mouth open. Celeste kicked him so he would shut his mouth before something flew in it. Finally, he said, "Wow."

Celeste gritted her teeth and rolled her eyes. Why did this dude always have to be so impressed with everything white folks said? He acted like they didn't go to Northwestern as well.

"Ed has a spot available immediately," Taylor continued. "Your beat will be entertainment."

Every writer she knew was trying to work their way to New York, and certainly the beat that kept an entire newspaper staff envious was Entertainment. Not that she had worked hard at her craft to review movies, but, she considered Entertainment as a nice diversion ... for a minute. If for nothing else it could be her introduction to the number one market. All she could say was, "Wow."

Quickly she returned to her business sense. There were a few questions to be answered before getting all starry-eyed.

"What's the pay for a gig like this, Mr. Reed? I mean, New

York is a very expensive place to live," she reasoned.

"Unfortunately, salaries are a drawback of the Big Apple in the publishing business. The pay is lower there because the expenses are higher and more people are needed in order to run an establishment. Chicago is known for paying the highest salaries in the business. But to answer your question," he said quickly, sensing her irritation with his explanation and noticing she was writing in her notepad, "you would be upped from $32,000 to $40,000. I had to fight with Eddie on that point because your $32,000 here is a managing editor's salary in New York. I told him that you'd never take a cut in pay even for the big time. I also told him you were a woman of exquisite taste and class, and you won't stand for any of his shenanigans, or anyone else's for that matter."

"And what did he say to the truth about me?" asked Celeste.

"He wants you to start right away."

Ed's no fool, Celeste thought and looked at Wayne for a response.

The look on his face told her, Don't be crazy. Wayne had been trying to get to New York ever since they were at Northwestern. He spoke of nothing else but making it to the Big Apple.

"I need two weeks from today," she said finally. "I mean a girl's got to pack her cedar trunks, let alone find a place to live in that town. I don't know a thing about New York. I need two weeks and that's all there is to it. I'm sure you can arrange it, Mr. Reed. Can't you?", she asked and blinked once, very slowly.

"Of course I can, it's no problem," Taylor smiled, "no problem at all."

The private line in Ed Townsend's office rang, and he dismissed his assistant before answering it. "Well how did we make out?"

"Two weeks," Taylor replied, "She needs two weeks to get settled. Call them off, Ed. She gave us no problem. This girl is not stupid. I mean, call them off."

"T, you're getting soft in your old age. Don't worry," Ed as-

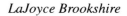

sured him, "everything's under control. You have done your part, now let me do mine. All right, I will call everybody off and hopefully her attention will be diverted. I'll speak with you tomorrow."

FOUR

C eleste decided to leave the office early. As she boarded the Number Six Jeffery Express bus, she thought about how much her life would quickly change. She took out her pad and began to write down the things she would need to purchase, the things she needed to do, and the order in which she needed to do them. This bus ride was the most relaxing part of her day. The 20 minutes riding down Lake Shore Drive by Lake Michigan was what helped her to think- and to dream.

When the bus hit the Hyde Park section of the city, there were kids in front of her alma mater, Kenwood Academy, who boarded the Number Six. She marveled at how well dressed they were for high schoolers, but the "Kenwood Cuties" always did have a reputation for dressing like they were in a daily fashion show. Their conversations were the same, too: "Who's driving tonight?" "Are we going to the Jack and Jill set or to the Warehouse?" "Tell me now so I will know what to wear!"

Those conversations thrust Celeste back into her youth for a moment. It was on this very bus line her first boyfriend told her he was in love with her. It was also on the same bus line he told her it was quits. The Number Six was where friends swapped homework, gossip, and meals from McDonald's.

She had to laugh when she thought of the first time she and her neighbor and best friend, Dippy, cut school to go to the

One Day Sale at Marshall Field's. One of their mother's mutual friends saw them on the bus downtown during school hours, and before they could get home this woman had already called in the information. So when they stopped at Dippy's house to further glare at their wares, her father Poppy was waiting for them.

"Ladies how was school today?" he asked suspiciously, hoping they wouldn't lie, as he loosened his tie after a hard day at work.

They both chimed, "Oh fine, Poppy!" Dippy went on about some activity of the day at school and Celeste stood there smiling and agreeing, until Poppy cold-cocked them both with a backhand and screamed, "Dippy, you go to your room! Celeste, you go home so your Mother can finish you off, or you can go to Dippy's room with her!"

Celeste ran across the street terrified as she heard Poppy screaming, "I'll teach you two about lying and cutting school to go shopping! Both of you are just too spoiled. Just two little spoiled butts! You have no business having your own telephone lines, your own credit cards, and Halston perfume. Y'all are too spoiled!"

Before Celeste could get to the door, her Mother was holding it open for her with that 'you're gonna get your tail whipped today' look on her face.

It seemed so funny to her now, but Celeste remembered she and Dippy took the whippings and punishments like champs because their purchases were worth it. Even in high school, they were shopping pros.

Celeste climbed the steps to the Toussaint home in Pill Hill, where she'd lived her entire life. In their neighborhood, the kids stayed at home until they were married or moved to another city. There was a comfort level which had developed over the years within the neighborhood. It was a loving, nurturing environment that produced effective adults. If it weren't for the new job, she would have gladly stayed put.

Suddenly fear struck her in the heart because she would have to tell her parents about her new transition. It wasn't the opportunity that had her fumbling for her keys at the front of their huge double doors, the advancement is what they'd be proud of, no doubt. It was the fact their baby girl was moving to New York that had her in a severe panic.

How will I tell them? she thought, *Mommie, Daddy, I'm moving to New York. Nah too blunt.*

Mommie, Daddy, I've been transferred ... to New York. No way don't lie.

Mommie, Daddy, remember the request I put in for a new beat? ... Well I got it. No too Valley Girlish. Just go for it, girlfriend!

The house, decorated in classic white oak furniture and plush wedgwood blue carpet, was, as always, immaculate. Today the house smelled of seafood gumbo and resounded with warm kitchen conversations. She took a moment to look at her loving parents. Her folks had been married for 30 years and they had always looked alike. Both had hazel eyes, sandy hair, skin the color of coffee with cream, and very long legs.

"Hey everybody!" Celeste said leaning in the doorway of the black, white, and chrome kitchen. "What's going on with my favorite dish in here? What's the occasion?"

"The occasion is My Gal Friday and the killer story on page one today. That's what is going on in here," said her father, Charles, as he dug into a crab leg, and motioned for a kiss on the cheek.

Her mother, Annie Mae, chimed in. "Here, here!" and clanged a fork on her water glass. Celeste took a bow to her mother, "Thank you," and a bow to her father, "and thank you."

"Sit down, child, and allow me to serve your Mommie's famous gumbo," exclaimed Annie Mae. "We want to hear all of the details."

Her father jumped in, "What your Mommie is really trying to say is, we hope this story was the reason why you've been so cranky, frustrated, irritable, non-communicative, down-right bitchy," he paused, looked over his glasses, and sucked the juice out of a crab leg. "Should I continue?"

"No, you don't have to continue," Celeste sighed and looked around the kitchen where she had shared plenty of good and bad news with her folks. The kitchen at the Toussaint home was more than a cooking and eating room, it was where the most serious conversations of her life had taken place.

Celeste closed her eyes for a second in silent prayer, then explained, "I'm sorry, about my behavior these last couple of weeks, but I have some great news. I got a new job out of the disaster at the Board!"

"That's marvelous, darling. It is a promotion I hope," said Annie Mae.

"Yes, it is," said Celeste slowly.

"All right, Princess, keep bringing home the bacon because your people are hungry," said Charles. "How much more will we bring home a week?"

"Don't you even want to know what the job is, Daddy?"

Charles cracked a crab leg between his teeth. "Of course. What is this new job and then how much more is it paying?"

"OK everybody," Celeste beamed, "my new beat will be Entertainment."

Annie Mae jumped up to slap a high five with Celeste. "That's my girl!"

Charles did not even look up from his plate. "What's the bottom line, Princess? What is the bottom line?"

"The bottom line, Daddy, is I have to move to New York," she said while squeezing her eyes shut. The only thing that made her open them was the sound of her Daddy choking and his spoon clanging to the floor.

Celeste ran to his side, slapped his back real hard, and helped him sip lemonade out of his favorite jelly jar. "Are you going to be all right?" she asked.

"Only if you promise to be all right," said a smiling Charles, knowing the number one market is what she deserved because she had been working hard.

"Oh yes, Daddy, I promise. I promise."

Annie Mae knew this day would come: When their only child would finally leave home. She had always been an overly protective mother ever since she failed to carry two children full term before Celeste. She was Annie Mae's miracle baby the doctors had said.

The other babies were unable to develop properly because Annie Mae insisted upon keeping her job as a teacher in the worst school district in town. Never believing that you could teach kids from behind a desk anyhow, Annie Mae knew that the way to keep one-up on her students, who were categorized as doomed for life, was to stay on her feet. *And* to prove the so-called experts wrong, of course.

Determined and unwavering, she put herself in jeopardy by taking on too much stress and not sitting more as instructed during her pregnancies. Annie Mae had finally resigned herself to the fact that she and Charles would continue to consider her students as their adopted kids, until Celeste came along and brightened their whole world.

Always and forever an exuberant child spoiled too much by Charles, and pushed just a touch before it was to be considered too much, Celeste was Annie Mae's personal project. Annie Mae prided herself on Celeste's aptitude in English and journalism.

Smiling at how a little push from Mommie never hurt anybody, while choking back the tears, Annie Mae asked, "What can I get for you, super star?"

Celeste gave her parents an obvious reply: "A couple of new cedar trunks."

Charles rolled his eyes. "And several new things at my expense to go in them."

They laughed and Annie Mae said, "As soon as we finish our dinner, let's drive out to River Oaks and get those trunks packed!"

FIVE

T he morning Celeste was to leave for New York, she woke as usual to take her four-mile walk around Stony Island Park. It would be the last time she would meet and walk with the ladies she'd known for an eternity. Suddenly the things she'd been accustomed to were magnified in her mind. She was so used to living in a neighborhood with people she had known all of her life. For the first time, she was worried about the people she would encounter in the big city. How different would they be from her? How different would she be from them? Would she be able to find someone to love in that place?

Now *there* was something to consider. Telling her parents had been a cinch, but as for telling boyfriend Frank, it was not as easy. Maybe it was her timing. Celeste and her mouth had gotten her in deep trouble with Frank when she chose to tell him about the move after they had made love.

It was bad enough he complained all of the time that she did not spend enough time with him. He loved her with all of his heart, but for Celeste, it was her work that she loved. Frank often referred to her work as "her lover." He would get angry with her and say she should try to get off on the words she put on paper. Maybe then, she would not need him.

Men. When Celeste was busy, she could live without them.

She wanted Frank's tender lovemaking to be their goodbye. She also knew him well enough to know he would not speak to her again before she left. So she decided to stock up on some good loving before taking on her new town.

These were her thoughts as she took a brisk stroll around the park. Her thoughts were intruded upon when she saw the car with the same license plate number for the third time that week: WBB 923. Celeste had an unbelievable memory for numbers, and the plate was so easy to memorize, it was juvenile. But it was that car. The neighborhood of Pill Hill was entirely residential. Strange cars were easily noticed. A black Town Car with tinted windows and a license plate which was virtually a nursery rhyme, puzzled Celeste as she sprinted from the park to her backyard to complete her last workout at home.

SIX

Annie Mae and Celeste were sitting knee to knee at O'Hare International Airport's Delta Terminal in a mother-and-daughter conference.

"Well, this is it," Annie Mae said tenderly. "You call if you need anything. Aunt June and Uncle Jim promised you your own room but you install your own phone line you hear Miss Chatty Cathy."

Celeste forced a smile. "I hear."

"Don't worry baby, Uncle Jim will watch out for you."

"Mommie, I just hope I'm doing the right thing." There, she finally voiced her little flicker of doubt that had been dancing in her head for two weeks. Celeste had the feeling something was not so great with this deal. She had tried her best to conceal those thoughts from her family. If they even had an inkling of her fears, she would have been hog-tied to her bed and spoon fed for the next five years.

Annie Mae looked at her strangely, as she had never heard that tone in her daughter's voice before. Celeste noticed her Mother's all-knowing, all-seeing eye on patrol and quickly made an about-face.

"What I want to do," she explained, "is to make a name for

myself, but mostly to make the family proud."

"That's a given, sugar," Annie Mae said reassuringly as she took Celeste's cheeks in her hands. "Now you listen and listen good. The foundation laid for you by this family will never be broken by some two-bit town that calls itself the greatest city on earth. You know your heritage, you know yourself, and, what will help you above all in that place is, you know your craft. So you dry those teary eyes, because your Mommie and Daddy are only a phone call and a flight away. So if you don't charge your credit cards to the hilt the first week you're there, and if you find you can't stand the town, buy yourself a ticket back home," she smiled.

"Not necessary," said Charles, kneeling down alongside of them, "I bought you a round-trip ticket with an open return. You can come home tomorrow if you find you miss me terribly."

Celeste threw her arms around his neck, "Oh Daddy!"

He pulled her to her feet and said to Annie Mae, "Please excuse us while we go have a Daddy-and-daughter talk."

Every time Charles made that statement, he would issue Celeste one of his famous warnings. They walked hand in hand to an empty waiting area, and sat in a corner next to the window.

He began very slowly, "Now Princess, New York is a mean place. Your Aunt June and Uncle Jim live in Harlem, and, well, I want you to be careful at all times."

He dropped a leather case in her lap. As soon as the weight of the case hit her, she almost jumped out of her skin. The look on his face told her to be very cool.

"You've already gone past the metal detectors," he pointed out factually, "and don't use the nose for news you've got by trying to figure it out on me. Just tell me if you remember how to use this thing."

She whispered, "Of course."

How could she ever forget? It was a ritual in their household to load the gun and shoot it out of the window into the backyard every New Year's Eve at midnight. And when they went down to

Louisiana, they would take the shot guns and go hunting for all kinds of game. Even more fun was when they would find bottles and old cans to use as targets. Charles would brag, "That's my girl! This child has a perfect eye!"

Charles saw her drifting into the past. "Celeste, you must tell no one I have given you the gun. It's our secret."

Charles Toussaint, Esquire, could not believe that he would actually have to phone in any of those favors for Celeste that he'd stock-piled for half a century as head legal counsel for the City of Chicago. There was no way he was going to let his Princess slip off to New York without an untraceable piece in her purse.

From what his brother Jim told him constantly of the New York streets , they were not to be taken for granted. Not too far off from the streets of Chicago, but in their home town Celeste never knew the entire police force was aware that she was his child.

Charles came from modest beginnings in Houma, Louisiana, where he and Annie Mae met at Terrebonne High School. The two then attended Southern University in Baton Rouge, marrying immediately after graduation.

Attracted by the postcards he'd seen, originally sent to a professor of his, of Chicago's Lake Michigan and it's skyline glistening against the water, Charles lured Annie Mae away from the security blanket they called home, with vivid dreams to be actualized in an undiscovered territory.

He had promised her the world and after only five years as an assistant district attorney, he was able to keep his promise when he was elevated to top dog. Now "Toussaint," as he was affectionately called by his peers, was retired, but still handled only a few "delicate" cases. He was the only legal counsel in the history of Chicago's political machine to survive four regimes. Because Charles Toussaint knew where the skeletons were hiding in everyone's closet and even where others were buried. His most admirable quality was that he knew how to keep a secret, a quality he instilled in his daughter.

The loud speaker sounded, "This is the final boarding call for Flight 22 to New York's LaGuardia Airport at Gate G-8."

"I'm ready," exclaimed Celeste and stood up to walk to the gate.

Annie Mae said, "Okay, everybody, group hug and prayer. Lord watch, between me and thee, while we're absent one from another. Amen."

"Amen," chimed Charles and Celeste.

"I love you Mommie. I love you Daddy," Celeste declared as she walked toward the jetway, waving. Charles ran up to the door and put an envelope in her hand, blew a kiss, and waved goodbye.

When Celeste was settled in her seat she opened the envelope, finding a stack of one-hundred-dollar bills and a note. "Here is $3,000 emergency cash for my Princess. Even if those emergencies come in the form of Ralph Lauren, Chanel, or Gucci. I love you.

Enjoy ..."

A smile came across her face the same time a tear rolled down her cheek as she thought of the family she was leaving. The family who knew her so well.

SEVEN

LaGuardia Airport was a horror show! Celeste could not believe the assortment of characters sleeping on floors, and begging for change, or the con cabbies trying to hustle up customers. She was watching the luggage carousel go 'round and 'round with antennae up in the back of her head, when a voice snuck up beside her.

"So you've finally made it to the Big Apple. Bet you never thought it would have looked like this, didja?" It was her cousin Sammy. She had not him seen since they were kids.

Celeste threw down her coat and bags and Sammy swung her around just like when she was little. "Whoa, girl," he said, "you ain't as easy to pick up as you used to be!"

"And you ain't as young as you used to be," she said, picking at the grey hairs around his temples. The last time she had seen Sammy, he was terrorizing all of the little cousins at their Grannie's house with a stocking cap over his face and Noxzema rubbed in on his cheeks; the perfect picture of the Boogey Man to an eight-year-old. But he was still as handsome as she had remembered. Good looks ran in the Toussaint family. Folks always wondered how their immediate family ranged in so many different hues. Celeste had her theory, and it went all the way back to slavery.

Sammy was a gorgeous chocolate Hershey's bar in color, but he had to lose the rough-looking hair-do he called a "cold wave." Too bad he was a cousin, but on the other hand it was a good thing because Celeste knew he had to have some fine friends. He was dressed to the nines, too, sky blue silk shirt with ivory silk pants and ivory leather loafers with no socks. *Tres* L.A.

He took the streets up to Harlem so he could show Celeste the sights. They passed through the Village, which he said was the most popular place in town for artsy fartsy folks, gays, and those who wanted to express themselves freely.

There was the Empire State Building and Macy's on 34th Street. Lord & Taylor's was on 38th and Fifth Avenue, and the huge Main Library was on 42nd Street and Fifth Avenue.

"And here is where you'll be working," announced Sammy, "One Times Square Plaza. This is the building where they drop the ball on New Year's Eve, you know."

"No, I didn't know," said Celeste in awe. "Well I mean, I know they drop the ball on New Year's Eve, but I didn't know that it was from the building where I will be working. Where are we? What part of town is this? Where is it in relation to the airport and how far is it from Uncle Jim's?"

"This part of town is called Times Square, it is considered Midtown Manhattan. We're quite some ways from the airport which was in Queens, and Uncle Jim lives in Harlem, which is only a 20-minute subway ride on the Number Three train.

"It's not that easy to get lost in this town, but you've just got to remember a few rules," Sammy continued.

Rules for directions, thought Celeste, but she didn't say anything, her eyes did. With Sammy being a family member, he read eyes.

"Just listen. Even streets run East, 40th, 38th, 36th, etcetera. Odd streets run West, 41st, 39th, 37th and etcetera. With the exception of the main streets, like 42nd and 34th-... they run both ways.

"Uptown is North. Downtown is South. Fifth Avenue is the dividing line between East and West. The odd Avenues Ninth, Seventh, and Fifth run downtown. The even Avenues Tenth, Eighth, and Sixth run uptown. Remember what I said and you'll never get lost. Also remember these rules go out of the window from the Village on down to the Brooklyn Bridge.

"Now, on your subways it's as easy as arithmetic and your ABC's. The Red line: numbers 1, 2, 3. Green Line: numbers 4, 5, 6. Purple Line: number 7. Blue Line : A, C, E. Orange Line: B, D, F. Yellow Line: N, Q, R. Green Line: the double G and the Grey Line is for the shuttle train between Grand Central and Times Square."

Celeste looked at him incredulously. "Do you think I will ever remember any of these directives?"

Sammy whooped, "It was a test my dear couz. You're the hot-shot reporter. You were supposed to either write it down or remember it."

"Oh, don't get smart with me, Sam," she teased, "I want you to know you are older now and I can probably run much faster than you. So I won't hesitate to chase your butt down until I can tickle you until you pee on yourself," she said reaching for his underarm, the area she knew was his most venerable spot.

"And for your information I'm not at work. I thought I was just chillin' and crusin' with my couz. So therefore I was not trying to memorize any rhetoric about some directions after being in town all of thirty minutes," she added and snapped her finger.

Sammy looked calmly and said, "Well couz, in all seriousness, I wrote out the directions for you. It's no fun getting lost in this place. And no two people will give you the same directions if you do.

However, I said all of that to say, without saying, you cannot afford not to be on your P's and Q's at all times. This is not, I repeat, this is not Chicago," he warned.

"Do not let anyone tell you all big cities are alike. I will say it again on the record, that is reporter lingo, isn't it? This is NOT Chicago.

"From this day forth you have got to shift gears into overdrive. You are gonna have to take off those damn high heels and put on some sneakers when you're in the streets. And you're gonna have to get yourself a little side hustle to stay alive."

"What's a side hustle?" Celeste asked.

"Girl, you better stick close to me if you don't know what a hustle is," cautioned Sammy. "It is when you have a part-time job of some kind. You know finding a way of earning some extra money. Everybody does it. Even me. I've got my nice cushy job down at Con Edison in customer service, but I drive a yellow cab on weekends picking up all of the touristy folks and telling them things about my city like I'm trying to tell you.

"And look at my dad. He drove a bus for forty years. Now he's a driver for a real plush private car service. So he gets his pension and he gets a salary from the car service. He's getting over, that's his hustle."

Celeste thought she had better play this back the way she thought she heard it. "Sammy, I can see you with a little hustle, you know, you are a young man with no wife, no kids, but you've got your serious party life to maintain."

"Ya got that right."

"But are you saying Uncle Jim worked forty years at his job, retired, and now he has another job?"

"Right."

"And you call that a hustle?"

"Right."

"I call it crazy, Sam. Who wants another job after putting in their time for all of those years?"

"Girl, how'd they raise you back in Chicago? I'll spell it out for you real slow, OK? My dad doesn't claim the money he makes on his new job. So it's extra", Sammy looked at her, nodding his head vigorously as if to say *'Got it dummy'?*

"It's not 'on' his job, it is 'at' his job," she said, correcting him, frustrated with the entire conversation. "And I still say Uncle Jim and Aunt June should be somewhere enjoying themselves on the Beaches of the World. And I'm not wearing any tennis shoes in the streets for anybody."

"Listen to me. This is your big couz Sam talking to you. Who needs them beaches when you got everything you would ever need in New York? We got Reis Beach, Orchard Beach, Long Island Beaches, and the Jersey Shore. We don't ever have to leave here if we don't want to," Sammy boasted. "New York has it all!"

"Hey, dude. Tell me, when was the last time you ventured past Times Square, The Village, and Harlem? Please don't tell me it was when you were last in Chicago when you were, what, 18 years old?"

"I was 17, Miss, when I graduated high school."

"Sam your English, pleeese. You are sorely missing a preposition. C'mon repeat after me: graduated *from* high school," she lectured.

"Yeah, yeah. Graduated, graduated from, whatever, who cares. But as I was saying here, before English 101," Sammy recalled, "come to think of it, that was the last time I left town. The trip was a present from my Mom. But with all of the cultural diversity right here at my fingertips, why spend the airfare?"

They hollered all the way to Harlem. When they pulled up to Esplanade Gardens on Lenox Avenue and 146th Street, Celeste stared amazed at the building. "No one told me your folks lived in the projects."

Sammy answered defiantly, "These buildings are not projects, my dear couz, they are co-op apartments. Where have you ever seen projects with balconies?"

"All day long at home. How do you think so many Negroes get killed up in the projects?"

"I don't know. How?"

"They go flying over the balconies."

"Well, these ain't no projects. They even have a doorman 24 hours a day for your protection. Now say good evening to the man."

"Good evening sir," she said to the doorman as she thought, *They still look like the projects to me.*

EIGHT

U ncle Jim and Aunt June welcomed Celeste with open arms. Aunt June had set up her room so nicely, with a Laura Ashley bedspread and curtains to match. All of those flowers were far too prissy for Celeste's taste but she was more than grateful to have a place to lay her head that did not cost an arm and a leg.

She had never lived 26 floors above anywhere. Worked, yes, but lived, no. Living so high up would take some getting used to. Out of her bedroom window was a terrific view of the Harlem River, Yankee Stadium, and a well-lit Yankee marquee flashing the time and temperature.

"Did your cousin lay out the rules of the city?" said Uncle Jim. He was the sweetest man she had ever known, next to her Daddy, of course. Uncle Jim had a solid-built, coffee-colored frame. His face was friendly, compassionate, and wise, which gave one the impression that he earned each and every grey hair upon his head. He possessed a baritone speaking voice which sounded the same when he sang.

The family bragged often that he studied opera at Juilliard. Celeste could confirm that Uncle Jim had a glorious singing voice, but she could not understand why he worked driving a cab instead of singing to earn money after being retired. This was New York City; the artistic mecca. He had at his disposal the Met, Carnegie Hall, Lincoln Center, Broadway, and even off-Broadway as avenues to showcase his talents. Well, she'd always heard New York was a very expensive place to live and her guess was Uncle Jim is in-your-face-proof it was, indeed.

"Yes, I got my pure unadulterated version of the dos and don'ts of 'New York according to Sammy.' So Uncle Jim, when are you going to show me around? And Aunt June, you must take me shopping to show me how the ladies do it around here," Celeste said enthusiastically.

Aunt June put her hand on her perfectly-rounded hip and replied, "Honey, around here the young ladies save their money to put it on the rent."

Celeste thought, *You're kidding right? Cause that is not what I heard.*

Her dear aunt had always been known as the most prudent woman in the family and, as a result, she had money stashed all over their apartment and in banks all around town. The family said Aunt June had it written in her will that she wanted to take it with her, for real. She also wanted to be buried in her one and only fabulous sequined gown, with her diamonds on every finger, and in her full- length mink coat. The only thing of great value she willed to anybody was a mink jacket and stole to her favorite relative. No one knew who it was specifically, because that was not to be disclosed until the reading of the will. The whole family guessed that it had to be Celeste because Aunt June never let any family member live with them in their beautiful, gigantic, four-bedroom apartment. Spend the night, no problem. Live, hell no. She even kicked out Sammy, their only child at 18.

Aunt June was 60 and still had the figure of a 25-year-old. Celeste could see she was still knocking 'em dead with her steel-grey eyes and matching hair, that bright smile, and peaches 'n' cream complexion.

"Now honey," Aunt June said, "we promised your Mommie and Daddy we would take good care of you, so you be comfortable and get acquainted with the city before you go rushing off to spend your whole salary on an apartment. You are perfectly welcome here. If you want to help out a bit with food and all, it will be enough."

Celeste thought, _I could spend my whole salary on many a thing in New York City, but never would I lay down the whole lot for an apartment._

"Oh no, Aunt June, I couldn't stay here for nothing, I have to pay some rent."

Celeste saw a hint of a glimmer in her eye, "You get settled first, then we'll discuss it, OK."

Sammy barged in the door and shouted, "What are you doing?"

"I am hanging my suits before they wrinkle," she said as she carefully placed her blazers in the closet not touching one another.

"Leave your bags, we can get them later. We have a party to go to, but I have to stop at home first and I want you to see my pad."

Celeste knew she had better explain some basics to her couz. "Sam, maybe you throw your clothes around like nothing, but I take care of my things, sweetie. We can leave when I finish. Where is this party anyway? You should have driven over to your house and then come back to get me."

Uncle Jim grumbled from the living room, "He has done enough driving of my car today, thank you."

"Well Sam, where is your car?" asked Celeste. Everyone in the room laughed.

Sammy started again, "Listen up, couz. New York City 101: Unless you have a parking space available to you where you live, a car is a hassle. We have a dynamite subway system, which we are about to experience right now."

"For your information," Celeste began, while selecting an all=white outfit in celebration of the last official weekend to wear white before Labor Day, "I was told that before I came here by several people, which is why I sold my car. So let's roll."

They ran across the street to the 145th Street station to catch the Number Three train. Celeste could not wait to get on board the train to escape the smell of the dank underground. In all of her life, her senses had never been so offended. She covered her nose with her silk scarf to escape the odor.

Sammy said, "You'll get used to it."

She looked at him as if to say, *"IT" what?*

"The smell," he said.

She doubted it very seriously.

Just then Celeste noticed something scurrying around an over-flowing garbage can and demanded, "Sam, what's that?" She pointed toward the two huge, unidentifiable rodents.

"Oh that, my dear, is the local wildlife."

When they boarded the train, Celeste could not believe her eyes. There it was, the graffiti everyone talked about. It was a unique artform, but it was everywhere. On the floor, on the windows, on the ceiling, and on the seats.

"How dare you bring me down here to this dungeon?" she said to Sammy through clenched teeth.

"Sit down," he said, "we've got a long ride."

"If you think I am going to sit on that seat with all of that spray paint on it in this white dress, you should stop breathing right now. I don't care how far we have to go, I will stand, thank you," she huffed.

After she was jerked around in every which direction, she thought about all of the people who gave her the bad advice to sell her Thunderbird. Celeste began making a mental note to see each of them personally when she went home, so she could kick their tails good.

Ed Townsend was at home with his wife and two children in his Park Avenue penthouse tri-plex when his portable phone rang.

The family left the room so he could answer.

"Tell me Rick, what's the story?" Ed stood at the window facing Central Park as Rick recounted moment by moment, beginning from when Celeste stepped off of the plane.

"She's living in Harlem? Are you sure? Oh, we'll see how long Miss Priss lasts up there. But you know, Rick," Ed said, pacing back and forth now, "her living arrangements may actually suit us fine. This way Miss Toussaint will be living quite some way from the action, so this may be just perfect. Good work, Rick. Pick her up again after she leaves my office on Tuesday."

NINE

The party was a throwdown! They went to a club called Leviticus, which was considered the hot spot for all of the Black movers and shakers. Sammy knew everybody in the joint and before the night was over Celeste did, too. The special party was for a group called Chocolate Singles that published a magazine of the same name. There was a fashion show, and a wonderful MC with the smoothest, deepest, and sexiest voice Celeste had ever heard named Vaughn Harper, from WBLS radio. Sammy told her he did a show nightly called the "Quiet Storm." Celeste locked in that information. She loved her some slow jams.

"So this is Saturday night in the city," Celeste yelled in Sammy's ear as she sat down exhausted from 10 songs in a row on the dance floor. "There are so many fine men here I don't know who to talk to first."

Sammy stroked Celeste's hand very calmly while swirling his Remy Martin and said in a "Father-Knows-Best" tone, "You take your time, there will be plenty of opportunities. You're the new girl in town and they want to know who you are just as much as you want to know them."

"Give me Uncle Jim's phone number, I definitely want to give it to the brother who I have been dancing with all night."

"I don't know, couz, he looks like he might be a little light in the loafers."

Celeste had not even pondered the thought. "Who cares. I'm not looking for a husband just a permanent dance partner," she said, while rocking to the music.

"That woman he's with, now she is fine!"

"I bet you they are just friends."

"Well, Miss Fine sho' has some moves. Mmm. Mmm. Mmm," he commented as he stared a hole in the woman.

"I hear from the family you're a dancer, and from what I see you've got some moves, too, girlie," Sammy continued. "Is it true you've had your Equity card since you were 15 years old?"

She nodded yes while sucking up her virgin strawberry daquiri.

"I don't know why you didn't come here to dance on Broadway. Instead, you've come here to review it," Sammy shook his head. "That's a trip. Wasted talent girl."

"You point me in the direction of a fantastic dance studio that has African dance with some live drummers and I won't disappoint you," Celeste announced and sauntered off into the crowd with heads turning in her direction as she passed.

"Lord help the brothers," Sammy said aloud, and downed his glass of Remy.

Before Celeste could find her dance partner, he snatched her and dragged her onto the floor. In the midst of burning it up, she asked him, "What's your name?"

"Maurice Franklin," he said, "and you are ..."

"Celeste Toussaint," she answered thinking about Sammy's assessment of her dance partner. He was such a cutie. She loved them tall, tan, and tempting. And this here Maurice was just her style.

"I love your energy and you actually smile when you dance. What do you do?"

"I'm an entertainment reporter for the *New York Daily Courier*, but I don't start until after Labor Day. I just got to town today. And you?"

"I'm a radio producer for a syndicated network. Where are you from?"

"Chicago."

Maurice stopped dancing, "So am I."

They hugged each other and jumped up and down.

"Where did you go to high school?" Celeste asked, so glad to have found a homie in less than 24 hours.

"Kenwood Academy, Class of 1975," announced Maurice proudly.

Celeste screamed, "Kenwood Academy Class '80!"

"I want you to meet my friend, Renee Poteat. Renee, meet Celeste."

Renee hugged her, "Nice to meet you, Celeste. Girl you two are over here getting down!"

"No, Miss Girl, I see *you* over there doing your thang," she complimented.

"Can you believe we went to the same high school?" said Maurice.

"Yep I can," said Renee pointing a finger in his chest, "because this dude can be in the room with a thousand people and he'll find the one from Chicago. Do you Chicago people have some special markings that only you can see?" Renee teased.

Renee was a very beautiful woman. Her features were very fine and delicate, with skin that was like a perfectly painted, tawny matte canvas. She had thick black eyebrows that matched her coal-black eyes and hair. Celeste was delighted to have met two people she might be able to call friends.

They danced all night, and when they weren't dancing they were swapping stories about their Kenwood days. Maurice said he made the mad dash for New York City to escape his family's dry cleaning business eight years ago. He had been having a ball ever since.

Finally, at four in the morning, Celeste woke up Sammy, who

was sleeping on a couch in the lobby, to go home. When she stepped to the curb to hail a taxi, Sammy walked in the direction of the subway.

Celeste ran down the street to grab him. "What's wrong with you? Does the subway have you on auto pilot or something? Get yourself in this here taxi."

Sammy pulled out two tokens, saying, "Girl your couz is all spent out, I ain't got no cab fare."

"Well when your drink of choice is 10 dollars a pop I guess you are all spent out. Let's take the taxi."

"Don't worry about the time. There will be half of the people from the club on the trains. Come on, you'll see."

"No Sam. I don't want to see," she protested, took off her pump and shook it in his face. "My dear, your couz does have the fare, don't worry. You just get your tail in the taxi and don't ruin my wonderful evening with the threat of getting on the train. I do not consider that hell-hole dessert."

Sammy read the eyes and reluctantly got in. Celeste gave the driver the address and noticed his identification tag read James Flint. As she eased back into the seat and reminisced on the evening, her precise thought was truly, *Home, James."*

TEN

The sun was shining so brightly into Celeste's face when she awoke, she was not glad that she had to go to work today. Her Mommie warned her she was going to want to start work one week later so she could explore her new territory. Celeste and Uncle Jim did quite a bit of walking all day Sunday. After church he really showed her some of the sites that made Harlem USA world renowned.

Uncle Jim was a New York historian. Celeste learned more on her walking tour than she had heard about the city in a lifetime. The tour began with Sunday morning service at the Abyssinian Baptist Church where Uncle Jim was a choir member. It was founded and formerly pastored by Reverend Adam Clayton Powell. The church itself was a historic site with its arched interior and circular pulpit, and the service was conducted in a true dignified Baptist manner. Even when the choir sang and Uncle Jim led the solo, which had Celeste totally filled with the spirit, the parishioners acknowledged intermittently with controlled "Amens." She clapped and shouted loudly when Uncle Jim finished his solo. Everybody turned stiffly to look at her.

After church, they walked down 137th and 138th Streets admiring the lovely single family homes. Uncle Jim explained that these blocks of beautiful brownstones got the name Strivers' Row because in the 1950's when Black professionals were striving to do better and got an opportunity to purchase the buildings, they all landed on these two blocks.

He had taken her to the infamous Sugar Hill on St. Nicholas Avenue, an area that was once a very high-rent district. "Sugar" was slang for money. The homes and apartment buildings had been occupied mostly by Jews. When they all fled Harlem, land-lords rented to Blacks who could afford to pay.

Sammy lived on Sugar Hill in Aunt June's first apartment from the late 1940's. Her name was still on the lease and Sammy only paid $220 a month because of the city's rent control law. The law, instituted in the 1950's, was enacted when elderly tenants needed younger relatives to move in to help care for them. The rent control law championed this cause, whereby rent could only be in-creased seven percent a year because of the act of kindness showed toward a relative in need.

"I tell you, Celeste," when Harlem was in its heyday, on Sun-days people would stroll the avenues just like we're doing now. Showing off their Sunday best. Then they would go and stand in the line for some good home cooking at Sylvia's," said Uncle Jim. After waiting in line at Sylvia's an hour, Celeste ate some deli-cious salmon croquettes, macaroni and cheese, and collard greens. Uncle Jim had the smothered pork chops, sweet potatoes, and string beans. She was more than pleased that it was all worth the long wait. Especially the sweet potato pie.

Exhausted from her first few days in the big city before even one day of work, she considered calling the office with an excuse. As she sank into her bubble bath wondering what to wear, she decided not to delay the inevitable.

Uncle Jim was in the kitchen singing gloriously with that bari-tone voice and cooking breakfast for all, including Aunt June's lady friends Miss Diane and Miss Audrey from down the hall, who ate together at one apartment or another each morning.

"I saw you at church yesterday," said Miss Audrey, an usher at Abyssinian. "Hope you enjoyed the service."

"It was nice," Celeste answered politely. "Especially the singing," she said, complementing her uncle.

"Well next week, I will take you to Convent Avenue Baptist Church, where *I've* been a member for years," said Miss Diane.

"What's it like?" asked Celeste, who decided from now on she would inquire about the type of service beforehand.

"Not too quiet and not too loud. Convent has just the right amount of 'Hallelujah' and 'Have Mercy' to let you know you've been to church without having to struggle to stay awake," said Miss Diane looking over at Miss Audrey.

"Sounds nice," said Celeste, calmly sipping her tea. It was as if Miss Diane had read her mind.

After breakfast, Celeste cruised out of the door to catch the limited-stop bus to her new office. She had said to heck with those whacked-out subway instructions Sammy gave her; Uncle Jim had given her the bus routes to take in Manhattan. After all, he did drive a bus for 40 years. Celeste could not imagine herself doing anything for 40 years. Not a job, not a hobby, not even a husband. She'd have to take the time to ponder the psychology of that thought later. Now it was time to mentally prepare for the sharks.

Celeste found the bus to be was such a nice ride to midtown, not at all the hustled feeling she felt even on a Saturday in the subway. She had decided the bus was the mode of transportation for her or she'd end up crazy and stressed before she got to work everyday like the rest of those folks down there.

Celeste entered the office of Mr. Ed Townsend on the 18th floor of One Times Square Plaza. He was the publisher of the number one newspaper in the country. That was power.

"Hi, I'm Celeste ..."

"Toussaint, and you have a 10:30 appointment to see Mr.

Townsend," interrupted a perky co-ed in black leggings and a Metallica T-shirt. "Well, you're ten minutes early. Have a seat."

"Yes, I am. Yes, I do, and yes, thank you, I will sit," replied Celeste, annoyed this greeter would not let her get a word in edgewise. "Your name is?"

"Jane Silverman, executive assistant to Mr. Townsend," she said looking at her nails, obviously very pleased with herself.

"Oh, really," Celeste said, wondering how the publisher of the number one paper in the country could allow his executive assistant to wear leggings and any old T-shirt to the office to greet his visitors.

"I'm sure you are terribly busy around here," Celeste said trying to make small talk.

"Well," said Jane, smiling as she put a stick of gum in her mouth on top of the wad she already had, "the production and editorial staffs, sure, they stay crazy down there. But you see, up here," she said, leaning over her desk and whispering to her guest, "we tend to the executive matters, and of course to Mr. Townsend's outside business interests."

Celeste cleared her throat and forced a smile. "But of course." She was seriously thinking, *OK, Daddy, I know you said give the situation my best shot, but this was ludicrous.*

Celeste politely picked up the morning edition of the New York Daily Courier so she would not have to continue to make small talk with The Jane. The office door opened and in walked a gentleman with a beard and a backpack.

The Jane giggled and kissed the man on the lips, "Morning, ET This here is Celeste Toussaint."

Ed Townsend walked over to her as she peered over the top of her paper not believing her eyes. Here stood the Ed Townsend in full cowboy regalia. Ragged blue jeans, cowboy boots with spurs, a turquoise and silver belt, topped off with a dusty cowboy hat.

Celeste screamed in her head, *Daddy!!!* , before she stood up all smiles and shook the infamous publisher's hand as poised as you please, "Good morning, sir. It is certainly a pleasure to meet you finally."

"Likewise, Miss Toussaint. You come with me." Celeste snatched a look at herself in a wall mirror and was quite pleased with the way she looked in her red suit. As she walked behind Mr. Townsend, in his rodeo outfit, she wished she still had on her Mickey Mouse nightshirt.

The publisher sat behind his mahogany desk and threw his beautiful boots on top of it, reclining in his chair. "I want you to know your reputation proceeds you, Miss Toussaint."

"I hope that's good," she said as she wrote in her notepad.

"Obviously or you wouldn't be here. You see, we only have the best minds working for us. However, the nature of your coverage will be more fun than the education beat, but certainly more grueling and time-consuming as well.

"The entertainment beat is unlike no other. You'll have to attend everything from screenings, to formal openings, to lunches and showcases. The business demands a personable, enthusiastic, energetic presence, who won't compromise her craft or take any shit from those trying to sell it. And from what I am told by my good buddy, that indeed is you."

"Thank you sir, I'll do my best."

"And cut the 'sir' shit. Everybody calls me ET, got it?"

"Got it ET, sir, I mean ET."

"And while you're writing, make sure that's ET with no periods in between. Got it?"

"I've got it, ET," she smiled.

"Your editor is Marcia Mason, one of the best in the business. You will report directly to her. When you find the workload overwhelming, just let her know and she will let you have a day off and assign a freelancer to your beat. Weekends are a must most times and you will find yourself so busy that this will become your life." He was uncomfortably aware she didn't blink.

ET continued, "With this job, you will be under a huge spotlight attached to an even larger magnifying glass. Every move you make will be scrutinized. Now we have a contract for you to sign," he said pushing it toward her.

Celeste folded her hands in her lap firmly, crossed her legs, and peered at him so intensely he looked away for a moment. "What contract," she said, not taking her eyes off of his.

"It's strictly a formality. It states that you will be paid $40,000 per annum, and you are not to write for any other paper. Not that you would have time to anyway, but all of our department editors have to sign this. It protects us from someone stealing you for one year, and it protects you from getting caught up in the changing of the guard, if there is any while your contract is in effect."

"May I have this reviewed by my lawyer before I sign? I can have it back to you by the end of the week," she said with butter.

Ed didn't like her not signing the contract on the spot. Taylor had told him she was not a desperate lady. In fact he remembered his words exactly: "If you mess with her, Ed, she is the type of woman who would tell you to kiss off and then go to have a manicure."

"I expect your counsel to look this over before signing it. It's the right thing to do."

"Thank you," Celeste said kindly, while thinking, *Now, go ahead and fall out of your chair, cowboy.* Attorney Charles Toussaint had taught her to never sign a legal document. Her Daddy would tell her if it was legit.

ET buzzed Jane. "Will you take Celeste to her office and tell Rick to get a move on it after lunch," he said and escorted her to the door. "You have a good first day and don't hesitate to talk to me about anything that may be of importance to you. My door is always open."

"Thank you for the invitation."

The Jane popped her gum. "That's a pretty color, that suit. Your editor Marcia, she wears pretty clothes, too."

What kind of talk was that for a grown woman, "that's a pretty color, that suit," Celeste thought and stared at her before answering, "Thank you," while praying, *Oh yes, Father in Heaven, thank you for one somebody with a fashion sense around this place.*

When the 10th floor elevator doors opened, the sound was deafening. People were shouting, phones were ringing, faxes were receiving, and everyone was moving super fast. It was a mess! Celeste just shook her head, thinking she had expected more than such chaos.

Jane knocked on Marcia's door once and opened it while ushering Celeste into the immaculate space. "Mason, this here is Celeste Toussaint. I'll see you around, just come up if you have any questions, I'll be glad ta help ya."

Celeste nodded thanks to The Jane and exchanged pleasantries with her new managing editor. Marcia, as she said she liked to be called, was in her late 30's but looked like she was in her late 40's. Marcia had thick brown hair that she played with when talking, putting on and taking off her headband. She had worked for ET for 10 years, beginning with the same job now held by The Jane. The *New York Daily Courier* was her life. She spent every waking moment at the office. As a result, she had never married and now, since she was so used to being alone, not only did Marcia doubt that she would ever get married, she doubted if she would ever want to join such an institution.

Celeste knew anyone who was so dedicated to their job was going to be a task master. "I just want you to know," Marcia said, "I am considered the old maid around here, because this job is my life. You will also hear nasty rumors about ET and me as a couple. Don't pay them any attention, they are just rumors," she said, satisfied she'd convinced the reporter of her innocence, and put on her headband for the 11th time.

"Thank you for the warning," Celeste said, wondering if she had a sign that read "Boo-Boo The Fool" plastered on her forehead.

Marcia took off her headband and began to braid the end of

her thick mane. "I'm sorry I won't be able to introduce you around the industry this week, but I had to cover your empty seat and I have three pieces to complete," she said, enjoying the additional work.

Marcia obviously had a heavy work load, but the only signs of her being frazzled in any way was that nervous twitch she had of playing with her hair and hair accessories. Otherwise she was as "done" as the divas Celeste knew back home in such positions.

"But don't you worry, they all know your name and they know you start today. In fact, here are a stack of messages for you already. You're invited to a luncheon for Whitney Houston at noon, and I have already called in your R.S.V.P.

"I want you to feel free to suggest any story ideas to me. I am quite open to different creative angles," Marcia said while unbraiding the braid she just braided. "Keep your eyes open for any and all twists on the entertainment beat. For instance, the luncheon today is at B. Smith's Restaurant. It's owned by former model Barbara Smith. I know there is a good feature there. So that's the kind of thing I'm looking for from you."

"I'll do my best," replied Celeste.

"Also, you should know the entertainment beat is the most coveted position on the staff and every writer, except the two who do homicide, were all dying for the opportunity. So there is a tremendous amount of animosity toward you already."

"But why?" Celeste asked incredulously.

"Honestly?"

Celeste's eyes said *Spit it out, sister.*

Marcia couldn't answer fast enough, "OK, the truth is that you're an outsider coming in and snatching out the most valued position right from under those who have been here and put in their time. If I were you, I wouldn't worry about it too much. These kids bounce back fast. Just be your charming self and everything will be fine. Because when it comes down to it, the only two people who really matter around here to you are ET and me. The paper may be owned by him, but I run the show. Got that?"

"I understand clearly," Celeste said, relieved.

"I got you an office *with* a window, which will also cause envy. But with all you're going to be doing, you will need to close a door for quiet when you need it."

"You should be running on over to the luncheon now. When you come back, I'll have your calendar for the rest of the week including a lunch with just the two of us," smiled Marcia. "Here are your business cards."

The cards read: Miss Celeste Toussaint, Entertainment Editor.

Someone was really paying attention to detail. Celeste was impressed and she liked the managing editor *and* her whip. Celeste knew that working in the number one market would be no cakewalk. Marcia didn't seem a bit conniving the way Wayne had turned out to be back home. No, this Marcia was straight-up no-chaser from the beginning. She and ET are allies. The only thing she didn't reveal openly up front was that relationship part between the two of them. No problem, because where Marcia got her socks off was none of Celeste's business anyway.

"Thanks for everything, Marcia," Celeste said warmly. "Do I look presentable enough to attend a luncheon with Whitney Houston?"

Marcia laughed hysterically. "Let's just say your press colleagues will be impressed. You'll see."

ELEVEN

C eleste stepped out onto Times Square and looked up at the building where the ball has been dropped on New Year's Eve as far back as she could remember. Walking west on 42nd Street toward the Port Authority Bus Terminal, it took Celeste only a few minutes to realize that the stretch between Seventh and Eighth Avenues were among the seediest, dirtiest, and most risque she had ever seen. What she couldn't figure out was why triple X-rated video shops with live nude dancers, peep-show joints and prostitutes were casually lounging out in the midst of the heart of the city.

She continued to walk in amazement at all of the lewd activity taking place in broad daylight. Even though she knew she looked like a tourist, Celeste peeked into several of those places to see exactly what was the attraction and was not listed as one in any "Welcome to New York" brochure.

Celeste finally got up her nerve to walk all the way into the Show Time Lounge. Her first thought was, *You're kidding, right?* There were men all over the place watching women dance nude. Women were dancing on the main stage, dancing on table tops, and wiggling in men's laps. The men were absolutely drooling, and had looks of complete satisfaction on their faces.

Upon second glance at these women dancing, Celeste saw that some of them looked like they were not women at all. Some looked like they were children in women's clothing, or pieces thereof. Some were women old enough to be her mother but with bodies that put even her bottle-shaped frame to shame.

She walked slowly around the sex shoppe smelling for the angle of this story that should be exposed first. In one corner there were two young women with suitcases, negotiating "day rates," Celeste overheard the manager say. It was painfully obvious these girls were fresh off of the buses or trains that dumped thousands into the world-famous Times Square each day.

In another corner was a young white girl who looked no more than 18 years old, playing hostess to the men who walked in the door. She escorted each of them to the fantasy of their choice. The strangest thing of all was, 95 percent of the men were dressed in business attire and carried briefcases. It was as though this den of iniquity was just one of their casual pitstops before cutting million- dollar deals.

Celeste pretended to look at the Triple-X videos lining the walls and counted the men in suits. Out of 48 patrons, there were 42 in suits who decided to have sex for lunch first. She couldn't believe that they chose a very public establishment versus one more private. The biggest angle to this story was going to be who owned these joints. She could smell it and it stank. Yes indeed, it stank.

Just as she headed for the door, Miss 18-year-old Hostess Without The Mostest on her overdeveloped young body stopped her, "I saw you come in," she said breathlessly, "but I had to take care of my regulars first."

Whaaaat! thought Celeste, *42 men in ties were regulars, this is going to be explosive.*

"My name is Muffin," she said with a slight Southern accent. "I haven't seen you in here before, what's your name?"

Muffin's Southern hospitality shocked her. Celeste recovered quickly knowing she'd better lie about her name.

"My name is Monica, and I just got to town today. I was passing by and decided to pop in."

"Well, Monica, is it work or pleasure you seek today?"

Celeste was too surprised at the question to speak, so Miss Muffin explained.

"I see all types, honey. Some ladies think that to get a job in this joint you have to dress up in a suit like you to apply. You know, looking for a little hustle on the side. And some ladies in suits come here for just as much pleasure as these here men," she said flinging an arm beyond her where the action was in full effect.

Get out! thought Celeste while grinding her teeth together so her mouth would not fly open.

"I've been here long enough to have seen it all," Muffin advised, getting back to business, "So Monica, which is it, work or pleasure today?"

"Neither," said Celeste/Monica, thinking about the ladies in the suits looking for a hustle, "I'm totally playing tourist at the moment."

"OK, if you say so. But if you change your mind, we have three spots open immediately. Decide quick, though, because with a Greyhound pulling in down the street at the Port every five minutes, there's always a new face."

"What exactly is the application process?" pried Celeste, curious now.

"You come in to see Sal, that's him over there with those two gals, and if he thinks you might be good, he'll take you in back for the screening."

"What happens in the screening?" asked Celeste, afraid to hear the answer.

"Well you know, Sal needs to see the goods."

The look on Celeste's face read, *What goods?*

Muffin answered, "He needs to see, you know, your stuff. You stand on this platform and perform for him. Right down to your birthday suit," she giggled.

"And then he decides who gets the job. Right?"

"Right. You've got it, Monica."

"I see that you guys are busy in here," Celeste said with a tone that showed she just might be interested in a screening.

"Every day," Muffin huffed. "During lunch and after work, this place is really buzzing. Our clientele is mostly professional. That's why Sal has to screen the gals. We have to be able to have intellectual conversations with them *if* it's conversation they want," Muffin giggled again.

"And just how long have you been greeting customers and having these intellectual conversations?" Celeste whispered real girlfriend-like.

"I started out two years ago behind the glass, then after a year I worked my way up to the stage and now I'm the official greeter. I've been here longer than anybody. So I know all of these Johns from those days. Sal never had nobody greeting the Johns before. I convinced him it would be a nice touch," she said looking around pleased that everyone had been dedicated her personal attention.

"You learn a lot," Muffin continued without a hint of remorse, "talking to these guys every day about what they want and what they don't want. And besides, by talking to everyone who comes in here, well you know, many of them are powerful. And one day I'm gonna be a star."

Celeste's mind processed the info but her face read, *You look too young to even be here.*

"Don't worry, Monica, I am of age. My youthful appearance is part of my appeal. There are many things that go on here but hiring gals under age ain't one of them. If one of them is under 18, they lied to Sal. Honey, around this place, no ID, no job."

"I see. Thank you very much for your time, Muffin. I will stop in to see you again, let me get up my nerve. Don't forget me."

"Oh I won't, that's another reason why Sal has me here on the door. I never forget a name. And I betcha you don't either."

"You're right. Have a good day, 'bye now," Celeste said, walking out of the door back onto the street, totally amazed at the lunchtime education presented to her by Muffin. That little girl should have been at home with her family somewhere south of the Mason Dixon line with "Muffin" embroidered on a local sports team uniform, versus "Muffin" being a moniker attached to her because of some sexual performances. The idea of this whole nude dance club thing had Celeste's blood pressure on the rise. By this time she was 30 minutes late for lunch with Whitney Houston.

TWELVE

Walking in the direction of the restaurant, Celeste heard a man and a woman having a tense argument in the doorway of a restaurant. The man kept slapping her face every time she tried to speak. When it looked as though she was going to scream, he covered her mouth to silence her. Several people simply walked past, just as though it was planned-and-paid-for street theatrics. Celeste ran back a block to a police car she'd seen parked there.

"Officers! Officers! Help! Come now. There is a woman down there who looks like she is in trouble and nobody is helping her!" she said frantically.

The fat bald officer spoke, "What do you want lady? This is Times Square," taking a bite of his white-powdered donut, leaving the residue all over his mouth. He continued to talk while chewing, "I'd be surprised if someone did stop ta help," taking another bite of his donut. "See that's hows I can tell you're not from here, because you ran ta get us."

Celeste was perplexed by his response. "You're trying to tell me just because this is Times Square, nobody would report anything to you because this kind of thing happens all of the time?" she said sarcastically.

"That's what I'm tellin' ya!"

"And you're trying to tell me, the woman who is back there who looks like she's about to get her teeth kicked in by a man in broad daylight, is not worth you doing anything, because you're having coffee and donuts?"

"No ma'am, that's not what I'm tellin' ya. Listen, did she actually call for help?"

"Well no, but ..."

Fatty interrupted her, "See there, she hasn't called for help. So ..." he said taking another bite, "I'm tryin' ta say, she is probably a whore, and he's probably her pimp. And she probably didn't give 'em all the money. So that's why there's a fight. We can't goes a runnin' everytime some pimp slaps up his whore."

"Excuse me officer, but are pimping and whoring legal anyhow? Hypothetically if I were the one back there, just an average citizen, you, Mr. Policeman, would think it must be another pimp-and-whore fight?" Celeste was dazed beyond belief by his indifference.

She narrowed her eyes and fired hot sauce in his face, "How dare you make such an assumption? There clearly might be a life on the line."

"Here we go chasing a maybe." He reluctantly snatched up the radio and phoned it in to headquarters. Celeste was seething, "So you choose to call it in, instead of walking your fat butt back down this street less than 100 steps?"

The cop was irate with her now, "You got it," he said and stuffed the rest of his donut into his mouth defiantly.

"No, I've got *you* Officer Janus, shield number 8820 of the Midtown South Precinct."

"And what do you plan to do with that?"

"You'll see when you read it on the front page of the newspaper tomorrow. You know what, Officer, this will be exceptionally juicy news if that woman, whom I can identify, turns up dead all because you chose to be the clean-up crew instead of the prevention crew, now, won't it?"

"And who do you think you are that you can manage getting it on the front page tomorra if she does turn up dead?"

"Only one of the *Daily Courier's* editors. That's who," Celeste said and smiled her best now-fuck-you-smile.

She was storming down the street when she felt someone grab her arm. After what she had witnessed in this town she had one hand on the pistol her Daddy gave her.

"I'm sorry Officer Janus was so rude to you. Please allow me to apologize for him."

He was absolutely the finest man in blue she had ever seen: Six feet four. Smooth paper-bag-brown-colored skin. Chestnut eyes with long curly lashes. And this gorgeous specimen was holding her arm. For a minute she almost forgot she was pissed.

"First of all," she said, snatching her arm away so angry that her voice was just above a whisper, "how dare you walk up behind a woman you don't know and grab her on the street? Where I come from, that could get you killed. Secondly, I don't want your apology for fatso. Let him apologize to the people of New York City. And third, you should be apologizing for your own self. How could you let a white pompous dog talk like that to a Black woman? What's wrong with you, brother? Don't you have a mother or a sister?"

"You're absolutely right," he said, dazzling 32 gorgeous pearly whites, "I apologize for my behavior, my mother and my sister would have been appalled. But what I really had to say to Officer Janus, I would never have said in front of any beautiful Nubian sister such as yourself. And for using my manners, Mom and Sis would be proud."

Celeste almost melted in the middle of the street. "I accept your apology. As for fatso back there, he thinks because he has a pistol and a badge he has power. I have something equally as powerful ... a pen," and she raised her eyebrows to his confirming she was right.

"Do what you've got to about him, he's a prick. I'm just stuck with him for today. I could care less. What else can I say?"

"You can say you'll walk up here with me to see if this lady is OK."

"Let's go."

When they got to the doorway, the commotion was over completely. Celeste was devastated she thought, *That poor woman. God only knows what could have happened to her, or what the circumstances were that led up to someone treating her that way. The man had rage in his eyes.*

"I know," said the policeman, "I'm very sorry."

"I have got to get to a press luncheon," she said, conceding to the fact she was unable to help. "You keep your eyes open, you hear?"

"I hear. 'Bye now."

He walked away backwards waving goodbye when he shouted after her, "Hey, news lady. I don't know your name."

"You can call me Gal Friday," she said, trying to be funny. Taking into account all she'd seen in half a day's work at her new job, she doubted if she would ever tell anyone her real name. "And you?"

He laughed loudly and said, "Call me Officer Friendly."

They both waved to each other and she walked into the door of B. Smith's restaurant to meet her colleagues.

THIRTEEN

Beyond the madness on the streets directly outside the huge glass and brass doors, Barbara Smith had done a fantastic job creating a serene environment with art deco on the inside of her now famous restaurant. A tall elegant Black woman who looked quite familiar to Celeste swept across the floor to greet her.

"Welcome to B. Smith's, are you on the list for the luncheon?"

"Yes, I'm Celeste Toussaint from *The Daily Courier*," she said, finally glad to be able to say her own name.

"Terrific. I'm Barbara Smith."

"It's wonderful to meet you," Celeste said, recognizing the very popular former high-fashion model instantly now from years of magazine covers. "I've been in town all of three days and I've heard a lot about you and the restaurant. It's fabulous," she commented, looking around. The aroma of the foods wafted to her nostrils. It was wonderfully intoxicating.

"Thank you very much. We work hard around here," Barbara said with a pride that comes from knowing a job has been well done. "Come this way, they are saving a seat for you."

The mauve and tan tables were so warm and cozy. The high-backed padded chairs afforded patrons optimum comfort as they

dined. The waist-high gold vases with extraordinary floral arrangements added a very rich touch. Celeste eyed the delectable dishes
as she passed the tables and noticed each entree was presented
picture perfect. Suddenly she realized she was starving.

"When you're not too busy in the near future, I would like to
do a feature on you, Barbara."

"We can do it any time you like."

"Fantastic."

"Celeste Toussaint, this is Donna Jones, vice president of publicity at Arista Records. She is your hostess this afternoon."

Donna greeted Celeste. She took her to all of the tables and
introduced her to each reporter, writer, and photographer in the
room. She noticed how casually they all dressed and mostly in all
black. Was that the New York fashion trend? If it was, she would
always be over-dressed.

They finally made their way to Whitney Houston and Celeste
was seated next to her. The interview and lunch were wonderful.
By the time lunch was concluded, she felt like the two of them had
known each other from way back.

The gentleman on the other side of Miss Houston was Dre
Tyson, the entertainment editor from the largest Black weekly in
the country, *The New York Stand.* He was a hoot. Dre repeatedly
called them "girlfriend" and snapped his fingers at the end of every sentence. He had Celeste and Whitney rolling.

Dre was tall and rail-thin. He looked like a Mounds candy bar.
The whites of his eyes and his teeth glistened just like the shred-
ded coconut on the inside. His forecast on life was perpetually set
to sunshine. You had to love him.

Celeste was truly going to like this gig if luncheons with champagne and such good company at high noon were to be considered
work. Those were the kind of working conditions she could get
used to permanently.

Before leaving, Celeste and Dre posed for pictures with
Whitney. Dre dished out orders to his photographer. "You better

take an entire roll with me in it, brother man. Some on my good side. Some on my bad side. Because if you mess these up you're fired."

The two of them hugged Whitney before leaving and walked outside hand-in-hand.

"Come on, girlfriend, I'll walk you to your office," said Dre.

"Thanks, but promise me we won't walk down Eighth Avenue. Let's take another street," she pleaded.

"And why, may I ask, don't you want to partake in the sights and sounds of the Avenue?"

"Because I took the scenic route on my way here today and it's what made me late for lunch. If I can help it, I don't ever want to walk down that Avenue again," Celeste said and then shared the events of the early afternoon.

Dre stopped walking and faced her, placing his hands on her shoulders, "Do you know how big this story can be? You have stumbled onto something major. We New Yorkers have a tendency to overlook many things. I mean, these strip joints have been here for years but no one has ever really bothered to investigate them, not from this angle anyway." He was getting totally excited now. The sign of a good journalist.

"Listen, Celeste. This thing could be big. Imagine cracking one of the biggest scandals this town has ever seen. The patrons who frequent those places is what always bugged me out. Honestly, I never thought about their owners. It took you, an outsider, to wonder who owns those joints."

"I need to call a meeting with ET to ask him to let me do this."

"Be for real, Celeste. You are the entertainment editor. There is no way he is going to allow you to cross the line."

"You think so, huh?"

"I know so."

"Then you go for it, Dre. I'll give you the tiny bit of info I have so far. But whatever you need to know, Miss Muffin is the key."

"Don't tell me to go for it. You might be an entertainment editor now, but you know you're the investigative journalist of the year with that Chicago Board of Education scandal. Who would have thought school administrators participated in such dirty activity?" said Dre, shaking his head. "You, my sister, uncovered it well. The news of your work made it all the way to New York. So don't tell me to go for it. You stumbled on this thing, it's your baby. I'll give you the platform."

"I can't do that."

"Why not? I won't tell anybody. Besides *this* is news. It's exactly the type of story that *The Stand* would be delighted to blow out of the water all over page one. You can even write it under a pen name."

"I can't do that. I have a contract I haven't even signed here from ET, which I got only this morning. It says I cannot write for any other paper, and my beat is strictly entertainment."

"Come on Celeste, do this story in a series for me. Do it under a pen name, we'll think of something catchy. I'll offer you $3,000 to get started and $3,000 when you break this story wide open and we sell papers like crazy," Dre pleaded.

"I really don't know, Dre."

"Listen honey, how far do you think 40 thousand will last you here?" he said pulling on her suit.

She looked at him wondering how he knew what her salary was.

"Honey, I know everything, I am a reporter, ain't I?" he said, with a wink. "Listen sweetheart, everyone has a hustle in this town, and my advice to you is that you get one, too."

Celeste began to think there was really something to this hustle thing Sammy was trying to tell her about. "Yeah, you're probably right, and that's why there are young women down the street dancing in their birthday suits right now, because they need a hustle to stay alive."

"You see there," screamed Dre, "you even have a sentiment

toward those girls. This is Pulitzer Prize material, honey. I am telling you, Pulitzer Prize material. Plus six thou from The Stand for the series."

Celeste pondered for a moment, especially the extra money. The first thing she would do would be to invest it so her Uncle Jim could be comfortable in his retirement. She didn't like him driving that cab all hours of the night.

"Six thousand dollars to write one series?" she asked suspiciously knowing that was above the average rate for an in-depth piece.

"Yep, that's right," Dre beamed.

"Dre, I'm sure you're a stand-up guy, but don't come blowing sunshine my way when it comes to money, OK? I'm already thinking about how I'm going to spend it."

"I'm not pulling your leg."

"Well Dre, who are you to offer me that kind of money for a story? As a matter of fact, who are you to hire me for something like this? I know you're the entertainment editor and all. But I didn't know editors had so much power," she asked suspiciously.

"Can you keep a secret?" he questioned.

"Of course."

"I'm not just the entertainment editor. I'm also the publisher."

"I see," said Celeste trying to piece together his logic of hiding the truth.

"Now you're wondering why the publisher of a newspaper also masquerades as the entertainment editor."

"Yes, I was kind of thinking along those lines."

"I so thoroughly enjoy the theatre and any type of music, I couldn't ever imagine not rendering my opinions about them on paper. Besides, I could never find a reporter who could capture the true essence of the arts like I could," he said with finality and snapped his finger.

Celeste clapped enthusiastically, "I can tell you really mean it."

"Yes I do, girlfriend, and this is our secret."

She held up her right hand, "I'll never tell anyone."

"Good. Back to business ... the offer still stands for you."

"I haven't even written my first piece for *The Courier* and here we are discussing my moonlighting possibilities under an assumed name."

They laughed and walked downtown on Seventh Avenue looking at each marquee for the Broadway shows, while collecting flyers for all sorts of things. There were two in particular which caught Celeste's eye.

"Oh look Dre, a sample sale at Tahari and Donna Karan. What's a sample sale?"

"A sample sale is usually held in the showroom of the manufacturer where they offer their overstocked, slightly damaged, or off-season clothing to the public at substantial discounts."

Celeste's mouth hung open, "Get out!"

"It's true girlfriend," he said with a snap. "You can get serious bargains at those places. Living here, you should never have to pay retail prices again," he said in a real didn't-you-know-that tone.

"It's just like being on this entertainment beat," Dre continued his lesson, "You don't ever have to pay to see another play, concert, or buy another record."

"Why not?" asked Celeste.

"Because you are the entertainment editor of the number one paper in the country, chile."

"So," said Celeste, more interested in the way she had just discovered how to buy Tahari wholesale.

"So," said Dre, exhaling loudly, "sooo girlfriend, if you want to take your aunt and uncle to see *Phantom of the Opera*, you call them up, throw around your title, they ask you when you would like to go, and they will messenger the tickets to you!

"Or let's say you want the entire Whitney Houston music collection. You call Donna at Arista, who you just met back there, ask her for it, and it's yours. Baby, this beat is sweet. The perks are outrageous. Why do you think all of the other reporters want to work entertainment!"

Celeste still was not as impressed as her friend. "Dre, I would never use my position that way," she said, admonishing him for the thought. "I want to know how do I get on the mailing lists for these showrooms?"

"You aren't even listening to me," said Dre throwing his hands in the air. "You really are 100 percent femme, aren't you?"

"Dre, leave me alone, I was raised to be a diva, " she teased, impatiently stamping her foot. "Please tell me, tell me, tell me. The list. How do I get on these lists?"

"You have to go spend money there first," he said, stepping into the street.

"Ain't nothing to it but to do it," she said, happy with her new information. "Dre, don't walk against the light with all of these cars moving so fast."

"Honey, everybody stands in the street until the light changes. Relax."

"Well you are not everybody. Don't be in such a rush like all of these other people. Safety first."

He couldn't help but to laugh at her. "You stay just like you are. If you can manage to live here and not get caught up in the hustle and bustle of things, you'll live longer."

She very much enjoyed being with her new friend and was reluctant to leave him when they got to the door of One Times Square Plaza. He kissed both sides of her cheeks Hollywood style and promised to see her later that night for the Grover Washington Jr. listening party.

"I didn't know about a party tonight, what will I wear?"

"Wear what you're wearing, you look great, girlfriend. When I get to my office I'm going to call you with the calendar so you will be everywhere you need to be."

"How sweet."

"I'm trying to take good care of you, so you will know I'm

serious about that little thing we discussed."

"Yeah, yeah, yeah. I hear you. Let me get to work."

He put up the peace sign to her and left. In the elevator she tried to make some sense of the events. How in the world was she going to get her work done for *The Courier* and report for *The Stand* in between the lunches and concerts? It was already 2:30. She had better get her butt to writing about Miss Houston instead of thinking about Miss Muffin's hustle and her coterie of confused characters.

She got settled behind her desk and dialed Chicago.

"Hello," said Annie Mae.

"Mommie! Get Daddy on the other phone. Guess who I just had lunch with?"

"Who, baby?" asked Annie Mae, picking up on her daughter's excitement.

"Whitney. Houston," she said in a can-you-believe-it tone. Celeste just had to call her folks and tell them about her lunch because she was about to burst.

FOURTEEN

If Celeste had to say so herself, the Whitney Houston piece was sheer brilliance. It turned out to be easy writing about someone who was so talented and friendly. Whitney's concert was the following Friday night at Madison Square Garden and Celeste knew she would blow the roof off of the joint.

Marcia strolled into her office, sat on the edge of her desk, and unbraided her mane. "So what did you think of the gang?"

"They were great," Celeste said sincerely, "everybody seems so carefree and happy."

"Yes they are, until it's time for them to meet a deadline," said Marcia from experience. "And how else do you expect them to act when they're being fed the best food in town and pumped with champagne?"

Celeste agreed, "A fact, indeed."

"Speaking of deadlines, I forgot to tell you about a Grover Washington listening party tonight."

"I've already heard."

"Good, because the piece must be done by 10 tonight for tomorrow's issue. Fortunately it's right down the street at Chez Josephine's, so you can run right back and finish the piece. I want you to enjoy yourself, but hit it and quit it. Get the info you need, have the photographer take the appropriate photos, and come back with the goods. "

"Yes ma'amm," said Celeste, while saluting to confirm her marching orders had been received and understood.

"Oh, I almost forgot," said Marcia, reaching into her pocket. "Here are a supply of car vouchers. You can get a car home any time after 9 when you're out working late. Just call the number and give them the account information."

"Thanks," said Celeste. She had just been wondering how she was going to get home after working such late hours.

"Don't forget the deadline is 10 o' clock sharp," repeated Marcia before she slammed the door.

"Taskmaster," whispered Celeste under her breath.

Chez Josephine's restaurant was a narrow, delightful presentation of Josephine Baker's artform and her life. The restaurant was packed already when she arrived. The Columbia Records VP of publicity slid up to her to introduce himself and whisked her over to the saved seat at Grover's table. Celeste was keeping in mind Marcia's orders, so she concentrated on the sweet, saxy sounds piping through the speakers, already formulating an opinion on this new piece of music.

Celeste had just closed her eyes and began getting into the groove of the next cut when she heard Dre summon her from across the room. She peeled herself out of the reverie that had her so engrossed to check in with him.

"Girlfriend, don't be sitting over there all by yourself. Here, have some champagne. The party's over here!!!"

The crowd chanted, "Hey! Party's over here! Party's over here!" Celeste smiled and greeted her colleagues for the second time that day, from *The New York Times, The New York Post, Jet Magazine, Right On! Magazine*, and from various television programs.

"Maybe we should push all of these tables back and show these people how we Chicago folks can party," said a voice from behind her.

Celeste turned around and was face-to-face with her homie Maurice. "What are you doing here?" she asked, throwing her arms around his neck.

"I told you I was a radio producer. This is my turf, too," explained Maurice.

"We are also best friends," interjected Dre.

"Yes we are," said Renee, sliding between the two fellas and linking arms.

Celeste shook her head. "This is a small world. Renee I didn't know you were a writer, too."

"Oh no, Miss Girl, I'm one of those dancers on Broadway that you three get to write about," she giggled. "When I'm between shows, I get to tag along with these fellas as a date."

"Yeah, Celeste, I forgot to tell you earlier," interjected Dre. "You can always bring a guest to an evening function or to a show. But never to a lunch."

"Very cool," Celeste mused. "From now on, Renee, you can be my guest and let these guys bring somebody else. That way we girls can chit-chat about those dancing gigs. I dance, too."

"You do!"

"Yep, at home I was in a dance company and everything."

"Well girl, we've got to keep you in shape. This weekend I'll pick you up and we'll go to dance class."

"I'd love that!"

"It's African dancing with drummers lined up all around the walls. Can you hang, Miss Girl?"

"Can I hang?" asked Celeste and sucked her teeth. "You'll see."

Grover made his grand entrance with Phyllis Hyman on his arm. She was the featured vocalist on the album. Now that was a winning combination. Celeste interviewed Grover "The Great," and had *The Courier* photographer take photos all around. She tried to sip ever so slightly on the glass of champagne Dre had given her because it was 8:30 and she had a story to write. She took a grilled shrimp on a skewer from a floating waiter and slipped out of the door.

Sammy promised he wouldn't get in the way when Celeste agreed to let him watch the dance class she and Renee were going to take. She had made him promise to work on his rap and get rid of that cold wave as an even exchange because she knew her couz had the hots for Renee.

When they arrived at the Harlem YMCA on 135th Street and Lenox Avenue, Renee was already dressed and stretching at the barre of the LaRocque Bey School of Dance. Celeste was dressed underneath her sweats, so she peeled out of them. Since Renee had Sammy mesmerized, he volunteered to hold their things during the class. Celeste shook her head and could not help thinking that her couz was whipped already and the girl had not even touched him.

Mr. LaRocque Bey, the owner of the school and instructor, was fabulous. He had a style very similar to the Muntu Dance Company that Celeste was a member of in Chicago. LaRocque was impressed with how well Renee and Celeste danced side by side. When it was time for him to show the class steps across the floor, he put them in front to lead the lines.

Celeste had not heard such great drumming since her days with Muntu, and the class was even more rigorous than she'd remembered. It felt good to "emote", as Renee put it, during class, expending all of her pent-up energy and emotion. It had been a grueling week at work. Celeste could see a little bulge in her belly. A wicked combination of too many weeks without exercise, too much champagne, and way too many late-night meals. As she stared at herself in the full-length mirrors, she vowed off of those vices she had picked up during her first week in New York City before they became a habit.

Sammy sat amazed that Renee was flirting with him while she danced. He was also thoroughly impressed with the agility of his little cousin. A couple of times he said, "Go on, couz!"

After class, LaRocque called Celeste and Renee into his office. His walls were covered with photos from his career. He was a huge cinnamon-colored man, about six feet six and he weighing over 225 pounds, but his movements were balletic and poised. Each photo captured the essence of his skill and grace.

"Renee, thank you for bringing this lovely lady to class today. It is wonderful to have someone walk in here and catch on so quickly," he complimented and kissed both sides of Celeste's face.

"Thanks," she said.

"Now, tell me about your dancing experience."

"Muntu Dance Company, Ebony Talent Theatre, Joel Hall, and Mayfair Academy."

"Mmm," LaRocque mused, "a Chicago girl. Well sweetie, I'm from Detroit."

"Same camp," Celeste and LaRoque said at the same time and slapped high five.

Renee looked at Sammy with a do-you-know-what's-going-on-here look?

Sammy whispered to her, "That must be some Midwest thing."

"Oh," Renee whispered back.

LaRocque was positively beaming now. "Well, I won't take no for an answer. I'd like you to join the Company immediately. Rehearsals are on Saturdays after regular class and then on Tuesdays when a show comes up. Renee, you're between shows, aren't you?"

"Yes sir," she confirmed.

Renee whispered to Celeste while LaRocque took a phone call, "Every dancer in town is dying to be in LaRocque's Company girl, they get paaaid."

No, thought Celeste, *not another hustle. No wonder so many people in New York had one, they just dropped down from the sky like little rays of sunshine.*

"Well ladies, since you didn't know you would have to stay today, you're dismissed. But I will see you next week," said LaRocque authoritatively. "Kiss, Kiss," he said, going back into the studio to begin the company rehearsal clapping his hands for order.

"Drummers, a six/eight if you please. All right everybody! Five, six, a five, six, seven, eight."

The drums exploded and the dancers followed LaRocque Bey, The Godfather of Harlem Dance, across the floor just as if he were the Pied Piper.

Renee and Celeste skipped down the front steps of the Y arm in arm, unable to contain their happiness. "Let's celebrate," said Celeste.

Sammy even agreed, "I think a celebration is in order. You two are terrific. Celeste, if you quit that job at the paper, I'll quit mine to become your agent."

"Sammy, you're so sweet," she said, kissing him on the cheek, "but I'm already 20 something and I don't have much life left in these knees or in this back."

"I know what you mean, girl, cause I'll be 20-something-more in December myself. Well, let's have a grown-up celebration, shall we?" squealed Renee.

"And just what does a grown-up celebration consist of, Miss Dance Diva?" asked Celeste.

"Fried chicken and waffles," said Renee factually. "Wells, here we come, and I'm paying!"

"Hey, Hey, Hey!" shouted Sammy, "That's my kind of celebration. But you all are going to ruin the good work-out you just had."

Renee dragged them both down the street. "Well I guess we have to do it all over again next week. Won't we?"

Wells Restaurant was an official Harlem landmark located on 133rd Street and Seventh Avenue now renamed after the great Adam Clayton Powell. They were famous for their delicious fried chicken and waffles. Anne Wells was the widow of Mr. Joe Wells, and she had worked diligently to see that her husband's establishment became an official city landmark. When Harlem was in its heyday,

Wells was used as a showplace for guys to bring in their pretty gals, and for the gals to show off their fine clothing. It was also the one place that you could guarantee would be open after the Cotton Club closed and appetites were high. It was the spot to round off perfect evenings and lovely afternoons, and Wells' success was evident in their perpetual long lines that no one ever minded waiting in.

Sammy was the first to finish his food and burp. Celeste admonished him quickly, "Uhh, you pig. Excuse yourself."

Renee was about to explain how the food had that kind of effect on you, especially after eating it so quickly, when she burped.

"OK, Miss Piglet, you excuse yourself, too, " she chastised.

Renee and Sammy were doubled over with laughter, because as soon as Celeste sopped up the last corner of her waffle and swallowed it, she followed suit.

They walked from Wells to Renee's house on 145th Street and Riverside Drive. She lived on the garden level of a brownstone building. It was called a two-bedroom, but it was really one bedroom and a half.

Renee had the place done from front to back with antiques. The hardwood floors were covered with authentic Oriental rugs. Her kitchen was exquisitely modern. It had a lucite table and highback chairs, utensils and decanters on the counters, also in lucite.

"Your place is gorgeous, Renee," Celeste complimented her friend. "You have really spent a fortune on furniture."

"I admit, buying anything for the home is my weakness. You should see what I have in my three storage rooms," stated Renee. "Every week I run down to my antique dealer at Sotheby's to see what she's saved for me."

"Renee, you have your own dealer at Sotheby's?" questioned Celeste.

"Yeah, I've had her for years," answered Renee matter-of-factly. "I will have to introduce you to her. Then I'll introduce you to my jeweler, my personal shopper, my hair stylist who comes to the house when I need her, and my designer. And oh yes, today I'm treating you to a facial, body wrap, massage, and hair treatment."

"You don't have to do that, honey," assured Celeste, "I'd be glad to pay for the works like that."

Renee was adamant, "No. No. No. I am paying. I want you to really enjoy yourself, and then you will be hooked on those pamper sessions twice a week just like I am."

The only thought Celeste had was, *Where did a dancer get the type of money to spend on antiques, hand-made jewels, and spa treatments twice a week?*

Sammy was most impressed with the apartment. "How much are they hitting you for rent?"

Celeste nudged him, "Sam, you don't ask a lady how much she pays for rent."

"It really is O.K girl, it's a common question in these parts. The rent is 13 hundred."

"Not bad," said Sammy approvingly.

"Not bad!! Wait, back up," said Celeste, "you pay 13 hundred dollars a month for a basement apartment in Harlem?"

Renee schooled her on New York real estate "Celeste, it's not the basement, it is called a garden apartment because it is at street level."

"Listen up, couz," said Sammy in his lessons-about-the-city-tone, "This here is Riverside Drive. You've got the Hudson River 30 steps away, a view of New Jersey, the subway is right at the corner, and plus this is a brownstone!"

"Exactly," confirmed Renee. "Sammy do you know how long it took me to find a place like this? Look, I even have access to the backyard."

Celeste asked, "Does the rent include utilities?"

"Of course not," Renee answered.

"Thirteen hundred dollars for a basement apartment, excuse me, I mean a *garden* apartment that does not include any utilities?

" repeated Celeste, still unable to believe it. "All I can say is, you're a better woman than me."

Z Designs and Skin & Body by Georgiana were the personalized salon studios at 64th and Lexington Avenue that Renee had dubbed her Repair Center. Celeste was delighted to find the ladies who were offering these fabulous services were both Black, with their 'workshops' across the hall from one another.

Renee was starting at Georgiana's with a paraffin wrap. Celeste saw walls of articles from *Glamour, Towne & Country, Ladies' Home Journal*, and the *New York Times* about Georgiana's miracle treatments. As a Cuban native, Georgiana had learned to whip up concoctions in her kitchen, and the homemade paraffin was one of such concoctions that had helped make her extremely popular. Renee swore that it was not only her dancing but also Georgiana's two-hour treatments twice a week that kept her body sculpted.

Across the hall at Z Designs, the proprietor had created the most serene environment via aromatherapy, essential oils, walls of books on the holistic lifestyle, and Afro-centric gear. Z was a perky woman in her mid-30s with flowing, well-kept dreadlocks and freckles. Her place was filled with dried roses and the aroma was divine. Mostly Celeste liked being the only client, so all of Z's attention was focused totally on her. Never before had she been the only person in a salon.

Z did the one thing to Celeste's hair that no other person did but her mother, and that was scratch her dandruff before washing it. With deep conditioner in her hair, Celeste laid on a heated massage table. Z rendered a relaxing facial while her hands soaked up a treatment in heated mitts. She thought she had died and gone to heaven. Before dozing off, Celeste could not imagine what would be in store for her across the hall with Georgiana.

Renee and Celeste giggled like two school girls as they passed each other in the halls in their robes. Georgiana laid Celeste face-down on the table and proceeded to brush her body with what she said was a toilet brush that had been soaked three months in herbs. She told Celeste that the circular movements from the brushing is what kept the skin taught and smooth. Celeste immediately felt her cells being invigorated.

When the brushing of her body, back and front, was completed, Georgiana then painted on warm paraffin wax and kneaded it into her skin with her knuckles. Then Celeste was wrapped everywhere in Saran Wrap, covered with heated blankets, and told she was about to melt down.

Celeste was so hot and sweaty that she couldn't stand it.

Georgiana said in a thick accent, "For one hour, you melt. Relax and allow those toxins to ooze from your body. "

See there, thought Celeste. "One week in the big city and I'm already toxic. Nobody to blame but me," she sighed aloud and dozed off in a peaceful sleep.

Four hours later Celeste and Renee walked down Lexington all buffed up, relaxed, and definitely well-pampered. "What did you think?" Renee wanted to know.

Celeste knew she had been neglecting herself, but this afternoon was a reaffirmation of the need to reclaim herself. "I will never let myself get in such disrepair again, I don't care what's going on in my life. From this day forward, I promise to make time for me."

"That's what I'm talking about, my sister!" Renee agreed. "So what are you going to do about that?" she laughed, impulsively pulling Celeste into Bloomingdale's revolving door with her.

"I made a standing appointment for once a week."

"Good Girl! I'm warning you, it becomes addictive. I started at once a week for one hour. And now look at me, I'm a junkie," she said, picking up a man-sized Coolgie sweater for herself.

Celeste whistled a sign of approval at the very expensive sweater. "Renee, my sister, if I must say so, I love your taste in junk food."

FIFTEEN

The Hard Rock Cafe was the site of the press conference to announce the nominees for the Grammy Awards. Celeste, Dre, and Maurice were front and center and had placed bets with one another about who would be nominated. Dre won by a landslide and proudly collected a dollar apiece from his friends.

The fellas tried to convince Celeste to hang out with them after the nominations were announced, but today had been one of those days.

"I'm going back to the office, guys. I am absolutely champagned out for a few months, OK?"

"Girlfriend, one can never have too much champagne," Dre informed her as he drained his third glass.

"Huh, your little narrow tail can afford those calories," she teased, pinching his butt, "These here hips have started to scream."

"Yeah right! Chile, you've got just enough shake. Don't you worry," said Maurice, throwing in his two cents.

"Both of you nuts make your own schedules, I have Hitler to answer to. And just about now," she said looking at her watch, "Marcia is sitting at her desk with nothing on it, looking for something else to do, unbraiding her hair, and wondering where I am."

Maurice and Dre cracked up and mocked Marcia by playing in

Celeste's hair.

"Stop it," she said laughing uncontrollably while tying the belt on her trench coat. "Love y'all. I'm out."

She decided to walk from the Hard Rock straight down Broadway. Celeste loved walking in the city. She hardly ever got to walk for pleasure anymore. Uncle Jim refused to let her leave the apartment at 6 o'clock in the morning like she used to do in Chicago for her workout. It seemed as if she was always in a rush during business hours, which made it impossible for her to take leisurely strolls. Taxi's had become her transportation of choice. She felt a little guilty lying to her friends about needing to be back at the office so soon, but a girl had to be alone with her thoughts sometimes. Celeste wanted and needed to walk and think.

Waiting in the lobby for an elevator at One Times Square, Celeste saw two older gentleman huddled together looking intensely at something. They were making a great attempt at whispering, but it was now a difficult task due to their overindulgence of booze and cigars, the smell of which reeked from them both.

She heard the Black one say, "I don't know, T.J., this one just does not make sense yet."

The white, bald one spoke, "What's there to make sense of? This here gal is D-E-A-D."

"What's this city coming to, a pretty gal like this strangled to death and then thrown right on the street." The three of them boarded the elevator together.

"Yeah, it's real F'ed up."

"Hold that there picture up in the light wheres I can see it real good."

Celeste got a good look at the bludgeoned body as well and screamed at the top of her lungs. The two turned to look at this woman screaming over the unnamed woman in the photo.

Struggling to speak, she only pointed and gasped for air while looking at the horror she saw in the picture.

Finally, she said, "I saw that woman last Tuesday."

"Where did you see her?" said one.

"Do you know her?" said the other.

Celeste stumbled again for words.

"Was she with anyone?" said the first one.

"Who else saw her?" said the bald one.

Carefully, "I was on my way to B. Smith's, and I saw this man smacking her around in the doorway of this restaurant. And trying to keep her quiet."

"Yeah, go on," they said in unison while scribbling in their pads.

"I was wondering why all of these people were just walking by and no one was saying anything."

"This is New York," said the first one.

"So I ran back a block to get some policemen who I saw sitting in their patrol car to come and help."

"It's obvious they didn't save the day," said the bald one, holding up the picture.

"Save the day?" seethed Celeste, "he would not even get out of the car." She continued with the rest of the details of the incident.

"Well Miss ...", said the first one.

"Miss Toussaint. Celeste Toussaint."

The two stared at one another and said together, "Didn't you just start last week?"

"Yeah. Don't remind me."

"My name is Newt Pickney. It's short for Newton," said the Black one.

"I am T.J. Radcliff, and what it's short for is none of no one's bees wax," said the bald one.

Celeste was thankful for the formal introductions. In her head she had been processing T.J. as Curly and Newt as Moe. They really looked more like twin Columbos in their wrinkled suits, rundown shoes, and slouchy postures. Yeah, that was it - these two were twins separated at birth, one white, one black, same mind. They acted like two-thirds of the Three Stooges. She had to struggle to keep from laughing at her thoughts. The situation at hand was no laughing matter.

"Oh yeah, the homicide team. You guys have an excellent reputation," Celeste said, recalling that these two were annual Pulitzer Prize winners.

"Thank you very much," they said at the same time, reveling in the response to their reputation.

"Did you happen to get the patrol car number?" asked T.J.

"I did much better, I've got the name and badge number of the indignant fat dog they call an officer."

"My girl, my girl," said Newt, feeling extremely proud she was a smart sister.

"Who was the officer riding shotgun with fatty?" questioned T.J., sucking on his his unlit cigar.

"He was the nice one. It was he who eventually came down the street with me to check on this lady. But the whole thing was over when we got there. Do you know what bugs me the most about this?"

"No, what?" they said.

"I said to fatso, this whole thing would blow sky high if that woman turned up dead, and it would delight me to write the story and splash it all over page one of *The Courier.*"

"And now looky here," said Newt holding up the picture. "So what are you, psychic?"

"I doubt it, Moe," she blurted out and then covered her mouth, "I mean Newt. Hey, can I call you guys Curly and Moe? It has been my first impression ever since I laid eyes on y'all." They looked at each other and agreed to their new names.

"The man who was slapping her had rage in his eyes," Celeste continued. "I smelled trouble."

"You saw the man beating her?" the duo exclaimed at the same time. *See: Stooges. Curly and Moe.*

Celeste nodded yes, knowing what was coming next.

Moe snatched up the phone to call the art department for a sketch artist, "Baby girl, we've got an exclusive here."

"Not at the moment, you don't. I have to make the 10 o'clock deadline before Marcia hangs me. I'm sorry, fellas, but I have to complete my piece right now."

"Honey, ET will understand," said Curly. "He's all about selling the paper. You hafta write about the incident you witnessed."

"Baby girl, for less than 10 days on the beat, you walked up on some Pulitizer Prize shit today!" exclaimed Moe.

Celeste buried her face in her hands and thought, *If only he really knew.*

Marcia flung open the door to Celeste's office just as page two of the Grammy piece was coming off of the printer. Not saying a word, she snatched the goods spewing from the computer.

"You're pushing my panic button coming so close to deadline like this."

"It happens like that sometimes."

"Well get yourself on down to the ninth floor with Newt and T.J. so you guys can complete the story for page one."

"I don't think I should write the story. Can't I give them details like an ordinary witness would have done?"

"This *is* news, honey. You couldn't pay to have been in a better position to witness this thing. *The Courier* will do an exclusive. It's going to be the story of the year."

Marcia didn't know that this story was miniscule compared with the one she really wanted to write.

Celeste looked at her watch. "It's five minutes to deadline, how are we going to complete all of the details by then?"

"They are holding the front-page press for you guys, so get going."

"What's ET going to say about all of this?"

"Sell. Sell. Sell."

"All right. I get the picture." Celeste didn't like the picture, but she understood clearly where the lines were going.

Curly and Moe already had a skeleton of the story drafted and the sketch artist waiting when she arrived. He was amazing. Even though Celeste couldn't describe some of his features clearly, this guy filled in the blanks. The final product was completely accurate.

The artist held up the finished portrait. "Yep, that's him," she said.

"Let's roll," said Moe.

"Wait a minute," she said, "not so fast! Wait. A. Minute. Listen. Shouldn't we take this drawing and give it to the police so they can go looking for this dude before we go splashing his picture all over page one? Check it out ... Number one: he knows he did wrong, right? I mean, the girl is dead."

"Right," the fellas agreed.

"Second: so now he's on edge. In hiding. Waiting for the papers day after day and listening to the news just to see what's up. Maybe somebody reported this girl missing. She has on the same clothes she had on when I saw her," she said pointing to the Polaroid of the girl. "That was a week ago. The last thing we need to do is put his picture out before the police get to look for him. Give it to the police and let them input his face in the computer. I mean, what if he's done this kind of thing before? Somebody in this big city may know who this is," she said, out of breath.

"Besides, if we run the photo first, it gives him an opportunity to get out of dodge," she added.

"She's got a point," agreed Curly.

"A point! Come on, Curly and Moe. You know I am right!" she exclaimed, irritated.

Moe lit another cigar and took a swig of some brownish-looking oil before passing the bottle Curly. "I've got an idea. Why don't we drag this thing out for a few days?" he said now, snatching the bottle from Curly, who was trying to fill that dry spot in the pit of his stomach.

"Why don't we print this here Jane Doe's photo now," continued Moe, "along with my baby girl's story."

Curly caught the fever and picked up on Moe's thought. "Then tomorrow after we speak to the police, we print the drawing with some more details."

"And the next day, after we get Officer Fatso in a heap of trouble behind this mess. Print the bottom line about him not doing his job, backed up with promises from the officer's immediate captain, the Police Commissioner, and the Mayor," said Moe dramatically.

"This way we sell papers in record numbers for a week," said Curly, slapping high five with Moe.

They jumped up to do a little dance, "ET is gonna love us. ET is gonna love us," they sang.

Celeste said, "I'm glad you guys have got it all figured out, because it sounds like a major project. Well I better enjoy your company now, who knows when y'all will come up for air."

"You're gonna be with us," Curly said.

"Let's set some precedents here," Celeste said sweetly but firmly, "Celeste Toussaint is paid for one job, that's entertainment. I am still trying to determine how to get all of those responsibilities done without sleeping on the floor of my office. So don't go telling me I am going to help you guys complete tasks which fall under homicide. Remember, I'm just a witness."

Moe came to the rescue, "Give us the details about what you saw, Baby Girl, and we'll discuss the other stuff later."

"Sounds like a plan to me," she said, "but I know you're lying though that cigar."

"Don't worry, you can share the byline with us," said Curly, "we ain't greedy."

"Is the byline a good idea?" she asked.

"You contributing to this story, arent'cha?" said Moe.

"I am."

"So you should share the byline," Curly said.

Celeste sat silent for a few minutes and her words exploded together in fury, "Come on fellas, snap the heck out of it. You two are the homicide experts. Put that alcohol down and those cigars out, they are clogging your brains. This is Matlock 101. I'm the rookie here. Don't play crazy with me, with my tail on the line."

Pausing to finally take a deep breath, Celeste said, "I shouldn't have to figure it out for y'all. You know my name on this piece puts me in jeopardy."

"How?" they asked.

Celeste thought these guys must have thought she was koo-koo for Cocoa Puffs. She blew hot air through her clenched teeth to avoid screaming. Instead she cut her eyes so sharply toward them that if the eyes were knives, the Stooges would be dead.

"No, I take that back," said Curly after he saw her cut those eyes.

"You know she's right again," said Moe. "Her name being on this thing gives the perp an opportunity to come looking for her and do some damage."

"And it gives the policeman an opportunity to play tough guy with me if he knows who I am. If you could have seen the look on his face when I told him I was an editor, I'm telling you, he would have shot me square in the face to save his butt if he could have."

"Does he know your name?" said Curly.

"No he doesn't. I did not identify myself."

"What about the cop who tried to help you? Does he know your name?" asked Moe.

"Yeah, he does. He thinks my name is Gal Friday."

The tension eased and they doubled over laughing. That was their running joke for the evening while completing the gruesome story that was not so funny.

Ed Townsend snatched up his private line on the first ring, "What's happening?" he barked into the receiver.

Rick braced himself before answering his boss, "Nothing that concerns us, ET."

"It better not be, what do you think I'm paying you for? This gig ain't exactly recreational, ya know."

"I know, but listen here. You're gonna love what the Toussaint lady did today. It's gonna sell you a bundle of papers."

"Oh yeah, I'm listening," said ET while putting his feet on the window sill facing Central Park.

After Rick reported the incidents of the policeman and the dead girl, ET clapped his hands with glee.

"Where is she now?" asked ET.

"In with Newt and T.J."

"Rick my boy, call it a night. I can count on T.J. to take it from here."

"Whatever you say, ET."

Born Richard Bray, Rick was a flunkie in every sense of the word.

The young man from Idaho who left the potato fields in search of a better way of living in the city was fortunate to meet ET during his second week in town, just when his money was running low.

Rick lived to walk where Ed Townsend told him to walk. He had worked in the capacity of "head jerk" since *The New York Daily Courier's* inception. The powers that be knew how useful he was to the entire operation. Rick could go wherever ET could not be seen and, mainly, do whatever ET could not.

Rick was good at his job, but his main fault was not paying attention to details. A fault that only he knew was a fault. He had always been able to slime his way out of most situations. A lover of the not-so-finer things in life, like greasy cheeseburgers and fries, fleabag hotel houses, and their raunchy resident prostitutes, all satisfied his sluggish libido. Rick was fulfilled solely by his work.

Together Rick and ET had been through some perilous, hazardous, and dangerous times. For the first time in 16 years, Rick felt ET was making a terrible mistake by taking him off of Celeste Toussaint's trail.

It was well past midnight by the time they finished the story. Celeste was amazed at how well Newt and T.J. jelled together. She could understand why they worked on the same beat for such a long time. Celeste knew if she could find someone who had the same working rhythm as she, then certainly she'd keep them for a lifetime also.

Newt and T.J.'s first job with the paper was on the printing presses. They even started on the same day. Through many late nights together, they discovered a common dream to write which brought them to the *New York Daily Courier* in the first place. But the only jobs available at the time were those on the presses.

When one of their linemen was discovered murdered in the locker room, Newt and T.J. went to work to solve the murder. Knowing it was an inside job, ET had offered $5000 to anyone with information on the death. Not only did they solve the case, implicating the head foreman, but they wrote up a five-page analysis on his motive as well. Newt and T.J. turned down the $5000, but pitched for positions as homicide writers exclusively.

ET was so impressed that he granted the requests. They had been award-winning journalists for *The Courier* ever since.

"How much longer do you think I have to stay here, guys?" asked Celeste sleepily.

"Well around here, when you make front page, it's tradition to wait until the front page rolls to receive your piece hot off of the press," said Newt, who was now pouring the remains of the brownish oil into a cup of coffee.

"I haven't called home all day. I'm sure my folks are worried by now. May I?"

"Of course," the two answered.

Aunt June answered on the first ring, "Celeste, where are you?"

"And how did you know that it was me?" she said laughing.

"It had to be, everyone else has called here today but you."

"I'm working late on a story for page one."

"My, my," sang Aunt June, "a page one story. Congrats."

"Yes," Celeste said cautiously, "but it's not what you think. If you can stay up until I get there I'll share all of the details with you."

"Sure. I'm a night owl anyway."

"Where's Uncle Jim?"

"Remember he works nights, honey. He called a few minutes ago and wanted to know where you were. He said he'd be glad to pick you up."

"That would be wonderful," said Celeste.

"Good. I'll call the garage and ask them to radio him now. He'll pick you up in front of the building in what ... an hour?"

"Perfect," she said, "See you when I get home then."

"Wait, Celeste, before you go. You've had five phone calls from Chicago today."

Celeste said jokingly, "My Daddy called five times?"

"No, he called once. But Wayne Stephens did."

"What did that traitor want, and why didn't he call me here?"

"That was what I wanted to know," said Aunt June, "but he said he couldn't talk to you there and it was imperative that he spoke to you today. He also said the scandal with the Board of Education in Chicago was linked to Mr. Armani."

"Whaaat?"

"Celeste, do you know what he's talking about?"

"Unfortunately I do," said Celeste somberly.

"Who is Mr. Armani? I hope he didn't get you into some kind of trouble."

"I second that emotion. Just stay awake and I'll explain everything when I get home," said Celeste. "I love you and thank you very much."

She hung up the phone sadly, wondering if she had made some terrible mistake coming to New York.

"Fellas, I need to call Chicago."

"Sure," they said, picking up on her mood change immediately.

Celeste dialed Wayne's number from memory. A recording came on saying the number was being checked for trouble. The operator told her something was wrong with the phone line. Those were the words Celeste did not want to hear, because now she knew, something was very wrong indeed.

SIXTEEN

U ncle Jim was sitting in his car in front of the One Times
Square building, singing along with the tape of his favorite opera *Aida*, and having his lunch. He loved New York
City with a passion. Here was a man dedicated to driving the people
of the city from point A to point B. Only now instead of driving a
yellow cab, he drove a private car for an exclusive service.

His wife, of 33 years, June, had been ecstatic when he said he
was changing from being a yellow cab driver to the private service. "Now I can sleep at nights," she'd said, not that she would
anyway. But it was comforting to her knowing the calls he picked
up were only clients of the service and that he never exchanged
money while working. All passengers used vouchers. Thieves didn't
touch those types of drivers because they knew there was no cash
aboard.

The yellow cabbies had fatalities at least once per month. Jim
was a retired man now and that was not the type of pressure he
needed in his golden years. Jim's only objective was making this
additional money off of the books so he and June could be comfortable. One day he'd like to audition for a male role in *Aida*. As
he hit the high A-flat note from "O Terra, Addio" he smiled and
said aloud, "Oh yes, one day."

Jim was shaken out of his reverie when he heard the sound of someone knocking on his car hood.

"What are you doing here?"

Jim rolled down his car window to answer Rick, the man who showed up every Thursday at 12 noon with his check. "How are you, guy?"

"I'm fine, but what are you doing down here?" asked Rick, who appeared to get irritated.

"Hey man, I'm on my lunch," he explained so Rick would relax. This guy was not his boss, he just passed out the checks.

"I'm down here picking up my niece who works in this building. She's living with me and the wife. You know, looking out for my brother's kid. If that's all right with you," Jim added sarcastically.

"Oh yeah," said Rick, relaxing and lighting a cigarette, then blowing out the tension of the day into little ringlets.

"Yeah," she just got in from Chicago, and started working at *The Courier* last week," said Jim proudly.

Rick couldn't believe his ears. He inhaled on his filterless Camel feverishly. Jim continued, "Celeste is working late almost every night. This must be some job."

"I'll bet it is," said Rick, still stunned, and unable to believe this.

"Hey man, you read the *Courier*, don't you?"

"Of course, who doesn't?"

"Well, you look for my niece's articles in entertainment and don't forget her name: Celeste Toussaint."

"That's a name you can be sure I'll never forget. You take it easy, I gotta run," said Rick, dashing across the street and disappearing into the subway.

Rick ran to the pay phones to call the boss. He picked up several receivers only to find that the only working phone nearby was being occupied. He knocked some man out of the way to get to it first.

ET picked up on the first ring. "I thought I told you to go home."

"I was doing just that, and you wouldn't believe what happened. I think you better sit down for this one."

"No shit."

"No shit," repeated Rick, "this is guaranteed to blow your mind."

T.J., Newt, and Celeste were waiting anxiously at the foot of the press so they could receive the first copy as it rolled off of the gigantic printer.

The guys gnawed nervously on their cigars and Celeste went over ballet exercises to ease her tension. The copy of the first edition was a beauty. Their piece was sheer genius. They all took turns reading the copy aloud to ensure there were no words missing and everything was as they wanted.

"Gee guys, I'm almost sorry my name isn't on that byline," said Celeste, pouting, "It's a masterpiece."

"It sure is, but so are these," said T.J., holding up the entertainment page.

"Gimme that," she said, snatching her column, "Do you know with all of this hoopla, I forgot to look for my piece."

T.J. was right, her piece was masterfully written. "I'm taking this with me," she said while folding the paper and putting it in her bag, "my Uncle Jim is outside waiting, I've gotta dash."

Newt and T.J. rushed to give her a hug. She couldn't explain the warm feeling she had on the inside and goose bumps on her arms.

When she got outside, Uncle Jim was blasting music from his car and he was acting out the song on the street. She stood still as he reached the crescendo, lowered himself to his knee and spread his arms wide for the last note.

She cheered, clapped, and whistled loudly, "Bravo, Bravo, Bravo!"

He stood slowly and stepped forward to take a bow to his adoring audience of one, basking in the glory.

"You are *magnifique!*" Celeste exclaimed.

"Thank you my dear," said Uncle Jim while holding open the door to the car, "but we must get you home my lunch hour is almost over. Rick, the guy who passes out the money from the garage, saw me sitting here and he didn't look too pleased."

"I'm so sorry you had to use your lunch to pick me up. If I had known, I would have taken one of our cars."

"Nonsense, it is my pleasure."

"Uncle Jim, you sincerely must do something about that dynamic voice of yours."

"Oh baby don't worry, I have a plan. When I get my little nest egg in the bank just like I want it, I'll pursue it then."

"So what you're saying is, if you had the money, you'd pursue a career in singing now."

"I guess I would," thought Uncle Jim. "In fact I know I would."

"That's good, because I don't like you driving a cab at all hours of the night."

"No more than I like you working at that paper all hours of the night," he mimicked.

They both laughed at his humor. "So how was your first week?" he asked.

"Eventful," she said and told him about everything.

"Wow, some first week. The stories sound great. I'm very proud of you sweetie. Welcome to my city."

"What a welcome!" said Celeste as they pulled up in front of Esplanade Gardens.

"I'll see you later, and tell June I have two more runs and then I'll be home."

"OK you be careful," she said, jumping out of the car.

He tooted his horn twice and made a U-turn headed back down Lenox Avenue.

Celeste said "good evening" to the guard and thought she had better find out what was going on with Wayne first thing in the morning. She only had speculation he'd betrayed their friendship, with no concrete proof. Not a characteristic of a good journalist - she knew it was her emotions that had gotten in the way.

Wayne and she had been through some really hard times together while at Northwestern. The journalism program did not necessarily welcome Black students with open arms. It was more like with closed arms, and through your tenacity and intelligence you had to pry the arms open. Even then, the arms would only open because they could not ignore one's brilliance, not because they were accepting.

Wayne was number one in their class and Celeste was number two. They were both the type who challenged the administration if they thought it would affect them or other Black students in the future. Northwestern University became their playing field. If Celeste was not in charge of the activity that was most sought after, then Wayne was in charge.

Celeste made history by becoming the first Black woman to win Homecoming Queen, as well as the first one to be accepted into an academic sorority. Wayne became the president of the student body and his academic fraternity. That made history also. Because both of their skin tones were of a lighter hue, on the order of cafe au lait, many of the Black students claimed they were only excelling to be accepted by the whites. Neither of them could ever grasp such a silly concept.

Wayne and Celeste spent many days pondering over the plights of their people's acceptance and of their acceptance by the white folks too. They both wanted to be accepted on their own merits as individuals. If any of their people would have bothered to get to know them, they would have found two people who were truly proud of their heritage.

They made history also by receiving paid internships at the Chicago Daily Courier, and then being offered jobs upon graduation. Wayne became managing editor because he was summa cum laude. Celeste received the education editorship because she was magna cum laude.

Now as she exited the elevator on the 26th floor, she dearly missed her long-time friend and hated the way she'd ignored him before moving to The Apple.

Aunt June opened the door before Celeste could get her key in it.

"Child, you look tired," she expressed while hugging her tightly, "Auntie has fixed you a tuna salad and a bubble bath." Celeste locked the door behind her. She was glad to be home.

SEVENTEEN

The morning conversation around the breakfast table was quite lively. Celeste awoke refreshed and ready to tackle another day down at One Times Square. While getting dressed, she debated on wether or not to tell Uncle Jim she was going to take the free lance position with *The Stand*. The conversation she had with him last night confirmed she would to do the story for Dre.

Celeste convinced herself into it not just for Dre, but for Uncle Jim and his safety. What she needed to figure out was how to manage her time appropriately and without anyone finding out about her hidden agenda. She had even decided on a pen name, Chi (rhymes with sky) Woods, a condensed derivative of Chicago and Kenwood.

From the dining room, Celeste could hear Aunt June bragging about her stories in the paper today. She listened at the door of her bedroom for a moment to see if Aunt June was going to slip and tell her girlfriends about the story on page one also. Celeste had explained to her how important it was that no one disclosed her involvement at this time.

Celeste looked out of the window across the water at the marquee displaying the time and temp. It was 65 degrees and time to get the bus. She snatched a royal blue, light wool crepe pant suit and pumps to match. She thought, *We won't have many more warm days like this.*

She sprayed herself lavishly with White Linen perfume, looked in the mirror and said, "Go girlfriend."

As she fluffed her hair she laughed and thought of Marcia constantly playing with hers. Celeste had a nice head of hair, but if she played with it as much as Marcia did, she'd be bald.

The ladies were enjoying themselves immensely when Celeste breezed through, taking the toast and grapefruit on the plate prepared for her.

"Sorry, I've got to run," she said while gulping her juice, "I think today will be as crazy as yesterday so I need to get moving. Where's Uncle Jim?"

"He worked an all-nighter," said Aunt June shaking her head.

Celeste thought, *Not for long.* "See y'all tonight," she said as she made her way to the door.

"Keep up the good work," the ladies congratulated her.

"Thanks," she said as she went running to make her bus.

Celeste stopped up to ET's to return the stinking contract she had full well intended on breaching anyhow. It was too early for anyone to be in his office so she slipped it under his door. The elevator opened and Celeste found Jane standing there crying.

"What's the matter?" asked Celeste, concerned.

"She was my friend," explained Jane frantically. "I talked her into coming here in the first place. Her mother's gonna kill me."

"Calm down. Who's your friend?"

"*The Courier* calls her Jane Doe," sobbed Jane, holding up the paper, "Her name is Julie Ryan and her mother is gonna absolutely kill me."

Celeste was mortified. "Sit down, Jane. Talk to me. I won't tell anyone, this conversation is between you and me. The whole story slowly."

"I want you to know everything. Can I trust you?"

"I am here to help," reassured Celeste, "You can trust me."

"Well, Julie and I went all through school together in a little town outside Philadelphia. When I moved here she was dying to come with me. Her mother finally let her come two months ago."

"Go on."

"I taught her how to play the game. But Julie got a little greedy with the life, if you know what I mean," she said, shaking her head sadly and stating quite motherly, "I told Julie rule number one was never try to chump the players." She was sobbing into her hands.

"Jane," asked Celeste calmly, "what game are we talking about playing here and just who are these players?"

The elevator doors opened and the Fed Ex man unloaded a box of packages. "Good morning, ladies," he said.

Neither of them spoke.

"Listen Celeste, I have to take care of this. Can we have lunch today?"

"Sure, I'll clear my calendar. You pick the place and I'll meet you there."

"Fine," she said, opening the office door.

"Oh I almost forgot, I returned ET's contract. Please make sure he receives it."

"No problem. Is noon good for you?"

"Any time is good. Call me."

Celeste opened the door to her office to find a beautiful flower arrangement on her desk. She leaned into the roses to get a good whiff of their aroma. The card read: *Congratulations on your first successful week! We've been first in line at the out-of-town newsstand every day. We love you and we miss you. Mommie and Daddy.*

She felt truly blessed by the support of her family. There was a tear stinging the corner of her eye when Marcia barged in out of breath.

"Your Aunt June wants you to come home," said Marcia nervously.

"OK" said Celeste, picking up the phone to dial the number.

Marcia snatched the receiver and hung it up. "She did not say call, she wants you to come home. So don't ask any questions, just go!" she ordered.

"I'm going, I'm going." Celeste promised not to panic before finding out all of the details. She knew she needed to get uptown quickly, and as much as she did not want to, it meant taking the subway.

The door to the apartment was slightly ajar when Celeste arrived and was packed with people. When they saw her, all conversations ceased.

"What's going on in here?" Celeste asked. "Where is Aunt June?"

A neighbor pointed to the bedroom. Celeste walked into the bedroom and her Auntie had her face buried in a pillow.

"Aunt June, please, tell me what is going on here?" Celeste pleaded, her eyes filling with tears.

"Baby, your Uncle Jim. He's been shot."

"What! Where is he? Let's go to the hospital."

"No baby. We can't. He's dead," she said, barely audible.

Celeste fell to her knees with her mouth wide open and a scream which only sounded in her head. Aunt June tried to comfort her before she ran to her room, slammed the door, threw herself across her bed and wailed, "That cab! That damned cab!" She screamed and cried herself asleep.

Hours later, Aunt June woke her up when it was dark outside. The sight of her made Celeste break out in uncontrollable sobs. They cried and comforted one another.

"I know this is a stupid question, Aunt June," she said through the tears, "but why him?"

"I don't know, honey," said Aunt June, drying her face.

"I should call home, shouldn't I?"

"Your folks will be here tomorrow, and your boss called to say she wants you to take off the rest of the week."

"We've got a lot to do, huh?"

"Yes, but the first thing you've got to do is talk to the detective out here about last night."

"I hope I can be of some help."

The detective was looking at Aunt June's vast book collection when they came in the living room.

"Detective Hamilton, this is my niece, Celeste Toussaint."

The detective turned around to greet Celeste and they both almost fell out. "Well if it isn't Gal Friday."

"And how do you do, Officer Friendly."

"So you two know each other?" Aunt June asked incredulously.

"Sort of. Aunt June, this is the officer I told you about who tried to help me last week," said Celeste now trying to wipe her face so she could look more presentable. "You have a penchant for turning up just a little too late on a scene, detective."

"I'm very sorry about your uncle," said Detective Hamilton, "I'm also sorry about the lady you were trying to help. I saw the story on page one. I know Janus is peeing in his pants about now."

"Yeah, I bet he is," Celeste chuckled, "serves him right."

"You two sit down over here and talk while I make you some tea," directed Aunt June.

"You don't have to, Auntie, I'll get it."

"No. I need to keep busy," she said while wiping her eyes with her apron. "Go ahead, tell the detective what happened last night."

"Yes, please tell me what happened last night," said Detective Hamilton, "I do believe you were the last person to see him alive... before his killer."

Celeste cringed at the word "killer" and the tears poured out of her eyes. The detective offered her his handkerchief and let her cry until she was all dried up. It was only when she wiped the tears in her eyes, did she see a tear in his.

Detective Kenny Hamilton was thinking of his own father's

death. More than that, every time he went to work he played their last conversation over and over in his head. It hurt him more to investigate these murder cases than anyone knew. Kenny's father feared that one day he may have to have someone investigating his only son's death. *Very soon I will give up this life, but for now I have a murder to solve*, thought the detective, turning his attention back to Celeste.

"You know, I can't help but thinking this is partly my fault."

"Why would you say that?" he asked, concerned.

"Because if he had not picked me up at one o'clock in the morning from the paper, well, you know," she said looking away.

"Don't blame yourself."

"So what have we got, Officer Friendly? Hey, if you're a detective, what were you doing in the patrol car with Janus last week?"

"It was my last official duty as an officer, but I had to report to work anyhow. I officially became a detective the next day. It was Janus' last day before he retired so I got stuck with him."

"So is this your first case as a detective?"

"No, my third."

"Great."

"What do you mean by 'great'?" quickly jumping to his own defense. "I'll have you know I've been on the force for 10 years. I am very, very qualified to be a detective, and I have an unorthodox way of breaking cases. It's the reason why I made detective in the first place. You should not think for one minute that the NYPD goes around making Black officers detectives just for the hell of it."

Celeste leaned so close to him she could smell a peppermint LifeSaver on his breath and his Aramis cologne. She stared at him a long time before speaking. "I want the little jerk who put a bullet in my sweet uncle's head found and taken through the ringer. Now, if you boys in blue can't manage the task, I swear to you on his grave which isn't even dug yet, that I will do it myself," she said bitterly.

Kenny leaned toward her with the same intensity. He stared into her sandy brown eyes. The pain in them stabbed him deep in his heart, while the smell of her perfume totally intoxicated him just as it had the day he met her.

"I promise you," he whispered, "I will find the menace to society who did this. All you have to do is trust me."

"All right, if you say so detective. But from where I've been sitting since I got to town, that ain't the case at all."

Kenny didn't answer, because from her frame of reference, she was absolutely correct.

EIGHTEEN

All during the funeral, Celeste's thoughts were bouncing off of the walls. She had begun keeping a personal journal since her arrival in New York, and now she could not wait to record her thoughts and feelings. Annie Mae and Charles were comforting Aunt June, who had finally broken down during the service. Celeste felt much better now that her Auntie had let out her grief. Sammy had also finally released his pain. The tears which had his face puffy from being locked-up now poured onto the floor.

Celeste and Charles had a major argument when they arrived about his trying to take matters into his own hands. Jim was his only big brother. Charles had driven to town and he came packing with a nine-millimeter gun. He did not even get settled when he got into the apartment before strapping himself down to hit the streets.

Celeste blocked the door with her body, saying, "You must be a crazy man to think I am going to let you leave this house with that monstrosity, with no leads on where to look. There is no way I am going to bury my uncle and my Daddy in the same week!"

"Move out of my way, Princess. Better yet, get yours and we'll go out looking together."

She looked at him shaking her head, eyes saying, *Big mouth, everybody knows our secret now.*

Annie Mae jumped up and got in his face real good. " Charles, you promised me you had not given my child that thing."

"Well I lied," said Charles, "And it's a good thing too, look at what has happened, baby."

"I'm gonna baby you," scorned Annie Mae and dragged Charles into the back room by the ear. Argument over.

Later that night Celeste was so wound up she refused to close her eyes. She was afraid her Daddy would try to sneak out in the middle of the night while she was sleeping. Celeste had called Detective Hamilton, scared about what Charles had done. He stayed on the phone with her until the sun came up.

Dre, Maurice, and Renee were crying their eyes out at the funeral. Chi Woods had made her debut in *The Stand* with a piece about Uncle Jim. She was eternally grateful to Dre for giving her the opportunity.

Celeste was infuriated at the sight of Newt and T.J. in the church. She still could not believe her last conversation with them.

"We're sorry we are not going to carry a story on your uncle, but we can't write about every cabbie who gets killed," Newt had said.

"He's not just some cabbie, he was my uncle," she ranted. "I don't care if you say you can't carry the story. Amuse me. Go through the motions. It will make me feel better."

"What Newt is trying to say is, we're so busy with the series on the girl right now," said T.J.

"I'm not going to let you forget that it is a series you would have never ever written if it weren't for me," she reminded them. "Even if we wrote the story on your uncle, it probably would not make the paper," said T.J.

"No, what you're saying is that the city doesn't want to read another Black-man-dead piece," she screamed.

"Now, Baby Girl," said Newt, "how can *I* mean something like that?"

Celeste went ballistic. "That's right. Dust good, boys. Make sure you clean yourselves up, get some soap and water too, because you are going to need it. And do it before either of you ever thinks about speaking to me again." She screamed a bunch of other obscenities at them before slamming the phone in their ears.

She was staring them down so hard in the church, they finally looked up at her, and when they did, she rolled her eyes so hard angry tears fell heavily from them. Sammy rushed to her side to hold her hand, irritated that someone had the audacity to anger his couz at this moment.

It was time for the family to walk past the casket and view the body before exiting the church. Celeste knew she was not going to look into that casket. She wanted to remember the Uncle Jim who was singing arias from *Aida* and sharing his dreams with her.

As she turned her head from the casket, she looked right into the soothing eyes of Detective Hamilton. They pleaded with her not to worry.

He mouthed, "I'm here if you need me."

Yeah, she needed him all right.

Annie Mae and Charles had planned to go back to Chicago right after the funeral. Charles called Celeste into her room when they got to the apartment. She knew that confrontational tone, but she couldn't figure out what the confrontation was all about?

"Pack your stuff," he ordered, "we're leaving."

"I know you guys are leaving, but I can't go with you now," she said, making light of what she knew were their fears, "but thanks for the offer."

"I don't think you heard me." said Charles very slowly. "Get those trunks I bought, and the very expensive things I bought to put in them," he said throwing clothes on the bed from the closet, "and we are leaving. That means you, Celeste Michelle Toussaint." He was using his finger to push her head back.

"Mommieee, do something with him." squealed Celeste.

"Get packing," said Annie Mae sternly.

"No way! Not you, too. New York will not chew me up and spit me out in only two weeks. No way!" she screamed. "What happened to all of that 'I'm so proud of you' jazz, anyway?"

"It went out of the door when they threw your Uncle Jim in the street like a dog to die, that's what happened to it," Charles reminded her as he shouted in her face, while shaking her like when she was a little girl.

"I promise to be careful. I promise. I will help find the person who did this to Uncle Jim," she said through rattling teeth with tears streaming down her face. "I am not leaving. Not yet anyway."

The deafening silence in the room was disturbed by a knock on the door which Celeste gladly opened. It was Kenny, and she was grateful for his impeccable timing.

"I'm sorry. Am I interrupting something here?" he said apologetically.

"No. No, in fact, allow me to introduce you to my folks," she said sweetly. "Mommie, Daddy, this is Detective Kenny Hamilton, better known as Officer Friendly. He's assigned to Uncle Jim's case."

"It is my pleasure," said Kenny, rather formally shaking their hands while Celeste ducked behind him for cover.

"Well, we were just about to leave. All of us," said Charles, looking around Kenny to his daughter.

Celeste's eyes pleaded with Kenny to help her. "Sir, if I may interject. I know you don't know me from Adam, but I would never let anything happen to your daughter. I am committed to find the perp who killed your brother," he said.

Charles sat on the bed and listened to Kenny. Celeste took that as her cue to slip out of the room.

Aunt June and her lady friends from down the hall were holding court with Dre and Maurice. The fellas were flattering them all over the place and they were just loving them up. Celeste didn't care if they were gay or not. She loved herself some Dre and Maurice! Annie Mae and Charles did a great job raising her in that department. They always taught her not to judge folks on what they were color-wise, sexual preference-wise, or anything else so petty. It only mattered how a person treated you. Dre and Maurice treated her like the brothers she never had.

In the other corner, Sammy was desperately laying his lame rap on Renee. She looked like she was in need of being rescued, so Celeste hurried over to the couch and squeezed between them.

"What lie is my dear cousin throwing your way?" she teased, taking off Sammy's glasses and cleaning them for him.

"Oh, the usual," Renee said to Celeste as if he weren't there. They laughed as Sammy snatched his glasses, shook his fist at them, and got up.

"Thanks, I owe you," she said. "Why do all guys try so hard to impress you? He's really good looking, but his rap has to go."

"I keep telling Sammy he's stuck in the 1960's." They screamed.

Renee looked at her friend and felt her grief oozing from her being. "You know, Miss Girl, I think that you are in need of a dance class."

"Am I wearing my emotions all over my sleeve?"

"Yeah you are. It's time you did some emoting."

"Emoting, huh - that's a new word," she chuckled. "But being a dancer I understand how that means throwing your emotions into movement. Right?"

"Right. You've been through too much. I find dancing really sets me free," Renee said looking down in her punch as if the answer to what had her bound was at the bottom of the glass.

"OK Renee, it's going to be your responsibility to make me go. Just call me and say when," said Celeste, wondering when she was going to find the time to squeeze in more *anything* between her work at *The Courier, The Stand,* and now Uncle Jim's case.

She'd have to find the time because she did love dancing.

"OOH, you go, girlfriend," teased Maurice from across the room, while snapping his fingers at Aunt June's feet.

Renee laughed, "Your Aunt's in trouble now, they're just getting wound up."

Annie Mae, Charles, and Kenny came from the room arm-in-arm and all smiles. Celeste stared at the three of them looking so comfortable with one another, wondering just what was up with that closed-door conversation in her bedroom.

Charles pointed at Celeste and announced, "OK, you stay." Everyone in the room clapped. It seems that everybody had known Charles wanted to take Celeste back to Chicago but her.

She crossed her legs with a defiant look in her eyes and mumbled, "I was staying anyway."

Charles crossed his arms and said, "Be a smarty and you will pack up anyway."

She smiled the smile which always warmed his heart and leapt from the couch to hug her parents. She looked at Kenny and said, "I could kiss you."

He mouthed seductively and winked, "Later." Celeste turned three shades of red and had it not been for Annie Mae hugging her, she would have passed out.

Celeste felt sad as they packed up the car downstairs. Her Daddy would never change. He loved to drive their Lincoln Continental whenever they took long trips and on Sundays. Those were the only times that car left the garage.

Charles always said, "Not only is this car class, but it is the best ride on the road."

Celeste could still remember years ago the first time they brought the Lincoln home. It was the day before an Easter Sunday. She was in the kitchen dyeing eggs with the kids on the block. Charles came in with them and tossed one of their uncooked eggs high into the air, astounding the kids with his agility.

"You know, these here dyed eggs are for kids. Go look out front at a grown person's Easter egg," he had bragged.

Celeste ran to the door to look and gave a low whistle, "That's the prettiest green car I've ever seen. Where are my keys?"

Charles threw a raw egg at the back of her head, cracking it. "You must be crazy. I can't have a dag gone thing for you. Listen up, this here car is for me, Miss Missy. You will not be driving it and within six months have french fries and shit between the seats. You got that?"

The thought of the raw egg dripping down her back made her awfully homesick. Deep down she really did want to leave with them. Not that she would ever admit it. No way. She would come home on her own. If things worked out the way she had planned, that would be very soon.

Annie Mae was looking sadly at her daughter but decided it was much better not to press the issue. She issued a warning instead. "You be very, very careful young lady."

"I will, Mommie."

"Come on y'all, group prayer. Lord watch between me and thee, while we're absent, one from another. Amen."

"Amen." chimed Charles and Celeste. They exchanged one last round of kisses and hugs. Celeste watched them make the same U-turn Uncle Jim had made to go down Lenox Avenue. She waved goodbye until they were out of sight.

Dre, Renee, and Maurice bounced out of the building and found Celeste waving and crying at nothing. They hugged her tightly and she thanked them for being there.

"Chile, isn't it ironic that you would meet me and Dre separately and then find out that we are the bestest of pals," said Maurice pensively.

"I don't believe in accidents," said Celeste, "somebody bigger than all of us knows we are going to need each other."

"You better preach, sistah," responded Renee, waving her hand in the air.

"Amen," said Dre with all of the amount of appropriate reverence he could muster.

"Hallelujah," praised Maurice, doing his little shindig while Dre clapped his hands and stomped his feet to a beat only he and Maurice were hearing. Renee and Celeste shook their heads at the duo. They jumped into a gypsy cab and headed downtown, with the three of them waving wildly out of the back window.

NINETEEN

A fter the dishes were washed, dried and put away, Aunt June stated, "I'm putting on some herbal tea for you, and I'm going to bed. You go out there on the balcony with the detective."

Celeste put her hand over her mouth shook her head, and whispered, "Auntie, I forgot all about him."

"Well what's most important is he didn't forget about you. Now go on," she said and kissed her.

He was patiently stretched out in a lounge chair staring at the Harlem River reflecting the city's lights. It was unseasonably warm for a late October night. There was a hint of a muggy breeze blowing.

"Do you like the water?" he asked, as calm as the movement of the river, when he heard her step onto the balcony.

"Oh yes, I love the water. I know that's what I miss most about Chicago, being near Lake Michigan."

"I hope to see it someday."

"I hope you will too."

"Your Dad offered me free room and board when I crack this case."

"Oh did he?" she said thinking, *The nerve of him.*

"What's the matter? Don't you want me to see the house you grew up in?"

Celeste could not believe this. "Hey, what went on in my room and just how much did they tell you about me?"

Kenny sat up to face her. "Whatever happened in there? You get to stay in New York, don't you?"

"I was staying anyway," she said defiantly.

"Don't even try it. So just get rid of that tone, young lady, because I met your Daddy."

She laughed, "Am I obviously a Daddy's girl?"

He put his hand over his heart, "Painfully." He stared at her for a moment before speaking again, debating on just how much he should say. "Celeste, in all seriousness, I think I may have my first real break in the case."

"Yeah. So why didn't you tell me?"

"I'm telling you now."

"OK, I'm sorry. Tell me, tell me, tell me," she said, dying to hear every detail.

He smiled at her zeal, "Well the car stolen from Uncle Jim belonged to a fleet from the private car service, right?"

Celeste didn't know where this was going but she answered anyway, "Right."

Kenny rubbed his hands together while saying, "So how come the service did not report the car stolen?"

"Oh, Officer, I think you're onto something," she said getting excited.

"The most interesting part of this is ... Why was his car back in the fleet for business as usual?"

"Officer Friendly, I know you are onto something."

"We had to go there and pick up the car for evidence."

"Did anybody have an answer?"

"No. That's why the next part I have to do alone, but I will let you know when I need your assistance."

"Oh, so I'm the assistant now," she teased, taking the ornamented comb from her hair and throwing it at him, allowing her hair to fall heavily about her shoulders.

Kenny picked up the decorative item and held it above his head. At six feet four inches, it was definitely out of her reach.

"I like this little thing. I think I'll keep it," he played, holding it higher and higher.

"No way, Mommie brought me this comb from Puerto Vallarta," she said now reaching behind his back. "Give it to me. The next time I throw something at you I won't miss. I'm usually a good shot."

"If I give it back, do you promise to leave your hair down?" he asked running his available hand through the ends of her tresses thoroughly enjoying its texture, and looking into her expressive eyes.

"Sure, why not," she said, blushing and now painfully aware that their bodies were touching.

"Don't you owe me something anyway?" asked Kenny, scratching his head trying to remember.

"Something like what?"

"Well, I think it was you who told me you could kiss me after your father said you could stay."

Celeste swallowed hard. "Oh yeah, that. Sure. Thanks," she said and pecked him on the cheek. Before she could get away, he held her head tenderly and attacked her neck. The sensation had her weak in the knees.

"Why, Officer Friendly, are you on duty?"

"I haven't been on duty all day," he said through the kisses.

"Oh, that's good."

"Oh, is it really?" he said while tickling her neck with his tongue.

"No, I meant, it's good you are off duty."

"Well," he said, holding her face between his hands and staring into her eyes, searching for the same emotion he was feeling, "is it good?"

"Uh huh," she said faintly.

"And so are you," he said, covering her face with baby kisses before plunging onto her mouth with his tongue and all of his heart. She wrapped her arms around his neck so that she could be as close as possible to him, and he picked her up while they kissed for an eternity.

His kiss was as sweet as cotton candy. Celeste felt an intense passion in his oral caress. She had never been elevated to such a wonderfully emotional pleasure from just a kiss.

At that very moment, Kenny stopped kissing her and held her face sweetly. "I just want to look at you," he said.

"Kenny ..."

"Sshh," he said and kissed her passionately, "Baby don't talk." She shut up, not wanting to spoil their moment. His eyes danced with delight at the new feelings he had stirring inside of him. She knew something way down deep in Detective Kenny Hamilton had been awakened, that had not been tapped for quite some time. Celeste hoped he knew the same was true for her.

No one had ever aroused these sensations she was feeling. Kenny had something wonderful stirring on her insides. She didn't know what it was, but she knew she liked it.

Celeste smiled and sighed with pleasure just thinking about the warm feeling. "Can I hug you?" she requested shyly.

"So you like hugging, do you?" he asked, kissing the back of her hand.

"I do," she said, giggling at the tickling sensation going through her fingers.

"And just why do you like hugging?" he said, stepping way back to get full view of her.

"Well, for me," she began dreamily, "there is a tremendous amount of comfort in a hug, because you can't fake one, you either mean it or you don't. Hugs help me to feel safe, and warm, and when I hug somebody, I hope they feel what I feel."

"Now that's a dynamite definition," he said, flashing those

gorgeous pearly whites. Kenny slowly opened his arms wide to receive her. "So bring your beautiful self over here and hug me," he said warmly.

Celeste fell into his arms. "I'm so glad I met you," she said, crying because she felt so safe there, but knowing how violated she had been with the death of her Uncle Jim. She knew that safety was only temporary while in his arms.

"When I first saw you on the street, I knew you were somebody special," he said, kissing her tears. "I knew somehow, and someday, we'd be together like this. I just didn't know it would be so soon and under these circumstances."

They remained hugging, each lost in their thoughts for a long time.

"I'd like for you to come to my house for dinner on Sunday. Moms cooks like it's Thanksgiving every week and all of the family drops in then. It would be wonderful if you could join us."

"I would love that."

"Good," he said and snuggled her closer to him. "I can't wait."

They walked quietly to the elevator, each thinking of ways to sneak in just a few more moments.

"Officer Friendly, you know, for once in my life I think I am lost for words."

"Just say what you are thinking right now."

"In the words of Les Brown, it has been a plum pleasing pleasure to have ended this evening with you," she gushed.

"I don't think so, my darling Gal Friday," he said and kissed her forehead, then her nose, and then ever so lightly on her lips, "the pleasure has been all mine."

The elevator doors opened, he stepped on and winked at her as the doors closed.

Celeste ran for the apartment door and slid toward it in her stocking feet like a baseball player sliding in for a home run. "Yes!" she yelled as she ran to her bedroom, whipped off her clothes, and fell into a blissful sleep.

Kenny barged into the door of his family's massive great room. His mother and sister were sitting at the grand piano rehearsing for Sunday service singing "Amazing Grace." He came in grinning from ear to ear and leaned on the ivory Steinway.

"I have met the woman I am going to marry," he said over their singing.

"Well, do tell," said his mom playing the wedding march.

"Yeah, right. Who is it this month?" asked his sister Jacqueline suspiciously, standing to look in his eyes. "We have heard all of this before you know."

He shook his head and said firmly, "No, I mean it. Her name is Celeste Michelle Toussaint. She's the new entertainment editor at *The Courier.*"

"Where is this dream lady from?" interrogated Jacqueline.

"Chicago. And before you ask me, she is beyond gorgeous, that goes for on the inside as well as the outside," he beamed.

"I don't know, Mom, his eyes are all glazed over," said his sister after inspecting him. "This might be the one."

"The best part about all of this, is her father already gave me his approval. And don't worry, Mom, I wouldn't jeopardize anything, she comes from solid, successful stock."

Kenny bent over to touch his toes, did five jumping jacks, and then boxed at the air, "Yes. I feel good! Time to go to bed and dream about my baby. Good night, ladies," he said as he floated to each of them and planted a kiss on their cheeks.

"Mom, can you do me a favor and hit that tune for me?"

"Sure baby, which one suits what you feel?"

Kenny began to hum as Mom tinkled on the piano, *"This is my same old coat, these are my same old shoes ..."*

"Oh yeah, I think I know that one," said Mom, as she picked up the tune on the piano in his key and sang along.

"... It was the same old me, with the same old blues,
Oh then you touched my life, Just by holding my hand.
When I look in the mirror I see a brand new boy.

Just because of you, Just because of you ... "

Kenny danced off toward to his room singing.

Jacqueline confirmed his mood, "Yep, he does feel good," she said staring after him.

"He smells good, too," said Mom approvingly as she continued to play. "That Celeste Michelle Toussaint wears White Linen."

TWENTY

When Celeste finally got back to work after tending to the business of Uncle Jim's death, her office looked like a mini-flower shop. Marcia met her at the door to offer a hug and condolences.

"I saw you at the funeral, Mason, sorry I didn't get a chance to speak to you."

"Don't worry. I just wanted to be there."

"Thanks," said Celeste, looking around.

"I know this is overwhelming," said Marcia shaking loose her braided hair.

"Overwhelming isn't the word," Celeste said, looking at all of the flowers. She didn't think she knew that many people in New York yet.

"I can't even sit down in here," she said, noticing a heap of mail in the corner on the floor.

"Oh yeah, it's all yours," confirmed Marcia.

"How can I accumulate so much mail in only eight days away from the office?

"It comes with the territory."

"Just terrific."

"I'm going to help you sort through all of this and make a list for your thank yous, because you have to attend a luncheon today and a theatre opening tonight," said Marcia, picking up the mail.

"Marcia, I'll go to the opening tonight, but I'm not in the mood for champagne and any chit-chat this afternoon," Celeste said irritably, "and I must get some order in this place before leaving it again. I hope that's OK with you."

"I can dig it," sympathized Marcia, "I guess I'll have to cover for you."

"Good, then let's dig into this mess."

Celeste found she really did not even know most of the people who had sent so many nice condolences. That was really sweet. She thought, *Who said New Yorkers don't care?* Most of the flowers were almost dead, so Celeste rubberbanded those together and turned them upside down to make dried flower arrangements.

When the last vase had been emptied, an intern knocked on the door, bringing in a huge bouquet.

Celeste said, "This is mighty thoughtful of all these folks I don't know, but it's getting a bit ridiculous." She tore into the wrapping and found her favorite of all favorite flowers, white and yellow roses.

Marcia counted them quickly and flashed a bulletin real FYI-like. "Somebody spent a lot of money. There are two dozen of each here," she said with a hint of jealousy.

"They're beautiful," Celeste marveled taking a whiff of the delectable aroma.

"Well dear, the vice presidents and publicity directors you deal with have huge expense accounts, they can afford to send four dozen roses any day if it means staying on your good side."

The card read: *"Have a fantastic day. Mine is already blessed because it has been filled with thoughts of you. Please meet me for a brief informational encounter on the steps of the Fifth Avenue side of the Library at noon. Your Officer Friendly"*

Celeste could not conceal her joy. "Marcia, I'm very sorry to disappoint your theory, but these flowers are from a true blue, ardent admirer," she said smiling at her intended pun, looking at the card with the beautiful handwriting in red ink.

He must have paid extra to have someone write this, she thought.

"Let's tackle the mail now, shall we?" said Marcia, interrupting her thoughts. Celeste saw that she was clearly wondering, *How does she come to town and meet a man who sends her four dozen roses in less than a few weeks?*

"I almost forgot, here's your paycheck."

"Thanks. I've got to frame it."

"You mean frame a copy of it," Marcia corrected.

"No. I do mean frame it. I never cash my first check from any job. I have a frame full of checks."

"You know dear, are too young to have so many idiosyncratic ways already," Marcia laughed while opening all of the bulk packages.

Celeste stared at the woman who played in her hair constantly and envisioned it all falling to the ground one day. She chose not to comment she laughed along with Marcia instead. She didn't trust her mouth.

The official mail that Marcia was opening contained press kits, new music, invitations, and promotional materials. Celeste tackled all of the handwritten envelopes. She noticed a package with no return address. It was postmarked from Evanston, Illinois - home of Northwestern University.

The letter read:

My Dearest Celeste:

This is from Wayne, she thought. He was the only person in the world who called her "Dearest Celeste." Now she felt badly because she had forgotten about him with all that was happening.

I can't believe that I was so naive to think Taylor and I were becoming close. When you uncovered that scandal at the Board, you exposed only the surface. Taylor is at the helm of the entire operation. The pages included in this package is the info I man-

aged to dig up thus far.

The other part to this is that all of those boys who have <u>Courier's</u> across the country are a part of something nasty in their respective cities. Taylor's playground is the Board of Education. But thanks to you his people are not in place anymore. So that means he's got to start from scratch, and sweetie he can't be too happy about that.

I know your Ed Townsend is hooked up into some major dirt in New York, I just have no idea what it is ,however. You must be extremely careful. Consider this information, as you like to say, an official Dirt Alert. They are a dangerous and ruthless bunch.

I've been trying to reach you by phone, but I decided to put this package together and have my Moms mail it to you.

The final part to the whole thing is: If you have gotten this in the mail and we haven't spoken, I'm probably dead.

Remember I always loved you. Wayne.

Celeste balled up the paper, put it in her suit coat pocket, excused herself, and ran to the ladies room. Only then in the privacy of her stall did she uncover her mouth to vomit and let the tears stream freely down her face.

At high noon, Celeste sat on the steps of New York City's main Public Library branch and rolled the salt off of a gigantic pretzel she bought from a street vendor. Her eyes were so swollen and red from crying, that she had to buy the darkest shades she could find.

Kenny stood behind her looking at how lovely she looked sitting there picking at her pretzel. Celeste Michelle Toussaint-Hamilton, he thought smiling. He lightly touched her shoulder thinking of all of the warm telephone conversations they had begun having nightly.

She didn't jump or acknowledge him as he thought she would. Instead Celeste's severe depression had her glued to the library steps. Once he got close enough to her, he could see her tears even behind the glasses.

She handed him the balled-up paper from her pocket then buried her face in the fragrance from the yellow and white rose clipped from Kenny's arrangement that she wore on her lapel.

After he read Wayne's letter, Kenny ordered, "Meet me in five minutes in the stacks on the lower level." He got up and took the steps three at a time until he reached the library's massive doors.

The only noise obvious to Celeste in the stacks was the humming sound of the fluorescent lights. She hated the stacks in college for that same reason. The thought of college had her thinking of Wayne and all of their study sessions at Northwestern's University Library. Uncovering the scandal at the Board had done more harm than good, it had probably cost her friend his life. This would be something Celeste would have to eventually come to terms with ... and soon.

Kenny snatched her from the side aisle into a narrow row of books barely wide enough for them both. He removed her sunglasses and looked into her red, tear-filled eyes.

He hugged her tightly. "We've got work to do, Gal Friday. You've got a penchant for folks turning up dead around you."

She finally smiled, "Don't run my lines, I'll sue you for plagiarism."

"Have you confirmed Wayne's status?"

"No, I was too afraid to call his Moms."

He took out his cellular phone, pulling up its antenna. "Step number one."

She looked at the note Wayne sent and dialed the number where he said his mother could be reached. The phone rang one time. "Yes" answered the familiar voice.

"Hi Moms."

"Celeste. So you finally got the package I mailed," said a relieved, but tired-sounding Mrs. Stephens.

"Yes Moms, I received the package. Is ..? Is Wayne all right?" she said, clinging to Kenny to brace herself and be close to him all at the same time.

"Not quite."

"What's that supposed to mean?" questioned Celeste. "Wait. Before you answer, where am I calling? How do you know that your phone is not tapped?"

"Oh, this phone is one of new-fangled contraptions that plug into the wall and can take anywhere with you. I forget what you call it."

"Are you on a cellular phone?" asked Celeste.

"That's the name of it, baby."

"Good. Then it's OK to talk.

"Let's just say this whole thing was better than the mystery movie of the week, my dear," laughed Mrs. Stephens, "but don't be confused. They tried to kill my baby. His girlfriend was at the apartment when it happened. Wayne made her hide in the closet when he heard them coming. Those punks pumped two bullets into his stomach and covered him with the quilt I made for him."

"No!" Celeste said unbelievingly.

"Well honey, God was on his side, because his lady is a surgical nurse. She said when those fools covered Wayne up, that kept him warm, which was the best thing they could have done. So when they thought they left him for dead, she took out the bullets with tweezers and sewed him up with coat thread," she chuckled.

"What!" said Celeste, thinking, *This does really only happen in the movies.*

"Then she called his brothers, who came to get him. And I tell you honey, we threw one helluva funeral for him! Did obituaries in the paper and all. It was grand!!" said Mrs. Stephens cracking up. "I'm surprised that you didn't hear about it up there. The company was very supportive."

"I had a death in my own family," Celeste explained. "Today is my first day back in over a week."

"I'm sorry for your loss."

"Yeah, me too," Celeste got the strength to say. "But what about

Wayne?"

"Oh he's safe now with some of my folks down South. I'll only say he's somewhere down South safe, waiting for you and the police to make some sense of this thing and arrest that man at *The Courier.*"

"He does know he can't ever come back to Chicago, doesn't he?"

"Baby, Wayne said he doesn't want to come back here now to this inclement weather. We have taken the money from the insurance policies he had, and we're gonna start a paper and some other businesses down South. I leave tomorrow for good myself," she boasted.

"I know that Wayne had insurance policies at companies I have never heard of," Celeste remembered. "Wayne was always concerned about his family being cared for if anything ever happened to him."

"That's right baby. That's my Wayne. He had three policies for me and one for each of five brothers and one for his Grandma. His lady hooked us up with a death certificate and all."

Moms continued laughing, "Since his death was accidental we got paid double indemnity on every one of 'em."

"I'm sorry to hear about everything that happened, but this certainly has a happy ending," Celeste replied, relieved. "Can his girlfriend identify any of the men who shot Wayne?"

"No, because she was peeking out of the keyhole all she saw was their belts and winged-tipped shoes. But she did get the license plate when she looked out of the window."

"What is it? I have a friend who is a policeman who can probably help," she said, smiling up at Kenny and taking a pen from his jacket pocket.

"Sure baby," said Mrs. Stephens, "I'll never forget it ... WBB 923."

Celeste dropped the phone, hyperventilating.

Kenny picked up the phone. "Mrs. Stephens, I'm Detective Hamilton. What did you say to her?!"

Outside on the library steps, Kenny sat silently next to Celeste until she fully regained control of her breathing. The people of the city bustled about as usual and Celeste used the scene before her to clear her thoughts. She liked being surrounded by millions of people who couldn't detect her fears or pain, especially since at this moment she was consumed by both.

"Hey baby, are you feeling better?" Kenny questioned, concerned.

She nodded, "Let's walk down to Lord & Taylor's."

Kenny smiled, "That's my Gal Friday. I heard about you and your shopping escapades."

"Do you know that I have not been into one store or spent one dime since I've been here?" she mused. "How unlike me."

"Celeste, I've never seen anyone react to a license number quite like you did, what do you know about it?" interrogated the detective.

"Right before I left Chicago, I saw a black Lincoln Town car with tinted windows and the plate WBB 923 three times in my neighborhood. I could have sworn it was following me. In fact, now I'm almost sure it was following me."

"I have to run this number when I get back to the precinct," he said while holding open the door of Lord & Taylor's for her.

"In a way I am really afraid to find out who the car belongs to. I mean, what if it's somebody I know?"

"Let me share with you a little secret of the trade. In cases like these, it usually is someone you know," he said, scrutinizing an ivory pant suit on the reduced rack. "Do you like this?"

"Hey, how did you know that ivory is one of my favorite colors?"

"I didn't. I can see this looking really good on you."

"You know yellow and white roses are my favorites."

"Are they really? Guess what, they are mine too, not just for their beauty, though. White roses symbolize prosperity and life and yellow roses symbolize friendship," he pointed out, showing off his roses 99.

"How romantic, Kenny," she acknowledged, melting.

"So do you like this suit?" he said, trying to change the subject before they embarrassed themselves in public.

"Oooh yeah. I'll try it on with the rest of these," she said quickly, grateful for what he was trying to do, "I tell you, Lord & Taylor's reduced rack is always worth the trip."

"Celeste, can you think of why anyone would want to follow you around in Chicago?"

"Sweetheart, I wrote a story that sent 12 executives from the regime at the Board of Education to jail. They were sitting pretty in their cushy positions before I came along and uncovered their misappropriation of funds, extortion, nepotism, contract fraud, and several other things which have no place in the educational system," she said, giving him the history while piling outfits across Kenny's arms. "So go figure on who would want to follow me around."

"Wayne's letter said Taylor was at the helm of the activity," he said while Celeste held up a blue Calvin Klein dress for his approval, "I like it."

"Good, 'cause it's half price. I know whatever Wayne said about Taylor must be true. Now we can add him to those list of reasons, including why he wanted me out of his hair. Wayne also sent some paperwork that I haven't looked at yet," she said, picking another dress, this one in red.

"Lord only knows what dirt ET is involved in here. Maybe the two of us can review the information together?"

"Anything to be with you, my sweet."

Celeste spent the next half hour modeling for Kenny. He was a really good critic. For whatever he didn't like, he found suitable replacements. Her tally for sixteen outfits was an even one thousand dollars.

"I can't believe you have spent a thousand dollars in less than an hour."

"Hey, when you're a seasoned shopper like me, it only takes an an hour. And take my word for it, these are great bargains, or girlfriend would *not* be buying," she advised with a snap a la Dre.

At the cash register, Celeste counted out ten one-hundred-dollar bills.

"I'm shocked, Celeste. You're from Chicago, you know better than to carry around this much cash," Kenny reprimanded. "Baby, how long have you been carrying so much money around with you?" he questioned.

"Since I got here. Daddy gave me this emergency cash before I left home."

"So why are you spending your emergency cash for clothes?"

"Cause, honey, a sale like this is an emergency."

Kenny cracked up at this woman. She was truly a shop-a-holic. His sister was gonna love her. "Please don't carry so much money around, OK?"

"OK, but you know I am from the South Side. So let me tell you something, Officer Friendly, you New Yawkers don't want to feel this South Side thing run amuck all over y'all. Cause messin' with my money is precisely when it can just pop right out," she explained.

"Celeste. No more. OK"

"OK" she conceded.

"You keep your cash baby, let me buy these for you," said Kenny, pulling out his platinum American Express card, which Celeste eyed closely, thinking, *His credit must be A-1.*

"No way. My Daddy said to never let a man buy me clothes when I can buy them myself."

"Your Daddy didn't know me when he told you that."

"True. But Kenny, I have the cash. I can't let you spend a thousand dollars on me."

"Baby, I'll do for you exactly what you would do for yourself and more," he said, blowing a kiss at her and exchanging the cash for the credit card with the saleslady.

Celeste could only blush.

Walking back toward One Times Square, Celeste thought how much she enjoyed the company of Detective Kenny Hamilton. She felt the best she had in days with her new purchases in one hand and Officer Friendly's in the others.

"Kenny, your card on the flowers said you wanted to meet with me for an informational encounter. What information do you have?"

"Three things. Jane signed a confidentiality statement about her friend Julie and the details she knows. I'm sure there are several things she's hiding. I want you to get together with her so she can eventually open up to you."

"Aye aye, sir."

"Second, the perp who killed Julie is a circuit court judge from Maryland, and quite a regular down at The Show Time Lounge."

"Ooh, nasty little scandal. Case closed now?"

"Not quite. Talk to Jane first. Crack her like a safe, real girl-friend- like, and we'll see."

"Consider it done."

"Third, I go undercover tonight as a driver at Uncle Jim's car service."

"No way. Kenny, that is sick," Celeste said hoping he would reconsider, "please don't."

"It's going to be fine, and you are not going to worry," he said, pinching her nose. "Am I assigned to this case or what?"

"Right, don't worry. Tonight, I'm going to be rubbing elbows with New York's most socially correct at an opening of a Broadway play, while my sweetie goes undercover for information about my Uncle's murder," she said, flailing her arms in the air and stomping off down the street.

Kenny suspected how much she cared for him, even though she had not said so. This display of emotion proved she cared plenty. He caught up with her. "Celeste, don't ..."

"No, don't you," she said softly, trying not to get emotional.

"Forget about this whole thing tonight, OK and come with me to the opening of the play," she pleaded, trying to reason with him.

"No way, baby, I leave the socializing with the beautiful people entirely to you," he said, brushing her hair out of her face. "Save me a seat when Luther Vandross and Earth, Wind & Fire come to town. Tonight I have to snoop around to solve this case."

She felt defeated. As they walked in silence she knew he was right. This was a homicide case and he was the detective assigned to find the killer.

"Do you promise to call me no matter what time you get home?"
He crossed his heart.

She smiled at him, "You watch your step tonight, you hear?"
"I hear."

Celeste hoped he did, because she did not want to lose the man with whom she had fallen in love.

Jane's perky voice answered on the first ring, "Ed Townsend's office, this is Jane."

"It's Celeste Toussaint."

"I am sooo glad you called."

"Really?"

"Me and you gotta do lunch on Monday."

"Where and what time?"

"Noon at Cabana Carioca on 45th Street, upstairs, and please don't be late."

"I'm never late. Jane is everything OK with you?" asked Celeste, concerned.

"What do you mean?"

"You sound so ... I don't know ... stressed."

Jane was relieved she had picked up on her mood. "Good one, Toussaint. That is exactly what I am. See ya Monday. Gotta go."

TWENTY-ONE

The curtain closed and the audience roared for more. *Black and Blue* was a hit! All of the VIPs and press ventured across the street to Sardi's for the opening night party. Celeste longed for Kenny's company but had ended up going alone: she wished now that she had invited Renee.

The party was sensational with food and champagne in abundance. She was supposed to be working, but she really didn't feel like collecting interviews. The turn of events with Uncle Jim's murder, the news from Wayne, and Kenny's undercover assignment had her in a severe funk. Celeste stood in the back by the food table and tried hard not to mingle.

She was feeling quite pleased with herself - indulging in party favors, absorbing the sights, and, of course, not working - when the very handsome, and dressed to the nines, Dre and Maurice offered to relieve her load. They snickered at how silly Celeste looked trying not to be conspicuous, when she was actually attracting more attention to herself.

"Chile," scorned Maurice, "don't you *ever* think you can walk into a room, park yourself in a corner, and not be seen."

"Truly," chimed Dre, "you're the most fabulous looking woman in the place, and you're back here trying to hide."

"It won't work!" reasoned Maurice. "So get on out there and work the room," he said, pushing her into the crowd.

"I don't feel like working," said Celeste, giving them the official black woman's neck roll, "so I'm not going to. It doesn't matter what the cast says to me anyway. I already have my opinion for the review. Now when I'm ready to do a feature on some of these cast members, I will call the publicist. But for tonight, I'm not talking to anybody else in this room except you two, and that's because y'all won't leave me alone," she said and snapped her finger. *Uh oh, that snapping thing is becoming a habit,* she thought.

Maurice did his shindig, "Ooh, she read us."

"Yes she did, just like a trashy little romance novel," said Dre with a raised eyebrow.

Celeste warmed up to them now. "OK guys, I give, you two are sick."

Dre said pensively, "You know Maurice, you've been auditioning all over the place for a personable woman to co-host that radio show you're putting together with me, and she's been staring us in the face the whole time."

"Dre, you're brilliant!" agreed Maurice enthusiastically. "Celeste, you've got to be the one. Your voice and snippy commentary will go over tremendously well on-the-air."

She shook her head and said vehemently, "Can't do it. I can not do another thing. Dre, you know what I'm doing for you already."

"Oh yes, I almost forgot," said Dre, pulling out The Stand's front page splash of the series by Chi Woods that promised to rock New York titled "The Times Square Masacre".

"It looks great, doesn't it?" he said, holding up the paper hot off of the press.

"It does, but this is what I'm talking about," she said looking over the story. "Do you know I had to stay up until five in the morning to make your deadline, Dre? Add to this my Uncle's case,

The Courier, LaRocque's Company rehearsals, and now some radio show. No!"

"Our sponsors are Coca-Cola and Nike," Maurice threw in for leverage. "They would flip at the combo of the entertainment editors from the nation's number one black paper and New York's number one paper. The show will feature reviews on all of the things you're already doing for your day job," said Maurice convincingly.

"Who is doing the writing?" asked Celeste, curious now. Coca-Cola and Nike as sponsors meant really big time.

"We are," said Dre. "We can use our pieces from the papers and turn them into scripts."

Maurice jumped in quickly, "The program will be syndicated nationally, and the pay is tremendous."

"Yeah?" she said, thinking like the natives that another hustle might not be so bad.

"Oh yeah," said Maurice.

"And ET should be glad to let you do this," explained Dre, "because it means exposure for the paper and sales revenue as well. The publisher of my paper let me do it," he said, laughing as Celeste slapped him in the back of the neck, knowing full well he was speaking of himself.

"As executive producer of the program, I will be glad to make the official call to Mr. Ed Townsend. Only if my new co-host says yes?" said Maurice, obviously anxious for a "yes."

"I'll do it," conceded Celeste.

"Waiter," ordered Dre, "Moet all around, please. We have a celebration over here."

"And where's the diva, Miss Renee Poteat? She's missing from this little celebration," said Celeste, looking around the crowd for her friend as if she would see her at any moment.

"She had a show someplace tonight," said Dre. "Renee just said she'd share the wealth of her performance with us this weekend."

Across town, an emergency meeting was called by the Chairman. Each of the members had a copy of The New York Stand. They were all furious at the allegations made by Chi Woods and the promise to expose the entity who perpetuated the so-called evil of their livelihoods.

The Chairman stood to bring the meeting to order. "Gentlemen," he began calmly, "this meeting of our leadership has been called because we understand the financial ramifications of this story will be tremendous if we don't get to the bottom of it and soon. We'll go around the table to each member for your suggestions." The Chairman took his seat.

Member 1 from Dallas said, "I will not stand for such an inquest into our business dealings. We must eliminate the source and it's ear."

Member 2 from Los Angeles said, "We clearly have a leak amongst our staff somehow. I call for a thorough examination now."

Member 3 from Philadelphia: "This is an outrage. We are simply businessmen trying to earn a living from the sexual pleasures of others. I say we castrate the bastard who is responsible for this."

Member 4 from Chicago said, "You should strongly consider finding the source of this. I am confident that when you do, you will eliminate the problem, not just on this business issue, but on many others as well."

Taylor Reed was very careful not to say "we" or "our" in his statement. He knew the source all right. Chi Woods was not a stranger to him. He had watched her work for quite a few years. Her writing style was evident to him.

Taylor was sick to his stomach with the violence his Committee had displayed recently. He had always been a more sensitive man than his business partners. It would be only a matter of time before she revealed their identities. Celeste was a thorough journalist and he liked that most about her. He needed to get away, and soon, but he could never let his pals know his true feelings.

Taylor Reed was raised on Chicago's Southwest side in a poor

Scotch-Irish neighborhood. At an early age, Taylor's father recognized his aptitude for logic. Pop Reed decided that the genera-
tional curse of poverty would be broken with Taylor. He mapped
out the child's educational career and investigated the avenues that
truly brilliant children could take via scholarships.

With the education mission accomplished, Taylor had successful tenures at the University of Chicago's Laboratory High School,
Northwestern University for undergrad, and Wharton Business
School. With Taylor attending these Ivy League schools, his al-
ready- poor family were constantly over-extending themselves to
keep him well-dressed and in school clubs.

Taylor died inside because he knew that his family was making sacrifices of mortgage payments, light and gas bills to keep up
his facade in the Ivy League. It was his personal determination to
absorb everything thrown his way, academically and socially.

At Northwestern, an entire new world had opened up to Taylor. His roommate was the very rich and very sociably accepted
Ed Townsend of New York City. It was one of the happiest days
of Taylor's life when the group ET had formed asked him to join.
He was elated. Even more so when he discovered there was no fee
to join! "Pops will be glad to hear that," he remembered thinking.

Their group was the most elite on campus at Northwestern and
Wharton, with only five members - a select few. It did not take
Taylor long to realize that he was only asked to become a part of
their little group because of his knowledge. The rest of the fellas
were bright enough, yes. But Ivy League bright - no. They were
actually below average in the aptitude department. Period.
Two months in, Taylor not only realized that the elite paid their
professors but they had paid their way through undergraduate and
would do the same in grad school as well. Everyone catered to
them because their daddies were this or that, as if they didn't need
to ever think for themselves someday.

He lectured them regularly, telling the friends he'd come to
love that one day they would be thankful for the opportunity at an

Ivy League education. Who knew what the future would hold? Maybe someday they might just use a wee bit of the information gained there. Instead of taking heed, his friends laughed and scorned and left Taylor to do their papers while they partied the nights away.

"We don't need that book shit ,T, we've got your brains and we've got money. And as long as we've got money, you've got money. When you help us pass these tests, write these papers, and get our diplomas, we're all gonna have more money," they reminded Taylor constantly.

So Taylor dared not say more to the inflated egos, which had concocted all of those not-so-brilliant *faux pas*, that he constantly had to patch up behind them so they would not get caught. Taylor only continued to help them out of trouble because his friends had decided to implement the business plan he had created.

The business plan was a win-win situation for all. Since there was no money to be contributed from the Reed family, he would have to rely on the charity of his buddies to get his portion of the business rolling. Then he would finally be able to help his family.

Sitting now in this closed-door emergency meeting, he was more than irritated that he had been summoned to New York so he could once again devise the plan to dig them out of a potentially disastrous situation. Since they think they thought they were so smart, Taylor thought, this time, he'd let them figure it out for themselves.

Little did they know, Celeste Toussaint was on the case. The games were over. He knew it was time to consider their organization closed.

At half past midnight, Celeste waited in the doorway of Sardi's with Dre and Maurice for car number 12 to take her home. "Celeste, do you know you are the only reporter on the entertainment beat who gets a car home?" observed Maurice.

"All of the reporters at *The Courier* out late can get one when we're on the clock," said Celeste, "and that's no perk, it's a courtesy."

"I have to talk to my publisher about providing a car service for us reporters, too," mused Dre. They were hysterical at how easily Dre referred to his publisher as if he were another person.

Andre Tyson Webb's middle-class family totally abandoned him to avoid a scandal, once they found out he was gay at age 19. He left Pine Bluff, Arkansas, for the City of Lights via a Greyhound bus.

In the bathroom on the bus, Dre transformed himself into the vision of what he thought the gays in New York looked and dressed like: in full make-up and high heels. Upon his arrival, before he could switch his way out of the front door of Port Authority, he became a victim of a sexual assault. Two undercover policemen witnessed the act.

Dre wanted to go to trial, but the guilty party, a very prominent and drunk Park Avenue plastic surgeon, insisted upon settling at any price to keep the incident very hush-hush. Dre's price for the hideous crime was a measly $5 million. It was a reasonable price to pay for keeping the public *uninformed*, thought Dre.

Borrowing the Dre part of his first name and Tyson from his middle name, he became a new man by shedding that guy who he had changed into on the bus. With his newfound wealth at 19 in the big city, he purchased a building in Harlem using his given name, Andre Webb, and *The New York Stand* was born. Its premise would be "truth and honor for all Black people."

He hired the most established Black attorneys in New York City to handle his affairs. He brought out newspapermen from retirement, and those who were unemployed. He acted as managing editor until he was able to hire one and then made himself entertainment editor.

It never bothered the staff members that they had not met Andre Webb because they all knew his ailment of emphysema had him confined to the clean air of Sedona, Arizona. The charade was on!

After that first day in the city, the outwardly gay behavior was off. Dre only allowed his sexual preferences to be known in the company of a very select few.

"We are going up to Leviticus for a nightcap," said Maurice, "why don't you come with us?"

"Why don't you two go home to bed," she scoffed, "haven't you guys had enough for one evening?"

"Chile, we are just getting started," Dre informed her. "You see, we know how to enjoy the city. You know, take it for what it's worth."

"Yeah, just like you took Lord & Taylor's for everything but the men's department today," interjected Maurice, observing her bags.

"Leave me alone. I have been a good girl."

"Your car is here, mademoiselle," said Dre.

The uniformed driver held open the door for her. "Miss, please let me put your bags in the trunk."

She looked into the driver's face only after she recognized his voice. The look in Kenny's eyes read, *Play along.*

"Thank you very much, sir. Fellas, let the gentleman put the bags in the trunk."

"Oh, he's so cute," whispered Maurice to Celeste.

"Be nice," she said, thinking she would have to tease Kenny later about being "noticed" by Maurice. "Do you guys want a ride up to Leviticus?"

"Nah, Reese and I will go back in here and harass those left upstairs. Give us a hug and we'll see you later."

They did a group hug, which reminded her of a Charles and Annie Mae scene, "Night. Night guys. Y'all be good."

"You be good," said Maurice, looking in the window at the driver.

Dre mimicked her, "Y'all be good. She cracks me up with that 'y'all' stuff."

Kenny screeched away from the curb and headed over to the

FDR Drive. The silence was killing Celeste, but his demeanor was serious. She focused in on the blaring dispatch radio. At the 61st Street underpass Kenny slowed down the car to a crawl. The radio became static.

"I know you have several questions, Gal Friday, but just listen, because the answers to your questions are probably lengthy, and we don't have much time. I have a few facts to give you."

She took out her pad.

"First, it's obvious *The Courier* uses the same car service that Uncle Jim worked for. Second, the car in Chicago is registered to Taylor Reed, but it is also a part of a fleet of cars. Its full name is Service-WBB Inc., which is the same name of this company."

Celeste stopped writing. She could not conceal her fear for him.

"I don't want you to be afraid, baby. I am fine. If I can find out all I need to know tonight, I won't have to do this tomorrow. Third, Jane has called dispatch over 20 times ordering cars since I got on duty at 6 tonight. Find out what's up with that."

She mouthed, "OK."

"Listen now, no more talking when we come from under this overpass," he instructed.

The voices on the radio resumed. This was a side of Kenny she had not seen before. Totally on-the-job, authoritative, procedural, and secure. Even though she was scared, she liked this side of him. That little element of danger turned her on. Now she was curious as to what name he used, where he said he lived, and what kind of background he said he came from. How did a man walk off the street into a car service and get a job just like that? She couldn't wait to get the details.

They pulled up in front of Esplanade Gardens and he got her packages out of the trunk before opening the car door. He walked her halfway to the building when she stepped in front of him and kissed his lips lightly.

"Please be careful and promise me no matter what time you get home, you will ring my phone once."

"Celeste, it will be late."

"Please promise me. I will not be able to sleep until you call. Promise."

"I promise. But I have two more runs and then I'll be on my way home. You get some rest."

Celeste was frozen to her spot. Those were the exact same words Uncle Jim used when he dropped her off that last night. She stood in the doorway praying for Kenny's safety as she watched him make the same U-turn and drive down Lenox Avenue.

At approximately 4:14 a.m. the phone rang once and Celeste finally went to sleep.

TWENTY-TWO

Aunt June, Sammy, and Celeste went to a Saturday morning service at Convent Avenue Baptist Church. They
decided it would be good to do something uplifting together.

The sermon was titled, "When All Else Fails - Read The Instructions." It was a message of how to turn pain into power and
how to take control of bad situations and put them into the hands
of God through His word.

"My brothers and my sisters, when disasters strike," preached
Reverend Grant, "turn to the word. For you must understand that
the Bible is your diagram for living."

"Amen," chimed the congregation.

"When going through trials and tribulations," continued the
Reverend, "read the instructions, for it is in the instructions that
you'll find how to turn that trial and tribulation into a triumph.
When overcoming obstacles, the instructions will help you turn
them into an ovation. You all don't hear me," he sang.

"Well ..." responded the audience.

"The instructions of His word, my brothers and my sisters,
will touch you in that place of total surrender. I'm talking about
that place of deliverance that no man can touch. I'm talking about
the one and only place that a man can truly change. And that place

is in his heart. Oh, if I had to say Amen, I think I'd put it right
there," he preached and pounded on the podium.

"Amen," responded the audience.

"Somebody just ought to shout Glory!"

The congregation was on its feet now, in one accord with the
Reverend sending up a chorus of Amens. With arms lifted in a
worthy praise and voices raised in righteous hallelujahs, all in the
house of the Lord felt the message. Aunt June was shedding true
tears of understanding at the preacher's words; they were of a comfort to her in this hour of bereavement.

Sammy too was glad to be in this place at this time. Since
Uncle Jim's death, he had been non-communicative, had complained of not being able to sleep, and just wandered from club to
club. His face beamed with joy as Celeste saw closure ease into
Sammy's recently restless spirit.

Taking into account the reverend's sermon about following the
instructions, Celeste knew everyone in the Toussaint household
could now finally say "Amen."

Celeste arrived at LaRocque Bey's early to meet up with Renee
as planned. She was annoyed that Miss Diva was not there. It was
near the end of the jazz class and the instructor, Earlease, beck-
oned for her to join them. *What the heck, it will be a cute warm-up
before LaRocque kills me dead*, she thought.

Within ten minutes Earlease had her sweating and panting like
some 15-year-old dog who had never seen the inside of a dance
studio. The woman was brutal. Celeste was too embarrassed to
sit down before the class was officially over, so she allowed this
instructor to torture her.

"Who is she?" Celeste asked a classmate who was also against
the barre struggling to catch her breath.

"Don't you know?" the woman answered. "That's Earlease
Robinson. Head Broadway diva choreographer."

No wonder she was half dead! Before she even got to

LaRocque's class her joints were achy and her hair was sopping wet. Thank God for her appointment at Georgiana's and Z's later. _Yeah, 'think on these relaxing things and you'll survive this class,_ Celeste thought.

"OK everybody, I want to see _gran jetes'_ all the way up here," commanded Earlease, pointing to the ceiling and then showed the class she could do them herself.

Celeste bent over, putting her head on her knees for one last stretch, and prayed she didn't break her neck trying to follow behind Earlease.

Kenny set up all of his needed provisions within reach of the telephone for his conversation with Celeste. They had not engaged in their nightly exchange since he was moonlighting as a driver. This investigation was beginning to take its toll on him physically. He knew he would have more energy if only he could get his blast of love from Celeste daily. Their regular work schedules were becoming more rigorous and it was becoming a major production for them to simply get together.

The employees of the car service were not talking about how Uncle Jim's car made it back to the garage. No one seemed to know or care. It was time for investigative journalist Celeste Toussaint/Chi Woods to put the pressure on some of the staff. Kenny loved her skill. The entertainment column had become even more popular since Celeste took over the beat. She could get anybody to tell her anything.

The struggle Kenny had at present was how he was going to tell Celeste her girlfriend Renee was dancing in those strip joints she was investigating. He had picked up Renee three nights in a row from the Show Time Lounge at four in the morning, and drove her home. He needed to approach the topic delicately.

Celeste had mentioned that Renee was living very well as a dancer, with a $1300-a-month apartment, vast shopping sprees, and just an overall abuse of money that seemed to come from some endless source. He decided to be as up-front with her on this matter as she had been with him on others. Kenny knew for a fact, that Celeste was a woman who would be totally pissed if he withheld that type of information, even if the information was about a friend.

Kenny lit the fireplace and settled on his couch with the phone to call his Gal Friday.

TWENTY-THREE

S unday at noon, Celeste was boarding the Long Island Rail road train at Penn Station headed for Huntington. The ride was approximately 52 minutes, so Celeste luxuriously read *The Courier's* Sunday issue. The cover of the Arts & Entertainment section featured a photo of the *Black And Blue* cast and her piece. She really did enjoy that play, especially the dancing, which her review reflected.

Celeste was still in shock when Maurice told her ET was delighted at the prospect of his entertainment editor doing a syndicated radio program. She knew he was really most delighted at the presentation of the revenues, which would automatically be given to *The Courier* for lending their name and their editor. They were to begin production next week and Celeste's work load was mounting.

Even more of a shocker was the information Kenny shared with her last night about Renee. That one still needed to sink in good. As much as she and Renee had talked about secrets, never was there even a hint of her involvement in strip dancing.

Walking around Penn Station before catching the train, she could not believe all of the homeless people living there. In fact, there were a tremendous amount of homeless people in New York period. She tripped over them every day, on her way anywhere. With the exorbitant rents, Celeste knew why they lived on the streets.

Dre lived on 100th Street and Broadway, his rent was $1200. Maurice lived in downtown Brooklyn and his rent was $1300 like Renee's, but at least he had a duplex with three bedrooms. Even still, in Celeste's mind, that much money should be reserved for house payments.

What she could not understand was why there were so many people out of work. Every time she turned around someone was trying to give her another job. Maybe if so many people were not concentrating on trying to get over with a hustle in the city, just maybe, a few of the homeless people could have a share in some of those jobs. Heck, they could gladly take one of hers.

When Celeste got off of the train in Huntington, she noticed for the first time that fall was in full swing. The trees were gorgeous in all of their splendor as they began to change from green to gold and rust. She was able to inhale deeply and smell fresh air. Just now she realized she was not able to do that in the city so easily.

"Miss Toussaint," said a sleekly dressed, distinguished looking Black man, "I'm Winston. Mr. Hamilton has sent me for you. Right this way," he said, guiding her arm.

Walking behind Winston, Celeste played the "Shaft" theme in her head. She just knew that during the 60's he was a rebel to his heart. Even now, Winston was sporting those gorgeous tapered sideburns and ankle boots with the zippers on the side, polished to perfection. He exuded the "I'm a bad mother ... shut yo mouth" attitude. Thinking about it had her cracking up on the inside.

"Relax, you've got a nice little ride from here to Dix Hills," he said as he held open the car door.

In the back of the limousine, she thought that it was nice of Kenny to impress her with a chauffeur driven car, but it really wasn't necessary.

"These New Yorkers sure know how to waste money, with their thirteen-hundred-dollar apartments and limo rides to a Sunday dinner," she thought aloud. "I have to talk to Kenny about his frivolous spending."

Kenny was standing in the doorway of the gigantic center-hall colonial. He broke out with his kilowatt smile when he saw her. "I'm so glad you could come," he beamed, taking her coat. "You look beautiful."

"Thank you, sir," she said.

He stepped behind her and whispered in her ear while inhaling her scent, "... Mmm, just like dessert."

The little black dress with a lace scarf and pearls worked its magic every time, "You behave now," she said, thinking he didn't look too bad himself. "And thank you for sending a limo for me but you really should not have."

"It was no problem at all," he said, smiling at her prudence. "Welcome to our humble abode. One rule applies here in this house at all times, no talk of work. We were taught to leave work at work and when we enter this house, we are home." "Now that, I think I can manage," she said thankful for an offer not to think about what indeed was always on her mind.

"Come," he said holding her hand, "I'll show you around."

A pretty young lady, tall and shapely, bounced up to them with her hands on her hips. "So ... this is Celeste," she exclaimed with approval, walking around her.

"And you must be Jacqueline," Celeste acknowledged, unable to ignore the striking resemblance between brother and sister.

"Well K-Trey, you've outdone yourself this time. She's fab!"

Celeste looked at Kenny, teasing, "Oh, so at home we're K-Trey, are we?"

"I'm glad she passes the Crest Test, Jackie," said Kenny, pushing her out of the way playfully, "now scram!"

The Hamilton home was anything but humble. The Wedgwood-

colored formal foyer had a ceramic tile floor, a gigantic chandelier, and a wide winding staircase. The living room was done with
the most delicate Chinese antiques Celeste had ever seen.

Venturing to the other side of the foyer, Celeste could not contain herself, "Wow. Kenny, what a great room!"

He laughed heartily, "And that's why it's called the Great Room
because everyone walks in here and says the same thing."

This tri-leveled room with vaulted ceilings was done completely in ivory. There was a stone fireplace encircled by a sunken
conversation pit. The movie-screen- sized television was surrounded by four easy chairs of different colors and styles, obviously selected as favorites by each family member. The custom-
built pool table by the arched windows had balls spread over the
table, an indication of an ongoing game.

The same was also true for the backgammon table. The sounds
of a Ms. Pacman game table, all lured Celeste's immediate attention.

"I love Ms. Pacman. Are you up for a challenge later?"

"Miss woman, are you challenging me to a game in my own
home?"

"Yep. And the only Ms. I wanna be called is Ms. Pacman. I bet
you a dollar."

"Ahhh, it's on now," Kenny laughed. "Let me finish showing
you around."

The spiral staircase that led to the loft area, overlooking the
entire great room, was a music lovers' paradise. There was an
old- fashioned jukebox, all types of stereo equipment, and the walls
held built-in shelves with albums alphabetized.

They found his Mom in the Aztec-colored kitchen taking a
huge turkey out of the oven. Celeste rushed to lay the heat protec-
tors on the center ceramic counter. She put down the 20-plus-
pound turkey and sighed, "Whew, that was right on time. I like a
woman who can find her way around in a kitchen. How are you
dear? I'm Mom," she said, kissing Celeste's cheek lightly.

"It's a pleasure, I've heard wonderful things about you. Kenny loves his mother dearly," she said, feeling comfortable in Mrs. Hamilton's presence right away.

"Well he told us that you were beautiful, but his adjectives did not do you enough justice," said Mom, holding her hand and looking at her up and down, "you really are lovely."

"Thank you, Mrs. Hamilton."

"No dear, everybody calls me Mom. So that means you, too," she said, patting Celeste on the cheek.

Mrs. Hamilton was obviously from money. She was not only beautiful with her silver hair and cocoa-colored skin, but she was also extremely well kept. She did not look as if she had worked anywhere in her entire life other than in her own kitchen and that only because she wanted to. From what Celeste could see, she did just that, but only on Sundays.

Celeste snuck a peek out of the kitchen window at the perfectly manicured grounds, in-ground swimming pool, and what looked like a guest house further back. To the left she saw Winston wiping down the limo. Also she saw, at a quick count, what she thought was an eight-car garage. She was going to have to have a long talk with Kenny later about all of this, which he never told her. *And just when you think you know somebody*, she mused.

"Come on, I want to show you my favorite place in the house," Kenny said, dragging her by the hand.

They climbed a set of stairs off of the kitchen. On the first level up he rushed her through a tour of the six spacious bedrooms, each done in opulent colors and varying decor. Her favorite was the one in a burnt orange with a circular bed. Yummy.

Continuing up to the third level of the house, he opened the door to the ultimate bachelor's pad.

"This is bigger than Aunt June's whole apartment, Kenny."

The room ran the entire length of the house. He had windows for walls and the view of the colored trees at that level was spectacular. Kenny had shelves and shelves of motivational books, martial arts books, cook books, and awards. There was a work-out area with a weight bench, rowing machine, treadmill, and LifeCycle. His bathroom had a spa for at least four people and a dry sauna. The shower stall had glass doors and doubled as a steam room.

"Over here is where I sit when we talk," he said, lowering her onto a supple leather tan sectional facing a fireplace with a bear-skin rug. "This is where I wish you were with me, in the middle of the night."

"This house is spectacular, Kenny. All nine thousand square feet of it?" she guessed.

"Close baby, nine thousand, eight hundred square feet," he said modestly.

She punched him in the stomach. "Why didn't you tell me? I would not have treated you any differently," she said, though she knew why he'd chose not to say.

"I just wanted you to love me for me," he conceded, kneeling down in front of her, "because I love you, Celeste Toussaint. Daddy's girl. Miss Chicago. The most beautiful woman I have ever laid eyes on." He kissed her intensely. "You know it's been too long since I have had a chance to kiss you."

Celeste was breathless and only nodded in agreement.

"Hopefully one day when you are Mrs. Kenneth Lamont Hamilton the Third, I can kiss you all day, every day," he stated, searching for a response in her eyes.

"Is this a proposal?" she questioned, not really wanting to know the answer.

"It sure is," confirmed Kenny, "but the only question I want answered first is, do you feel the same about me?" He pulled her to her feet, closer to him.

Since they could not be together regularly, the phone had been their link to one another. Celeste and Kenny had come to know each other quite well and they both knew they were in love.

"I'm afraid I do," she said, happy to have verbally released her emotion.

Kenny was so happy, he picked her up and swung her around until they both got dizzy. She stood on her toes and kissed the lids of his eyes, before taking control over his mouth and exploring once again the same feeling she had that night on Aunt June's balcony.

"Let's go away, just you and I. Here," he said, handing her a leather bound book of various vacation spots, "you pick the place."

She flipped through the book, looking at each house and the snapshots of their interiors in every part of the world imaginable.

"Kenny, these places are gorgeous, but we don't have to spend ..."

"Sssh. Baby nothing is too good for you."

"I mean, for all I care we can get a suite at the Pierre for the weekend and pretend we vanished," she objected, financially speaking. "Traveling to any of these places requires airfare, and the rentals, and food, and ..."

Kenny put his hand over her mouth. "You worry about other people's money too much. Let me spend what I want to spend."

"Is there anything else you want to tell me about all of these gorgeous houses from here to East Giblip?"

Kenny was looking around the room to avoid her eyes.

"Kenny ...," she said, impatiently waiting with a raised brow, "No secrets between us ever, even if they are pleasant surprises. OK?"

"OK I confess," he said sitting her down on his lap. "Those are our properties."

"All of them?"

Kenny took a deep breath, knowing he must definitely be in love with her because he was about to divulge the family secret. "Yes, all of them."

Celeste's mouth hung open for a moment. Kenny saw her eyes dancing with shock, and he did owe her an explanation.

"You see baby, my Dad made a fortune in real estate. As a result we have properties all around the world at our disposal and a monthly income that is ... well, you can imagine.

"My Dad's philosophy was to buy up all of the land because there was never going to be any more. It's a philosophy the family business is still run by today. Jacqueline and other family members manage the real estate properties. I have never had an interest in the business. Dad was pissed when I passed up Yale for The John Jay College Law Enforcement program. What can I say? It's law enforcement that gets my adrenalin pumping."

He reached up to touch her velvety cheek with the back of his hand, feeling glad he had finally shared his secret with her.
"I'm sorry I didn't tell you before now, but you can understand why. My Dad also taught us to always pretend like we don't have a dime, that way you'll know who really likes you for you."

"I ...," Celeste began.

"I'm not finished," he said, holding his finger over her lips. "I haven't told you the details of my father's death because I needed to tell you all of the above first. He died last year in the plane crash of the inaugural launch of the company jet."

"Oh I'm so sorry," she whispered, stunned.

"Yeah, I was too for a while, but my father loved his company and he always said he wanted to go down blazing trails and not in some hospital bed.

"Just the day before he died, I promised him that when I found the right woman, I would give up chasing bad guys and settle in with the business. I totally understand being a detective is not the kind of life you should subject the woman you love to at all."

Celeste thought, *You've got that right pal.*

"Mom and Jacqueline have a hard enough time dealing with the late nights, undercover work, and even my carrying a gun. So you see Miss Toussaint, my complicated life has been waiting for you to walk in to uncomplicate it. Only when you're ready."

Mom's voice belted over the intercom, "Dinner is served. You two get down to the dining room, pronto!"

"Now, where would you like to go and when, my dear?"

Celeste flipped through the book to the spot in Negril. The stark white house against the blue water and white sand in the photo had her completely captivated.

"Kenny, I'm not doubting my feelings for you, I know they are real," Celeste reasoned, "but shouldn't we take some precautions first before we go traipsing out into the wild blue yonder?"

"I agree," he said earnestly. "When do we take the test?"

Celeste knew her mind could not be read so easily. "What test are you talking about?" she quizzed narrowing her eyes.

"The AIDS test," he smiled, "and don't tell me it's not what you were thinking, Gal Friday."

She had to laugh, "I was. I'm just really shocked that you knew, that's all."

Celeste was never going to let another man touch her intimately again without the HIV Antibody test. There was a 20-year-old receptionist at *The Courier* in Chicago who had a three-month fling with her first beau. When the girl tried to give blood at the annual Red Cross Blood Drive, three weeks later they told her she was HIV positive.

Celeste remembered thinking what a stinking way to find out you were going to die, by trying to help someone to live. That same day Celeste went down to the Department of Health to take the test, anonymously, of course.

"I knew exactly what you were thinking, Miss Toussaint," he said, pinching her nose. "We are meant for one another because we are in tuned that way. We can go to take it together."

"And when we get our negative results," she said, snuggling up to him and running her fingers down his back seductively, "here we come, Negril. No problem, mon."

He closed his eyes with pleasure. "Now you see, I told you we were meant for one another, 'cause baby you are reading my mind."

By the time they got downstairs, everyone was seated and served. The dining room, located in the center of the house was the only room with no windows. Their formal table accommodated twelve. The deep cherry wood dining ensemble glistened against the hunter green wallpapered and carpeted room. The crystal wall sconces and chandelier provided the perfect amount of light.

"Everybody, this is Celeste Toussaint," announced Kenny proudly. "Celeste, even though you won't remember everybody, this is Uncle Zeke and Aunt Betty. Uncle Cleon and Aunt Josephine. Uncle Lester and Aunt Nina, and Uncle William and Aunt Irene."

"Hello, nice to meet you," she said, feeling definitely overwhelmed.

"Here is your seat, sweetie, between Jackie and Uncle Zeke," said Mom.

Kenny held out her chair and took his seat at the head of the table. Everyone joined hands while Kenny prayed.

"Most gracious heavenly Father, we come to you once again offering thanks. You have been so good to us and we thank you. Thank you for the food we are about to receive for the nourishment of our bodies. Bless those who do not have as we do. Thank you for uniting us in your love. Through Jesus Christ, our Lord. Amen."

"Amen," said all.

That was the most beautiful prayer she had ever heard anyone pray over food. The passion with which Kenny rendered the prayer brought a tear to Celeste's eyes. There was nothing that she liked better than a man who knew how to pray. She said to herself, *Mmm that's my man."*

Kenny saw the look of pride on Celeste's face after his prayer. Their eyes locked and they longed to hug one another right across the table.

"So Celeste," said Uncle Zeke, shaking her thoughts, "we've been reading your column since we heard about you. You're a good writer."

"Thank you, sir."

"No, I insist you call me Uncle Zeke. That goes for all of us."

"Thank you, Uncle Zeke."

"Your story on the cover of the entertainment section today," said Aunt Irene, "convinced us all to go to see *Black And Blue* next month."

"You will absolutely love that show," confirmed Celeste, "I want to see it again myself."

"Then you and Kenny must come with us," said Aunt Josephine. "We're all going to stay in the city at the Plaza and make a weekend out of it."

"Can you recommend any other activities that you rate as a must for us?" asked Uncle William.

"Of course." she stated, "I'll give Kenny a list and do my best to get as many complimentary tickets as possible."

"Oh no, we'll be happy to pay," said Uncle Lester. "If you want to use your muscle, we only like to sit down front."

Everyone agreed.

"I'll start working on it tomorrow," she smiled, glad to be in the company of a family who did things together often and in grand fashion. Annie Mae and Charles were gonna love this bunch.

When Mom Hamilton was in the kitchen, the dinner conversation turned to real estate matters and the family seemed to know instinctively it was all right to openly discuss business in front of Celeste. Each of them worked in some aspect of the establishment. The Hamilton clan was adamant about keeping their assets amongst themselves.

From what Celeste could deduce, Kenny's father was the mastermind behind their success. He took his life savings back in the mid '50's and began investing it into apartment buildings that fell short on taxes. He worked as a clerk in New York City's Tax Lien department. Since it was against the law for an employee of that department to cash in on someone else's misfortune or late payments, Mr. Hamilton gave his money to the female members in the family to make the property purchases in their married names.

On the fifth occasion of these such transactions, the family called a meeting to organize a pool of their financial resources. Notlimah International Realty virtually became an overnight success. The company name was Hamilton inverted, which served as a nice camouflage of their nationality. It was an important factor to their success in the racist 1950's stateside. They did not have those problems abroad and Notlimah flourished there initially.

Uncle Cleon was the first to bring up business. "Listen here," he said in a hush, "I saw a sweet high-rise in the city down on the east side in the late 40's. It's ours if we want it."

"Even if we do want it, Cleon, you know the rule and this is not the place to discuss it," reminded Mom Hamilton, returning to the dining room with dessert.

"I think I know the building he's talking about," interjected Jacqueline, "and if it is the same one I'm thinking of, Uncle Cleon, you and I are going to have to take a little walk outside after dinner."

"We'll come with you," said Uncle Lester, speaking for the rest of them.

"You all are hopeless," said Mom, shaking her head, "you can't even keep the Sabbath day holy. K-Trey, help me out here."

Mrs. Hamilton was a practitioner of God's word. She was deemed the most righteous woman in the family, and knowing the word for themselves, they all followed her suit.

Kenny coughed, "Um, Mom, I can't help you this time. I have to work tonight."

Everybody teased him, "Uh oh. You're in trouble now, Kenny."

"Mom, hopefully I won't have to do the Sunday thing anymore. I'm almost done with this case."

Celeste perked up, "You are?"

"What case is this, son?" questioned Uncle William.

Mom broke up the conversation. "I can see you insist on trying to talk business in this house, so I'm ending it here. You all know better."

Jacqueline whispered to Celeste, "They try her every week, and guess what, they never get away with it."

Celeste's thoughts were miles away, considering Kenny's statement about the case. *He's almost done ...*

In back of the limo on the ride home, Celeste and Kenny snuggled up to one another in silence wishing for more time together. He would not allow her to ask any questions about the case and he did not supply any answers about his business for the evening.

Downtown by the Holland Tunnel, Winston pulled into a parking lot, and Celeste felt Kenny's whole demeanor change. She knew this was the on-the-job facade that he needed for survival.

Kenny held her face and saw the questions in her eyes, "Winston will take you home. I garage that old jalopy here and drive it to work."

"It doesn't look like it can make it out of this garage," Celeste teased about the green 1975 Dodge Charger.

"Oh, it will make it out and about the city, but that's as far as it goes. Yeah, it's just what you need running over all of the city's pot- holed streets."

"How do you get home?"

"Winston takes me."

"Every day?"

"Every day," he said, kissing her nose. "Oh, do I feel an interview coming on, Gal Friday?" He answered before she could ask, "You see, Winston is my secret weapon number three."

"Number three? What are numbers one and two?"

Kenny lifted up his shirt to expose the holstered nine-millimeter. "This is number one, and this is number two," he said, raising his pant leg showing off a .45 Smith & Wesson.

"Ooh Officer Friendly, that's just like mine."

"Just like yours?"

"So my Daddy didn't tell you everything," she said, laughing and opening her purse so he could view her piece.

He whistled, "I had heard you Chicago women came packing. For once the rumor mill was correct. Why didn't you tell me?"

"A girl has got to keep some things to herself," she said with a wink.

"Celeste, you really don't need that, you know."

"Oh yeah? Well my Daddy always told me that it is always best to be prepared, because he would rather I be judged by twelve than carried by six," she pointed out. "And would you agree?"

"I can only agree if you know how to use this thing. Sweetie, that's a pretty big piece for a woman."

"Come on Kenny, you met my Daddy. Do you think he would have given me the gun if I could not use it and use it well?"

"Yes beautiful, I agree," he conceded.

"So don't change the subject, you still didn't tell me how Winston is secret weapon number three."

"Woman, nothing gets passed you, huh" he asked.

She crossed her arms and waited for his answer.

"Celeste, when I joined the force my Dad wanted to ensure that his only son was safe at all times, so he hired Winston, a former CIA agent, to tail me when I'm on the clock.

"Winston was a specialist in espionage, explosives, and a master of disguises. He and his team single-handedly busted up the famed Cartel crime ring that would have unleashed two billion dollars of cocaine and heroine on America's streets."

The impact of the Hamiltons' power really finally struck her. "My goodness."

"Winston is more than our chauffeur and more than my secret weapon, he's my best friend. So, my darling," he said smothering her face in kisses, "when I tell you not to worry, I really mean it. OK?"

"If you say. Promise to call no matter what time tonight."

"Hey, what do you think, that I don't know the rules by now?

I can't even sleep myself until I call."

Winston knocked on the car window and pointed to his watch.

Kenny laughed, "He's also my timekeeper."

"I have had a wonderful day," she said, kissing both sides of his face. "Watch out for those bad guys, will you?"

"Most definitely, because it's you that I really want to watch out for, baby," he said, getting out of the car. "Oh, I want you to know something else."

"What do you want me to know?"

"I'm in love with you," he winked, and slammed the door.

Digesting what Kenny said and the events of the day, Celeste had to lay down to collect her thoughts. This relationship was full of surprises.

TWENTY-FOUR

C eleste walked into the Midtown South Precinct as Kenny instructed, so she could pick up Uncle Jim's personal effects. The two of them had discussed exactly how they would play the victim's relative and the detective roles. If Kenny's superiors ever found out he was romancing Celeste while the investigation was pending, he could be charged with conduct unbecoming an officer.

Waiting for Detective Hamilton, Celeste sat on the bench next to a young girl who had been beaten badly in the face.

The girl spoke. "Monica?"

Celeste looked more closely at her. "Muffin?"

"Yeah it's me," said Muffin in her now not-so-delightful Southern drawl.

"Goodness gracious, what happened to you?"

At that moment Kenny was standing over them. She spoke fast before he did, "Are you Detective Hamilton?" asked Celeste.

"Yes, ma'am and you are?"

"Monica Price," she said, standing to face him. "I came to report a robbery, but my friend Muffin here needs your immediate attention."

Kenny helped Muffin to her feet. "Please come with me, Miss," he said, not believing that "The Muffin" walked right into his precinct.

Muffin asked, "Can Monica come with me?"

"Of course," said a comforting Officer Friendly.

"I'm right behind you, Muffin. Right behind you."

Celeste watched Detective Hamilton take charge of tending to Muffin. He collected the necessary items so no one else would have to enter into his office. First aid kit, complaint forms, a pot of hot water, and several packages of hot chocolate. He placed a tape recorder in front of her so not one detail would slip by him. Kenny served the chocolate to the ladies, and after Muffin downed her cup in three gulps she was eager to share the details.

"This little episode all began when I first got to New York a few years ago from Macon, Georgia," she stated, totally at ease. "You see I am gonna be a star so the Show Time Lounge is the first place I go to get a job. I have been there ever since and things had been going just fine."

Muffin peeled apart an alcohol wipe and put it directly on an open wound in the palm of her hand. She didn't even flinch. Celeste winced for her.

"It started to get a little sticky around the place just recently."

"How recently?" asked the detective.

"Oh I would say in the last few weeks. But to be exact, it was the day after Julie was found dead."

Celeste and Kenny exchanged glances.

"Do you mean Julie, the girl who was strangled to death by the judge from Maryland?" said the detective, seeking specifics.

"She's the one," confirmed Muffin. "Remember the story in *The Courier* with the sketch of the judge and that picture of her dead body referring to her as Jane Doe before they knew all of the details?"

"Yeah. Go on," stated the detective, feeling this coming together.

"Well, I wanted to tell the police who she was. I mean, I didn't think there was any harm in letting them know what her name was. Julie didn't deserve to die as a Jane Doe."

"Uh huh."

"But saying anything to the police was out. They gave me a warning then to be careful of who I talked friendly to because they would be watching me."

"What makes you so sure they are not watching you this morning?"

"Because, Detective, they do their dirty work at night. They are like little vampires, you know. They don't make it to their offices until at least noon-thirty."

"OK, go on."

"They told me I better not say anything, even if I could identify her and the judge. They wanted to take me off of the door because they said I knew too much. But I convinced them that it's me they needed for the same reason. So they let me stay."

The detective overlooked for the time being Muffin's repeated references to "they." "What prompted them to do this to you now, then? That murder case has been solved."

"You see, they are a very jumpy bunch, Detective Hamilton. There was this story in one of them weekly papers, I think it's called *The New York Stand.*"

Celeste looked at the floor, she didn't want anyone to see the guilt in her eyes.

"I did not see the entire paper, they only let me read the article."

"You've lost me, Muffin," said the detective, even though he was nowhere near lost.

"Some reporter from this paper did a story called the 'Times Square Massacre'. It's some expose' series about what's going on in places like the Show Time Lounge."

"What does that have to do with you, Muffin?" questioned the detective.

"They figure that since I am on the inside and since my good friend is now dead, that I will probably talk to that reporter and spill my guts eventually. I mean somebody already talked. They know that if people on the inside keep talking, they will be exposed. So they *gently* came to warn me instead of killing me, to send a message to everybody on the inside to shut up. Whether I did it for the first story, or am considering talking for the next, don't matter. They don't want no more stories."

How dare they touch her. Celeste was pissed, "Muffin, you keep referring to they. Is it Sal?"

"No, no Monica," laughed Muffin, "Sal may look like he's in charge, but believe me he's a flunky. They roughed him up, too. No, they are very powerful and successful business men in this here city."

The detective wanted to get to the bottom of this. "I can offer you protective custody. We can literally make you disappear. I can also arrange 24-hour protection for your family in Georgia."

"May I have another cup of chocolate?" was Muffin's only request.

She sipped her hot cocoa with warm remembrances of her family at home. Whenever she or her brother would come inside from playing with a bruise or scrape, her mother would always fix them hot cocoa. She thought of all the lies she had told her family these last few years about her lifestyle. Her family only knew that their Muffin was making it big in the city. For holidays she always went loaded down with gifts for everybody.

Muffin's mother had told her often of how her success was the envy of the other moms in Macon. There was no way she could go home now and tell them everything she had said over the years had been totally a lie.

"You know, Detective, I am going to tell you, I really appreciate your offer. I want to see that they are taken down at any expense. Their operation is 20 percent legal and 80 percent illegal. But it won't be done by my hand alone. Don't you have some undercover people who you could put at the Show Time?"

The detective was thinking how he was going to play the scene so he would not be taken for a ride by this informant who just happened to walk into his precinct. "Sure, we can arrange an investigation," he said noncommittally.

"Good. I can be a lot of help on the inside. You see, Detective, I have led you to some very dirty water. We have this saying down home: 'You can lead a horse to water, but you can't make him drink.' I can not make you drink and I will not help you drink, either. It has been nice meeting you," said Muffin, collecting her things.

"How do I reach you?"

"I'll call you, Detective. If you have an message for me, send Monica. 'Bye now."

Celeste was lost in her thoughts. The gal was street smart, all right. She just bet that Muffin was going to get total satisfaction when "they" went down. Little Miss Muffin was probably laying and waiting for some big payday when it happened, too, and then she would go smiling her sweet Southern smile all the way to the bank. Was it worth subjecting herself to such dangerous people? It's one thing when you don't know, but when you do ... the thought of it gave Celeste the heebie jeebies.

"This is getting out of my jurisdiction, Gal Friday," Detective Hamilton announced. "In light of what Muffin just told us, this is a case for RICO."

"What's Rico got that you don't have?"

"No. No. No. RICO stands for Racketeering Influence Corrupt Organizations. It's a specialized crime unit."

She gasped, "Do you think what they are doing is racketeering?"

"Did you see that girl's face? Did you hear why she said they beat her up? All of their shit is to further their business dealings. It all spells racketeering" said the detective factually. "It sure ain't good business."

Kenny had a gut feeling that all of this hanky panky at the

Show Time tied in nicely with WBB and Uncle Jim's murder. All he needed to do was prove it, and he'd quit as soon as he signed his name on the final report. Now, he knew that was a promise.

Celeste saw Kenny was long gone, piecing this puzzle together in his mind as he stared at the city from his office window. He had gotten awfully comfortable in his high-back chair, with his feet on the window sill. She took the bag from a chair labeled "Jim Toussaint" and left without saying goodbye. Outside of her office she called the detective from a pay phone.

"Hamilton," he answered, irritated that he had been interrupted from his thoughts.

"I like the way you work, Hamilton," Celeste gushed sweetly.

"I'm sorry I wasn't more attentive."

"You're working. So you're forgiven. I left something in your top drawer that is sure to keep you thinking of me for the rest of the day."

"Now what could ...."

"I've got to run. Kiss. Kiss," and she hung up.

"Don't keep me in suspense," he laughed. "Celeste. Baby ..."

Kenny looked at the receiver, saying, "She hung up on me."

He finally opened his drawer and found her business card. "Thanks baby, a card for my wall at the office," he said and resumed his favorite position, chair facing window, feet up, when he saw the writing on the back of the card.

"Meet me at the test site downtown TONIGHT. Cause if I don't make love to you soon, I am going to explode!"

Kenny screamed to the top of his lungs, "Yes!" Two of his colleagues rushed to his office. "Hamilton, are you OK?"

"Am I OK?" he responded looking at the card. "Yes, indeed."

As promised, Celeste was right on schedule for lunch. It was Jane who arrived late. Celeste did not mind, for the one thing she could do was make herself at home in an eating establishment.

The Cabana Carioca was a traditional Brazilian restaurant. Its menu consisted of Shrimp Paulista, a Brazilian version of shrimp scampi; black beans and rice; Guarana, a popular Brazilian ale; and flan. The prices were modest and the portions were more than generous. Ever since Celeste spent a semester at the Universidad de Madrid, she had acquired a love of foods from other countries. Jane would never know how much the noonday environment revived her.

Celeste devoured the salad bar while Jane downed two Caidirinha's in a row. "Jane, you should really take it easy. You know that drink is nothing but pure sugar cane rum and a splash of lime," warned Celeste. "You *do* have to function the rest of the day."

"Haven't you noticed by now that over half of the people in this industry are functioning alcoholics. Toussaint, please, I need this extra boost," claimed Jane between gulping her third Caidirinha, "because the only way I will be able to justify spilling my guts to you is if I am stoned out of my mind."

Celeste did not want to interrupt the "spilling her guts" part and held up her Guarana. "Then let's have a toast."

"That's more like it," agreed Jane.

"Arriba, abajo, al centro, por dentro."

Jane was hysterical, "What the heck, Toussaint. I bring you to an ethnic restaurant and looky here, you done gone native on me."

"Not quite native, it's a Spanish toast. But I'm cheating a whole lot with my Brazilian version of cream soda here," Celeste referred to her Guarana.

After conversing for more than an hour, Celeste found Jane to be not quite the bubblehead she had made her out to be after all. In fact, she was educated and certainly had designs on moving her way up through the publishing ranks.

"If you haven't noticed by now, Toussaint, all of ET's gals come this way from the same training camp."

"What camp is it?"

"The Ed Townsend Boot Camp. There are those of us who

survive and get their foot in the door of the executive office like me," said Jane, pleased with her accomplishment.

"There are those of us who survive and climb the corporate ladder well, like Mason. Then there are those of us who get a little too greedy too soon and get themselves killed, like ..." Jane's voice trailed off painfully.

"Like Julie?"

Jane's eyes held big buckets of tears and her voice had lowered to a whisper. "Yeah, like Julie. She was my very best friend, since first grade."

Celeste produced a packet of Kleenex.

"You know what Julie's main problem was? Her Mom had this hold over her. I'm telling you, it was not natural," Jane said pensively. "So when she came ta town she just ran buck wild."

"When I saw you on the elevator the day after the story, I never got to say to you that I hoped you would call the police to identify Julie," Celeste prompted.

"I did go to the police. They had me sign a statement and everything. Then while I was there I got ta thinking, maybe I should not tell the police everything. So I didn't."

The detective was right. Julie was holding back more information, thought Celeste.

Julie continued, "The only statement I made and signed my name to was that I knew her from high school. I didn't say nothing about her coming to New York because of me, you know."

"Do you remember saying to me the first day the story came out that you told Julie not to chump the players?" questioned Celeste, eager to get to the facts of this ordeal.

"I sure do. That is rule number one," said Jane factually while snapping for the waiter to bring another drink.

"What does that mean? Who are the players, Jane, and what game is being played here?"

Jane downed her drink. "Toussaint, you ain't never been in the streets, have ya?"

"I don't understand what that has to do with the question."

"Let me tell ya something. These folks here ain't bullshittin'. Maybe you should stick ta writin' your little entertainment columns and leave this dirty business to someone who knows these dirty streets."

"Don't tell me what to do. Just because I don't know what you are talking about does not mean I can't help you."

Jane was about to tackle her fifth drink.

"How are you doing anyway behind all of those drinks?" Celeste asked, worried that Jane would be, as she put it, too stoned to go on with her story.

"Look at who is telling someone what to do now! Don't worry, I'm fine."

This chick is getting on my nerves, Celeste thought just as she decided to fire her up with hot sauce. "You know what 'fine" means to me? Fucked-up. Insecure. Neurotic. And emotional. If the dress fits, Miss Jane, buy it," Celeste walked away raging, then came back.

"I do believe that it was you who wanted to discuss this mess with me, so when I come from the restroom, if we are going to discuss it, I hope to see you here. If you have changed your mind, be gone."

The very attentive waiter brought another drink to the table. This time Jane waved it away and ordered a coffee. Black. She knew an apology was in order. Jane held these thoughts as she nursed her black caffeine.

"I see you're feeling better," Celeste acknowledged, her mood back to normal.

"ET had one thing right for sure, Toussaint, you're a lady even down to how you tell me off. The only reason I had even asked you to lunch was because I really trust something about you. I can't put my finger on why, but I do. I'm sorry..." Jane apologized.

Celeste held up her hand, "Apology accepted. For the sake of

time let's have it." *And for the sake of my patience*, she thought.
"I don't really know where to begin."

"Let's try introduction, body, and conclusion," she said sarcastically.

"Yes teacher." They laughed.

"Let me ask you this. Have you ever been in some of the clubs down on 42nd and Eighth Avenue, like the Show Time Lounge?"

"I've walked past them but I have not been in them," Celeste lied.

"Well. It's a whole different life in the game. You see, the game consists of gals and players. The players are men."

"Go on."

"The players come into these clubs to fulfill their fantasies. They see naked women dancing on a table just for them, watch the gals do anything they tell them to do from behind the glass while they get off, and then they can sit and have drinks with these pretty ladies later. They like it when the women on stage have them entranced. In short, the players are looking for a voyeuristic experience without the responsibility."

Celeste was lost. "Responsibility for what?"

"You know, male-female relationship basics, like taking out the trash and bringing the check home to the old lady on Friday."

"I'm with you."

"These men want to be doted on - made to feel like they're King of the Hill. They want to have a drink in peace without discussing some overdue bill," Jane explained expertly.

"Now the gals down at Show Time and other places, they enjoy it just as much as the guys do. In fact, the gals go looking for the players who can piss away a thousand bucks in a night."

"What does a guy spend a thousand dollars a night on in a club?" questioned a confused Celeste.

Jane patted her hand. "Toussaint, stick close to me. Honey, in these clubs you can do anything you want."

"Anything like what?"

"A-n-y-thing you want," she said, accepting a coffee refill. Jane was soaring from rum and caffeine. Neither of which affected her ability to tell her story. "You still don't get it."

Celeste shook her head.

"OK. For one, you can get high, you know, snort cocaine. Or, a guy can pay to see two women together. Or, ultimately he can end up in bed with a gal and it all happens without transacting any cash."

"Right, and he pays for it with his American Express card?" joked Celeste.

"Exactly!" cheered Jane, happy her student was catching on finally, "He can run a tab like in a regular bar. Just like if it were for drinks or for food."

"Unbelievable," Celeste said, aghast.

"You see, a woman only has to be totally female with a player who is high. She shakes her naked behind at him a few times, he gives her a hundred-dollar tip, and when she's done with her set, she'll milk him until the till, that means his pocket, is empty."

"Is that when she has chumped the player?"

"Almost, but not quite. You see the player knows that the gals will sit with them until the till is empty. He don't care. He goes there for a good time and to blow all the dough he's got. It is the barmaids' duty to tell the girls when the card is maxed out, or to watch for when his wad is depleted. Then the gals go find the next guy who made eye contact with them."

"This is crazy," said Celeste.

"Chumping the players is when you give a guy an indication that you are going to let him pay you to go all of the way with him. You know, more than just sitting around in his lap drinking. In essence, 'chumping' is when the gal leads him on. That's what Julie did. That's why she's dead."

"No man wants to be led on. Player or not," interjected Celeste.

"Exactly. Now you see, the judge was her regular. They all have regulars, by the way. The judge would walk in the door once a week carrying a gram worth of snow. Then when they tooted all of that up, he would buy I don't know how many hundreds of dollars more," Jane remembered.

"That's what I mean when I say Julie got greedy with the life. She loved cocaine. We nicknamed her Candy Girl.

"Julie was very popular, she had a *couple* of regulars for *every* day of the week. She was pulling down a thou a night in tips."

Celeste choked on her ice.

"And believe me when I tell you, she chumped every one of them.

If the judge had not killed her first, I can name you at least ten others who probably would have gotten around to it."

"I still can't believe Julie was making a thousand dollars a night," said Celeste in disbelief. "The IRS must have had a field day."

"Toussaint, be for real. No one claims that money," Jane schooled. "This business is 80 percent hustle."

Here we go with that hustle crap again, thought Celeste dreadfully.

"The business is taken very seriously. Many of these gals are paying for college educations, taking care of entire families, and more than you'd like to know about are married. They do it to make ends meet."

"Get out!"

"I promise you I am not lying. There are many gals who get lucky and just by talking to the right player, one day find themselves set up as a permanent mistress, set up financially forever or," she said hesitantly, "like in my case, set up with a decent job."

"Jane, you didn't."

"Yes, I did. I came here with no money, a degree, and dreams. Fortunately for me I knew how to dance and how to talk to men. That's how I got over. That's how I met ET. I owe him my life."

"I'm not going to judge you for your actions in the past. I promise," vowed Celeste. "What about your current actions? Remember the first day we met, you told me that you tend to ET's outside business interests."

"Yeah, I do," confirmed Jane.

Celeste waited a moment, hoping Jane would volunteer more information before she asked her next question. Jane did not.

"You said you owe him your life, but what else exactly do you do for ET? I hope you both don't know more about Julie than you're saying."

Jane smiled.

"What is it that he does exactly with his outside business interests anyway?" asked Celeste..

Jane snickered, "Now Toussaint, I can't tell you everything. I gotta leave something for you ta figure out."

TWENTY-FIVE

Renee Poteat was doubled over from a blow to her face that had temporarily blurred her vision. If she had known her comment about the article written in *The New York Stand* would evoke this type of action, maybe she would have kept her mouth shut. Her visitor did not take too kindly to her opinions. The way he constantly punched her in the face, she knew that his involvement ran far deeper than she had ever imagined.

Renee's only thought was to agree with her bedmate, for the time being. Yes, she would keep her mouth shut if asked any information about the article by those outside of her circle. After making his point, the sucker left her to mend her wounds.

"Fat chance, buddy," she said aloud as she looked in the mirror at the damage he had done to her face, "the information bank over here stays closed."

Renee couldn't wait to call Celeste and tell her she had been sleeping with one of Times Square's most guilty parties.

Celeste bolted out of One Times Square and headed toward the subway. She was entirely too excited for a bus ride downtown to the Department of Health's testing site. Jane had blown her mind earlier. She had to tell Kenny the details and to see his smiling face. She needed to get to dance class quickly. There were too many emotions dancing around on her insides, Saturday couldn't come fast enough.

Kenny was waiting at the testing site. He thought he was well informed about this testing business and such matters, but Celeste had really opened his eyes. When he said he wanted them to go to his family doctor to take the test she hit the roof and bombarded his fax machine with articles about why it was imperative they take it anonymously.

Reading the articles, he found out that when you sign your name to the test it gets listed on the Medical Information Bureau report. The MIB. He read that the MIB was the TRW of the medical world. And taking an HIV test was not something either of them wanted noted on their medical history reports.

He felt the prospect of getting a number and then calling for the results was so impersonal. He could stand an impersonal process; what he could not stand was the MIB getting too personal. There were several insurance matters pending with the family business, and he was not about to risk allowing something like this to leak onto his medical history. He added another item to the list of Celeste's many attributes. For Celeste did not suffer from an acute case of the N.I.M.B.Y. (Not In My Back Yard) Syndrome. No way. As usual, his Gal Friday had all of the facts.

The test was actually a painless procedure. The excruciating agony was a three-week wait for the results.

"Are you busy this weekend?" asked Kenny.

"After dance class I'm free. What's up?" she asked.

"Pack some casual clothes, I'll have Winston pick you up after class."

"Where are we going, Officer?"

"Someplace where we can talk for hours uninterrupted."

"Good, because the info from Jane will shock the living daylights out of you."

"Baby, nothing shocks me."

"I know," she said. "How masculine."

"Now, I'm trying to be good. So you be good."

" 'Be good' he says. 'Pack some casual clothes he says'," she teased.

"Don't worry, we will each have our own rooms," advised Kenny reluctantly, "Just don't leave any more notes in my desk drawer. I could not think straight for the rest of the day."

She smiled, "Mission accomplished."

He leaned over to kiss her when she stopped him. "Kenny, do you think I can stand to have your lips on mine without getting all hot and bothered?" she said seductively.

"I thought that was the purpose, sweetie," he said, countering her seductive tone.

"It is. Do you think we can try to abstain from any kind of physical contact until the test comes back?"

"Abstain! Celeste, that's three weeks with no kisses and no hugs from you?"

"Come on, it will be fun," she whispered, allowing her moist lips to barely touch his ear. "I promise when we get the results back, I am going to tear your clothes off."

He smiled his million-dollar smile, and Celeste knew she had his approval.

"Now I've got to get to the studio. Dre and Maurice will be angry if I'm late."

"I don't want to cause you to be late. They'll understand if you tell them you were with me."

"Maybe if you came with me to explain personally, they would really accept your apology," she tried to insist.

"No way baby, you go ahead and meet your pals," said Kenny, thinking of how Celeste told him the guys thought he was cute.

"Why, Officer Friendly, I do believe you are a bit homopho-bic."

"Call it what you like. I ain't going with you," said Kenny in protest. "Have a good show."

By the time Celeste arrived at the recording studio, Dre and Maurice were already doing sound checks. The guys had placed bets as to her whereabouts and Maurice collected a crisp $20 from Dre.

"My friend here thought you were shopping," said Maurice, snapping his new bill, "but I had the feeling you were with Officer Friendly."

"How do you know so much?" Celeste asked annoyed.

"Because Miss Thing, you always have that glazed-over look whenever you are with HIM," Maurice admonished. "Now that we've gotten that out of the way, don't walk into my recordings late again. I'm the Diva here," he quipped. "Time is money."

"Be quiet before I quit," she laughed, "I won't be late again."

"Good, because I can't concentrate with you two squabbling," said Dre, irritated. "Where is your script girlfriend? We need to rehearse."

Maurice donned his executive director position in the sound booth and discussed timing with the engineer. Celeste heard the theme song playing in her headset as Maurice gave the cue for them to begin.

"Welcome to *Entertainment Review.* I'm Dre Tyson," he began.

"And I'm Celeste Toussaint. Each week we'll feature a film, concert, or album offering our points of view."

"This week *Entertainment Review* goes to the Anita Baker concert."

"Stay tuned. *Entertainment Review* will be back after this."

Maurice ran out of the sound booth to adjust the mikes and hug them. Celeste and Dre held hands to calm their nervousness.

"Stand by," belted Maurice through the headsets, "Don't forget, keep your commentary light and lively. And three, two ..."

Dre began, "Welcome back to *Entertainment Review.* Anita Baker has become one of R&B's little darlings. Since her Elektra Records debut album *Rapture,* she has picked up Grammys for

Best R&B song "Sweet Love," Best Female Vocalist and for Best Gospel duet "Ain't No Need to Worry" with the Winans. Beginning her musical career at age 12 on the Gospel circuit, Anita's voice has cultivated a ripe, bluesy, jazz flavor that is undeniably unique. Now, this concert tour celebrates the release of Anita's second album, *Giving You The Best That I Got*."

"Dre, I have really enjoyed Anita Baker's smooth and sultry ballads on the vinyl and her songs are bound to become music standards, but her performance at New York's Madison Square Garden left me disappointed."

"I'd have to agree, Celeste. Anita's voice got lost in the Garden. She'd be much more effective in an intimate setting."

"As a result the audience was a little lost during Anita's attempt to show her versatility with a cover of Gladys Knight's song 'Love Overboard'."

"Those selections threw her performance overboard. And Anita kept saying, 'Come on New York, give me some!!' "

"Well Dre, if a performer knows anything about a New York audience, that is to never ask them for some because they give you none."

"How true, Celeste. But there is no denying Anita's talent. However, I'd rather not strain to hear her sing. I must admit saxophonist Everett Harpe and guitarist Ray Fuller actually saved the day."

"And so did Anita's rendition of 'God Bless the Child.'

Maurice gave the 30-second hand signal. Celeste wasn't quite finished with her commentary but she needed to wrap it up.

"Well just as Anita ran out of time while performing her number one hit, sorry, so have we. Until next time. I'm Celeste Toussaint."

"And I'm Dre Tyson. Thank you for joining us. *Entertainment Review* is a Windy City production."

The three of them doubled over with laughter. Maurice was so happy, "It's a take! It's a take! Look out world. *Entertainment*

Review is on-the-air!"

The tension that had mounted while preparing for their studio debut left them famished. They bopped down to the Village to Poppa's Place for homemade banana ice cream and Belgian waffles. Ever since the fellas had taken Celeste there, it quickly became her favorite spot for dessert.

Poppa's had every kind of the junk food from your childhood. Everything. From rock candy to candy necklaces. Pineapple upside down cake to a la modes and root beer floats. Even Alka Seltzer for the inevitable upset stomach.

Maurice knew the match between Celeste and Dre was perfect but he had no idea it would be sheer perfection. "Watching you two animated children has given me a great idea."

"Listen Reese, I don't want you to forget that pairing me with Celeste for *Entertainment Review* was my brainchild," warned Dre shaking a sundae spoon in his face.

"Hey guy, you get all of the credit, no problem," assured Maurice, "and when *Entertainment Review* debuts on national television, I'll tell the whole world about how the industry's dynamic duo was discovered."

"What debut on national television?" questioned Celeste. "I heard you just skip right on over that part like we're supposed to know what you're talking about."

Dre interceded, "Celeste, I like the national television part. So don't assault my brother here. I think you've been hanging out with the Officer too much."

"Ha! Ha! you're jealous," she sang with a mouth full of her ice cream waffle sandwich.

"So what if I am?" admitted Dre, being in love is where I'd like to be right now. But since I'm not, this national television thing will make it all better. What's the big idea, Reese?"

"While you guys were recording, I really couldn't believe how good you sounded. That's my job, to focus in on how this thing sounds, you know," said Maurice, excited. "So when I stopped focusing on the sound and started watching you two nuts, it hit me."

"You finally realized the essence of my true beauty?" joked Dre."Get to the point, man, you're killing me."

"Not only do you two sound good together, but you look even better together."

"Now we've got 'looks good' and 'sounds good' together," interrupted Celeste to help this along, "which equals ..."

"Television!!" shouted Maurice. "A package like this screams television and you two are perfect."

"Maurice, that's a nice idea, but can we get established on the radio first?" reasoned Celeste. "Build a following and then think about this super glitzy stuff? That's a natural order of progression."

"I'm with her, Reese," said Dre, considering his work at *The Stand.*

"Listen you two, I know what you're thinking and in terms of the work for television ... and you are absolutely correct," assured Maurice, "this is just a preliminary idea. Keep up the good work and let me do the rest. Checks like these are only the beginning," he said, handing them each an envelope.

Celeste peeped in her envelope, vowing not to get excited. "Maurice, is this check payment for the next few weeks?"

"What is enclosed in this check is what you will receive each week. So block out this studio time on your calendars."

"For two thousand dollars a week and a couple of hours of work," exclaimed Dre, "just tell me how many weeks you would like me to block out of my life?"

"You see, my best friend here understands the economics of a venture like this one. I'll executive produce the show, of course. Dre, you do the P.R. and Renee can do the choreography."

Celeste perked up, "Where is that fast child, anyway? I haven't seen her in a while. Have y'all?"

"Nope," said Maurice.

"I haven't either," admitted Dre. "You know how Miss Thing gets when she's doing a show. She probably hasn't had time."

"Listen you two. I don't care how busy I get, if you don't hear from me, come see about me, OK?"

"OK, I hear you home girl. What you mean is, New York ain't the place you should act like you fell off the end of the earth if you really haven't," said Maurice.

"That's it. I'm stopping by Renee's house tonight," said Celeste.

"Good looking out," said Dre, "that's a great idea."

Celeste had not shared with the guys what Kenny told her about Miss Renee Poteat's nighttime activities. In light of what she found out about the dealings at those places, she should have checked in on Renee a week ago.

Celeste knew by the sound of Renee's voice when she answered the buzzer that something was wrong. She stepped into a dark hallway. A frail hand led her to the bedroom, which was lit by a single candle.

"Renee, why are you sitting in the dark?"

"I do that sometimes when I don't want to face the world."

"Is that why none of us have heard from you?"

"Yeah."

"Lady, these streets are too crazy for you to curl up and pretend you don't exist," warned Celeste, "So the next time you don't want to face the world let somebody know so we won't be worried."

She smiled, but it hurt, "I promise."

Celeste could tell that she was in ocean-deep thought. Renee kept staring out blankly at nothing and fiddling with her hands. Celeste figured that since she was sitting in the dark, Renee had an assortment of things nagging at her conscience. Rule number one as a journalist was never to force someone to talk until they were ready.

They sat in silence on the bed Indian style. It was a long time before Renee finally broke down and cried her eyes out. She didn't do any talking, Renee's tears came first. Celeste comforted her until they fell asleep.

The next morning Celeste awoke to make breakfast and found Renee had enough food for an army.

Who in the world has this woman been feeding? Celeste marveled, going through her cabinets.

Celeste whipped up scrambled eggs, fried potatoes and onions, toast, and mimosas. Renee stumbled into the kitchen still teary-eyed, but it was the black and blue bruises on the side of her face that had Celeste horrified.

"Please tell me you shot the dog who bruised your pretty face," seethed Celeste, putting an ice pack on her cheek.

"There's something I need to tell you about me," said Renee, taking a deep breath through tears, "about my life, and about how I've been living foul. And ... and how something like this," she whimpered pointing to her face, "happening to me is not the first time, and unless I change courses, it won't be the last."

Celeste flopped into an antique wing-back chair like a ragged doll, afraid to hear anymore confessions about people and their hustles of how they got over, or the near-death experiences that came their way in the process.

"When I first came to New York from Connecticut," Renee began, "I never expected life to be difficult for me. My life never has been difficult. Dad was the lead singer of the group the Moonbeams from the 1950's. He had a golden voice. Everyone expected me to do well in the business, but my talent was not in singing, it was in dance.

"When I go to auditions, Celeste, I never tell anyone who my Dad is in the business, I don't want any special treatment. They only want to see that you can dance anyway, but a little mention of who you know, or in my case - who you are never hurt anybody. I haven't gotten as much work as I think I'm entitled to getting, because I've been stuck in this catch-22 situation. I am too light for roles that want darker black women and and my wavy hair and full lips give me away under the scrutiny for roles that I could possibly pass for to be played by white women. And believe me, I'm so desperate to dance, yes, I would pass just to get the gig.

"So while I kick higher, pirouette faster, tap slicker than any dancer in this town or any other, black or white, I can't get a job. It is a devastating reality to someone who wants so desperately to simply dance. I spend every waking moment of the day auditioning or taking class, therefore I can't get a temp job. And I would never call home for help. Of course I need money to maintain my bad habits," she said flinging an arm around her exquisitely furnished apartment, "so I have to do something. When I tell you what that something is, I hope you will still be my friend."

"I love Renee the person, bad habits and all," assured Celeste.

"I hope you mean it," said Renee sadly, remembering that the last few times she told someone her secret she lost them as friends. "The first part is I have been perfecting my dancing abilities a few nights a week at the Show Time Lounge."

Celeste did not blink.

"The money is great, I get treated like a queen. The owners send us home in cars every night and the whole bit. It's my nightly escape into a surreal experience. I throw on a wig, pile on the make-up, and play with various costumes. If I could do the exact same thing without taking off my clothes, though, I'd be much happier."

"The second part to this is, I've been having an affair with a very powerful mogul in the city. We have been having a wonderful time romping in the hay, going shopping, and you know stuff like that. It really turns him on to see me dance up there, but ever since the article that you did in *The Stand* came out he's been a raving lunatic."

"What do you know about that?" Celeste asked, monotone.

"Dre told me.   Don't worry, I would never betray my real friends to this secret life of mine," Renee confessed. "The fellas tell me everything. I haven't felt that I could be as honest with them as I am with you. They consider me their little sister. Well, you know how that goes.

"Anyway, my friend said that the article - and I quote - 'jeopardized the livelihood of the establishment that he and his friends enjoy tremendously and he would do everything in his power to see that there were no more articles,' unquote.

"I got really angry with him because I know all the parties involved, of course, and I threw up the freedom-of-speech part as well as how this nude dancing business would be fine if that was all that went on in those places."

"What did he say?" questioned Celeste.

Renee chuckled, "He didn't laugh. He expressed himself all over my face."

"That's it!" Celeste cried out. "Pack your stuff right now, you are leaving town. Renee, you just don't know. The lid is about to be blown off this joint. There is a woman dead because she worked in this place. There are more women than I care to know about being abused because of this place," she said, pointing to her and thinking of Muffin.

"I'm telling you, there are a team of folks working to blow this thing up right now and you don't need to be anywhere around."

Renee broke out in a cold, shaky sweat. Celeste laid her on the couch, covered her with a blanket, and took the liberty of packing her clothes in every suitcase and duffle bag she could find. Renee was definitely a dancer, there were plenty of duffle bags. Celeste scooped all of Renee's toiletries from her vanity and thought hard about where she could send her friend in trouble.

She already knew Kenny was in a closed-door, can't-be-interrupted meeting with RICO for the day, discussing just how far the Show Time Lounges of Times Square had gone over the line on the Nuisance Abatement Law. She was going to have to do this without him.

Celeste dialed the phone. "Winston. It's Celeste. I need your help."

"Talk to me," said Winston, ready for action.

"I have a friend in trouble. Can you meet me at Kennedy with the directions to the Hamilton's Negril property? And can you phone ahead and let the housekeepers know to expect company?"

"See you there."

Celeste dialed Sammy's number. He answered on the first ring. "What's up?" he belted, full of energy.

"Sam, this is an emergency. Save your questions for later. How much vacation time do you have?"

"Four weeks."His tone changed. Sammy recognized the seriousness of Celeste's voice.

"Call your office, make up any excuse, and meet me at the international check-in to Jamaica Airways at JFK in an hour."

"Celeste are you in trouble?"

"I'm not, but Renee is and she needs an escort. Are you in?"

"Damn straight."

"Good. Don't forget your swimming trunks and your passport."

"I ain't got no passport."

"OK then bring your birth certificate."

"Couz, I'm a little low on cash."

"I've got you covered. I owe you, so don't worry."

Renee finally got herself moving to Celeste's pace after she downed the leftover champagne straight out of the bottle. Celeste made a checklist of the items she had packed.

She opened her wallet to expose the selection of credit cards. "Take what you need," she ordered Renee.

Eternally thankful for what her friend was doing, Renee hugged her and cried because Celeste really did love her. Good and bad. A panorama of friends from the past played before her mind. Renee had already decided to tell her family that she had a gig down there. Hey, maybe she would find one. This was beginning to feel really good. Renee was even more thankful to Celeste for picking up on her desire to get out of town, even though she never said so.

Renee threw back an enormous Oriental rug in the center of her living room. "Thanks girl for your credit cards, but I do everything in cash. It's better that way. No trails," she said, lifting two boards in the hardwood floor and pulling out a strong box containing hundreds of $100 bills neatly wrapped and labeled.

Celeste was beginning to feel like Kenny; emotionless after seeing so many shocking things. "Don't tell me you made all of that money dancing?"

"A lot of it comes from my father's royalties. I get a hefty check every quarter. Not only did he have a golden voice but he had a golden pen, too. That's where the money is in the music business, you know, in writing."

"I can't believe you don't have that kind of money in the bank."

"Girlfriend I have two rules. Number one, I never let anyone know how much money I really have and number two, I don't believe in letting people use my money at five percent or less. I may as well keep my cash right here where I can get to it if I need it ... like now," she said while counting six months' rent for her landlord plus a bonus to keep her mouth shut and forward the mail. "I do keep a checking account with a couple hundred dollars just because."

"You're crazy."

They jumped into a bass-thumping gypsy cab to JFK Airport, which was blaring Latin music loud enough for the driver's relatives to hear back home. For a minute they enjoyed the thrill of their wild escape. Renee was more than delighted Sammy would accompany her. Celeste was not so surprised to find that the two of them had been intimate on more than one occasion.

All parties involved were at the airport on time. Winston handed over the keys, and the directions. He knew not to ask questions there. He too came with a travel bag full of cash. Celeste liked him. Winston was a man who came prepared for anything.

Sammy was in a rage when he saw Renee's face, but the ladies assured him the situation would be rectified soon.

Before checking in for customs, Renee pulled Celeste to the side, "Aren't you going to ask me who my friend is?"

"No ma'am."

"Don't you even want to know who did this to me?"

"Yes I do, in the worst way. I'm not going to ask you to name names."

"You're a good friend. Do you know that?"

"So are you."

"Celeste, my friend is someone you know."

"I find that hard to believe," she said dryly.

"If you ever spent time in that joint you wouldn't be able to believe who you might see there. But I'm not going to name names."

"I don't think I want to know."

"I do want you to know one name. The name of my friend."

"OK, if you insist."

"The only thing I insist is that you nail his tail to the cross."

"I'll try. Who is he?"

"ET. Ed Townsend."

TWENTY-SIX

Dear Mommie and Daddy:
I know I haven't been in touch like I promised but you would not believe the hours I have been working. I'm still trying to get adjusted to the city. You know, minor things: no car, the trash in the streets, the homeless people, Uncle Jim's death. I guess I sound like I'm complaining. Not really, but when I get used to these things the locals call minor, it will be time for me to come home. Not a day goes by that I don't think about how much I love you, but most of all ... how much I am loved.
Celeste Michelle.

Celeste was aching for her parents' affection. What she really wanted to do was jump on a plane and crawl into her own bed for a few days to work this mess out. There was nothing like the comfort of her own twin bed. She wrote the letter to her parents because if she dared to call they would pick up on her mood right through the phone from the sound of her voice. Her folks were always on radar patrol when it came to their baby girl. She could bet you a million dollars that they knew something was up anyway.

Luckily for Celeste, Aunt June and her friends, Miss Audrey

and Miss Diane, were totally star struck. They had been ripping and running in the streets with free tickets she provided for them to some event every day.

There was also a method to Celeste's generosity. Keeping Aunt June occupied kept her mind off of Uncle Jim. All of that movie, concert, theatre and museum-hopping had Aunt June so tired by the time she got home, all she could do was collapse. It gave Celeste peace and quiet in the apartment without being given the third degree.

Packing her duffle bag with casual coordinates as Kenny had instructed, Celeste got the urge to slip in a little something sexy. Then she remembered about the ridiculous promise that she had initiated regarding their intimacy.

No hugs and kisses until their AIDS test results came back sounded like a cute challenge at the time. But now as she thought of how this would be the first time they would be totally alone, Celeste was no longer convinced. At the moment she needed just a little dose of TLC. Instead of the naughty nightie she'd considered, she dug out her flannel pajamas with the feet attached.

During LaRocque Bey's class, Celeste danced so hard she gave herself a headache. She was glad to have a physical form of expression to release. As she moved across the floor she left her worries right there.

Dance class was much more than physical exercise for Celeste, it was an exercise of faith. Leaving her worries in the dance studio was, for her, like leaving her troubles at the church altar. The sweat of her labor was just as evident as a chorus of Amens. Even more delightful was the mere fact that she was surrounded by people who didn't know what she was going through. Personally or professionally.

After company class, LaRocque asked, "Where's Renee?"

He was the first person outside of their circle who had asked about her since the mad escape and Celeste was totally unprepared for the question.

"I haven't seen Miss Thing in a few days," she responded, trying to cover her uneasiness.

LaRocque narrowed his eyes almost shut. "I hope that whatever the two of you are up to works, 'cause I can't stand to see you leave your brains scattered all over this floor again."

Celeste was speechless. No he didn't read me! was her thought. She heard that LaRocque had a true spirit of discernment. Never thought she would have to experience it first-hand, though.

"You tell Miss Honey I have a major project for her to choreograph. So she should call me, and soon."

"See you next week," was all Celeste could manage to say. She didn't even bother changing into her street clothes before going outside to find Winston. Once in the car she thought of how much she enjoyed that class, but there was no way she would ever go back.

"Oh well," she sighed, "one hustle down. Two to go."

The sunset shimmered against the Caribbean as the breeze gently blew the sand back into the sea. Renee and Sammy pledged eternal love before God, their cook, and gardner in a last-minute ceremony.

Knowing both of their families would have a fit once they found out they had married, Sammy still felt good about the decision. His mother June had met Renee a couple of times. He had never met anyone in her family.

Nonetheless, Renee said "I do" three times before she was supposed to. They had found eternal bliss on the island of Jamaica, both vowing never to return to the dangerous big city again.

When Winston awakened Celeste, it looked as if she were dreaming. That was the best sleep she'd had in weeks. The scene of the mountains spread out before her looked like it was snatched off of a postcard.

The L-shaped log cabin sat nestled in the multi-colored trees. Beyond the house were even more mountains that appeared to meet the sky. Birds sang, rabbits scurried, and deer grazed as if they were accustomed to cohabitating with humans. The icing on the cake was the fresh mountain air, full-bodied due to the lush vegetation and absence of pollution.

Kenny galloped up on a gorgeous thoroughbred, carrying an axe and geared from head to toe in his mountain attire. "What do you think of my Shadow here," he questioned, kissing his horse all grins.

"I think you should consider being a catalog model for Eddie Bauer. And swinging that axe, you look prepared to sing that love song from *Seven Brides For Seven Brothers,* " she noted.

"You don't know that movie?" he asked suspiciously.

"Yeah, my Grannie hipped me to it."

"Mine too. Now it's my favorite!"

"Mine too. I even have it on video.

The two-story house was done in modern-day country furnishings. The decor gave the house such a comfortable feel that Celeste had shoes off and hair down upon her arrival. She sat on the floor and warmed her hands and feet in front of a huge stone fireplace with a roaring fire.

"So when are you moving?" Celeste asked seriously.

"You like it here that much?" said Kenny, surprised. "I don't know, Gal Friday, you don't strike me as the type who would abandon her high heels for mountain boots, or her Evian for well water."

"Don't tell me you have well water?" she said anxiously.

"There's nothing else out here besides this house for miles, of course we have well water." Celeste ran to the kitchen, turned on the faucet, and searched the cabinets for glasses.

"What do you know about well water?" he shouted after her.

"Were you sleeping during our phone talks when I told you how I spent almost every summer of my life in Louisiana?"

"No way, baby, I heard you," he said, reaching for the glass she'd prepared for him brimming with ice cold water. "But you didn't say nothing about having experiences with water from any wells. I would have told you then that it was yet another thing we had in common."

They were so cozy and relaxed with one another that they both hated to bring up the nasty little business they desperately needed to discuss.

"So when are you moving?"

"Baby, if you think I should move here, I will. Just remember that one day you will be living with me, too," Kenny stated, unafraid to remind her of his desires.

She got up to avoid the topic and the romantic atmosphere brewing, and walked outside to take in the sunset over the mountains. "Kenny. One question. Where are we?"

He cracked up, "What did you do, sleep all the way?"

"Yep."

"You're so easy to kidnap. Welcome to the Pocono Mountains," he announced with outstretched arms.

"The Poconos. As in Pennsylvania?"

"You've got it."

"Wow. It's gorgeous."

"And so are you."

After dinner Kenny and Celeste put on their P.J.s and settled in front of the fire. They had not talked at length for a few days and they knew there were hours of discussion ahead.

"You know when Winston told me how you maneuvered Renee's move out of the country, I was so proud of you," admitted Kenny. "I always knew my Gal Friday was smart, but a thinker on her feet, too. What more could I ask for?"

"Did you think I was incapable of something like that?"

"No. But listen good baby. From the first day that I met you, you have been on this emotional rollercoaster. Not that there's anything wrong with the timing of your emotions. They have been warranted. But the way you helped Renee showed me that you are capable of completing this investigation with me."

Celeste tried hard not to show she was getting mad. "So what you're saying is, if what happened with Renee had gone down another way, you wouldn't be soliciting my help with the rest of the investigation?"

"Right."

"So did you think I was just going to sit back and let you do this thing alone?"

"Negative. You were going home."

"Home? As in Chicago?"

"Affirmative."

The crackling sound of the fire consumed the room. Kenny put on his stone face. She knew he was serious.

"Did you call my Daddy?" she asked, grimly holding her breath.

"Only to say hello."

She exhaled gratefully. "Then let's get busy, Detective."

"You first. Tell me about Jane."

"Jane and Renee are linked."

"No shit."

"In more ways than one." Celeste gave him the full-length versions of both girls' stories. Kenny had easel paper taped around on all of the walls. As she talked he made flow charts and arrows. This snooping around magnified how terribly she missed meaty journalism. Entertainment was cute, but this was mental stimulation.

"What you say about Jane confirms what I figured. She places the orders for the cars every night for the girls who dance. And they all know her very well. Now I see how."

"Really."

"You know the owners of this operation are some very clever thinkers. They always insist each girl have their own car. Even if they live in the same building."

"How odd. That's a tremendous expense."

"I thought so, too, until a couple of the gals got in my car one night. When one of their cars didn't show on time they hopped in together with me. They chatted for days about this and that regarding the business, which helped me with my diagram here. But the one thing that I hung onto was their mention of a dude named Rick who pays them."

"What does it mean?"

"I get checks from a dude named Rick, too."

"But how many guys around town are named Rick?"

"Hundreds. Now the question is how many are seedy, reek with smoke, are sneaky, and ever so faithful to 'the boss.' The girls described to a T the Rick I know at the garage."

Kenny calculated and drew more boxes and arrows on his flow chart. He also figured that Rick knew each detail of Uncle Jim's murder. Especially how the car managed to find its way back to the garage.

As sunlight forced her to awaken from a deep slumber, she saw Kenny standing next to his masterful artwork clearly looking like he had not slept.

"This is the preliminary plan," he announced. Celeste carefully examined the ten sheets, taking a mental photograph of each one.

"We will need a few weeks to get prepared. As we continue to investigate, let's meet out here every few days and fill in these blanks until it's time to take action," said Kenny.

"Hey, Detective, will this really work?" she asked ruefully.

"Why not, it works great on paper."

"You're so smart, I bet your head hurts," she commented and planted a kiss on his forehead. "Enough of all of this work, what are we going to do today? Just me and you."

"I have a big surprise. We've got to get dressed and back to the city if we're ever going to make it," he shouted as he ran upstairs to change.

"I love surprises," she screamed back, "but at least tell me what I should wear."

"Strictly dungarees and sneakers, baby!"

"Oh you mean jeans and gym shoes."

"Celeste. When in the East do as they do," he instructed. "Now repeat after me, dungarees and sneakers."

"Listen here K-Trey," she teased, "I do want to go home some-day and I don't want a tiny thing like vocabulary to give me away to having picked up y'all's bad habits," she said, bolting down-stairs.

"Wait a minute, you say y'all every chance you get, and you've got the nerve to talk about someone's bad vocabulary?" Kenny defended.

"How do I look?" she questioned.

"Don't change the subject on me, Gal Friday. Get in the car," he laughed.

They arrived at Madison Square Garden at the start of the sec-ond quarter. The New York Knicks were playing the Los Angeles Lakers, and the visiting team was down by ten. Celeste was ec-static. She loved basketball and knew the game well. The Lakers had always been her favorite NBA team, second-place favorite after the Chicago Bulls, that is.

Kenny was a season ticket holder as were all of the Hamilton men. They took up the entire fifth row under the basket. Dyna-mite seats! Celeste was the only woman among the male family members and their guests. She was able to hold her own with the vast knowledge she possessed of the game and of the team mem-bers' stats.

Madison Square Garden was on its feet cheering the Knicks as the Lakers were the champions and undefeated thus far this sea-son. By half time the Lakers were down by 13. Kenny was amused at how salty Celeste was that her team was losing. It was a delight to his core that he now had a lady who not only shared an interest in his favorite sport, but one who really knew the game.

Uncle Lester picked up on Celeste's mood also and shouted to her from his seat at the other end, "What's the matter, baby, can't stand to see your boys go down today?"

"That's right, there's nothing that can help them now, our boys are hot!!!" screamed Uncle Cleon.

Celeste stood up. "You all can gloat now, because come fourth quarter, y'all won't have a prayer."

Kenny shushed her, "Don't jinx us now baby."

"I'm not jinxing anyone. Here are the facts: Your quote, un-quote "team" is not hot today. Patrick Ewing is," she said, pointing to the board which posted he had scored all of the points except seven.

"Patrick's hot all of the time," said Uncle Zeke, "what are you talking about?"

"He's not this hot, Uncle Zeke. So what is going to happen is this: The Knicks are going to run the same line-up after the half because it's working. Riley is not going to let the all-time rival beat them on their turf, so he is going to turn up the power."

Kenny was intrigued, "How's he gonna do that?"

"He's going to run Magic, Michael Cooper, Kurt Rambis, Worthy and Kareem straight through to the fourth and it will be bye-bye Knicks. Because by that time, Patrick the Boy Wonder will be tired."

The Hamilton men laughed at her for selling big wolf tickets, bragging so vocally. One-dollar bets were exchanged.

Celeste warned them all, "I'm telling you there is no way Riley will go home with a defeat from the Knicks. No way. Not this day!"

The second quarter began with the Lakers line-up exactly as Celeste had predicted. The Lakers slowly closed the lead and by the end of the game the Lakers were the winners by six. Celeste gladly collected her dollars from the lot of sore losers.

"All I want to know is, how you were able to predict that, baby?" Kenny asked, scratching his head.

"It's called good basketball strategy, my dear. Stick with me, sweetie pie, and I'll show you how to pick up on it too. I learned from my Daddy, it's simple," she shrugged, kissing his mouth tasting the residue from the cherry icee he had.

"Tasty. I'm starving."

"I've got the perfect little spot for a Sunday meal. It's nothing fancy but it is gooooddd," he said, pulling her up Seventh Avenue.

The restaurant was in back of a bar on 37th Street just off of Seventh. Kenny was right, it was nothing fancy at all. Just plain red patent chairs and tables with plastic red-and-white checkered tablecloths. Their menu was written up on a blackboard and listed good old fashioned soul fixin's with peach cobbler to boot. Kenny ordered for them both. Spicy fried chicken wings, potato salad, baked macaroni and cheese, string beans, and homemade lemonade.

There was a D.J. up front playing some serious slow drag music. Blasting from the speakers was the Isley Brothers, "For The Love Of You." Looking one another in the eyes, Kenny asked her permission to dance, for which the reply was yes.

She wrapped her arms around his neck and he held her tightly by the waist, singing sweetly in her ear the melody of her favorite of all favorite slow jams.

"Drifting on a memory. Ain't no place I'd rather be
than with you. Yeah.
Loving you, well, well, well.
Day will make a way for night, All we'll need is candlelights
and a song, yeah, soft and long, well.
I'm glad to be here alone with a lover unlike no other.
Sad to see, a new horizon slowly coming into view.
I wanna be living for the love of you.
All that I am giving is for the love of you."

They each held the other so tightly that Celeste was glad she didn't have her dinner first or she would have exploded. She did not mind being held so snugly by him. She loved feeling his heart-beat next to hers. She loved the sweet sound of his voice singing what she knew he wanted to say. The masculine scent of his per-spiration was driving her wild. And after a while, they were not dancing at all just standing and swaying.

Kenny tried to get closer to her with each breath. The softness of her body reminded him of the pillow he held when he wished Celeste was with him. He had dreamt of the moment of their first dance, but the dream was nothing like this moment - passionate, inviting, and for real. He too was aware that they were now only rocking from side to side. As far as he was concerned, they did not need the music.

The D.J. also saw how much they were enjoying their moment and he played the entire side of that Isleys' album. It contained the three most lyrically intoxicating love songs to have ever been penned. The two never said a word but danced through all three of the songs that Kenny sang to her while looking in her eyes.

By now their dinner sat on the table cold. All they could feel was the warmth in their hearts.

TWENTY-SEVEN

T he death toll of cabbies killed while on the job soared to
eleven in the month of October 1988 alone. Ed Townsend
called a meeting with his homicide reporters to discuss how
the *New York Daily Courier* could capitalize on the entire sce-
nario.

"Think revenue, fellas. What will sell papers?" ranted ET. "I
don't want our cab driver death stories to be just stories. No. No.
No. How do we make them features?"

"We turn them into human interest pieces," said Newt.

"What's the human interest side to a cab driver getting killed?"
quizzed ET.

"The reactions from the cabbies' families and their stories of
how they are now surviving without Dad, hubby, uncle and
granddad," said T.J.

ET clapped his hands with glee, "Exactly! I tell you, yous guys
are terrif. Now," he continued, pacing the floor, "You know, I like
that uncle part," he said snidely, "do you follow me?"

"That's an excellent idea, " said T.J. who picked up on his
thought. "I can see the headline now, 'Courier Reporter Grieves
Cabbie Uncle's Death'. It's a good angle."

Newt chimed in, "We can piece together a lot of this story

without even talking to Celeste, we were at the funeral you know."

"No, I didn't know. That is good," said ET, "you can write from an outsider's point of view. However, I still want you to interview Celeste for her personal reactions as well as her aunt."

"We have one problem, the piece on Celeste's uncle has already been done from that angle by Chi Woods at the *New York Stand*," informed Newt.

Chi Woods' third piece on the "Times Square Massacre" was just printed and her name rang a nasty bell with ET. He flinched. "I have heard about this Chi person. Do you know if it is a him or a her?"

"No," they said.

"So you haven't met her or him?"

"No, I haven't had the pleasure. I'm just a faithful subscriber to *The Stand*. But Chi has been writing some deep shit ever since he or she started," said Newt.

ET was almost in a blazing rage, "Did I hear you say you subscribe to *The Stand*?"

"Damn skippy," said Newt, sucking his cigar and matching ET's controlled anger. "That's the best black paper in the country, and there is no way you can fault me for keeping informed on what's happening with my people. There is just no way, ET."

ET changed his tone, he needed to have Newt cooperate. "Hey man, no hard feelings OK. I'm sorry. Now back to Chi Woods. I think I want to offer that writer a job. See if you guys can dig up whoever it is. Meanwhile, I want that story done on Celeste's uncle anyhow. the *New York Daily Courier* way."

T.J. cleared his throat, "We have another little problem, sir. Celeste ain't speaking ta us."

"And why not?" asked ET.

"She is mad because we didn't cover the story from this very same angle when her uncle was first killed," explained T.J. "I mean, sir, she told us off, cussed us out, and rolled her eyes at us right there at the funeral. She ain't talking ta us, boss."

"She cussed you out?" ET couldn't help but laugh, "Is that a fact? Well I think Miss Toussaint is professional enough to put her personal feelings aside and get this story done."

He needed Celeste to put her personal feelings aside so he could get next to what she was thinking. Ed Townsend had not been able to sleep. Sicking Newt and T.J. on her was far easier than anything else ... for now.

"But you are asking her to share her personal feelings with us," said Newt. "I'll tell you what would possibly score points with her, is if we investigated the murder."

ET went out of control. "Listen fellas, that aspect of the story is weeks old."

"Yeah, man, you know that," said T.J. to Newt.

ET continued, "I understand the police have even closed the file because they have no suspects and no leads. The only reason why we're digging it up now is because of the recent driver deaths," he pointed out, taking his seat and putting his cowboy-booted feet on his desk.

"I have outlined the story angle for you plain and simple. Follow it carefully. Submit it by the end of next week. That settles it. Meeting adjourned."

Newt Pickney and T.J. Radcliffe hit the ground running under ET's order. Newt's first call was to the *New York Stand's* office for Chi Woods.

"Chi is not in. She is a free-lancer and doesn't keep regular office hours," said *The Stand's* receptionist.

"Oh, so Chi is a woman," he responded.

"Yes she is. May I take a message please."

He left an urgent message for her to call him at *The Courier*

Newt lit his cigar and replayed the scene in their publisher's office. He did not like the ET explosion that had just taken place at the mere mention of investigating the murder, nor T.J. backing his decision. He reflected back to what Celeste said about them not wanting to cover Uncle Jim's story, because it was "just another black man dead piece."

Newt laughed out loud, "You know, baby girl, you were right."

He did not want to make the call to Celeste but he was certain T.J. was not going to call her. Too chicken.

"Toussaint here," she perked into the receiver.

"Hey, baby girl, Newt here. Remember me, Moe?"

"State your business."

"ET wants to do a piece on your uncle now and he wants us to interview you," he said straightforwardly.

Celeste looked at the phone in disbelief before slamming down the receiver. "Newt Pickney. Kiss my be-hind!"

He had spent weeks trying to figure how he would make his exit from The WBB. Now Taylor Reed had summoned his pals to Chicago to discuss serious business.

"My friends. My dear friends," he began somberly. "We have been through it all. There are times when I thought we were invincible. I understand these days that is not the case. We may have the ability to cover up many things, yet some of the things I have painfully come to know are unable to be masked. In front of each of you are three opinions from the best oncologists in the country."

"What the hell is an oncologist?" said Member Two.

You see your stupidity is exactly why this is all happening, Taylor thought.

"An oncologist is a cancer doctor. My friends, your T has terminal cancer of the prostate. The doctors have only given me a few months to live." His associates were shocked. Taylor slowly recorded each response.

"I gathered you here today to officially turn over my part of our business interests to each of you. I am retiring from my post as publisher of the *Chicago Daily Courier* effective the minute this meeting is adjourned.

"It would please me greatly to spend my last days in Florida.

I hope you wish me well. I don't want you grieving for me, we've had a good life. So let's party tonight so you can remember your T as he was. Vibrant. Strong. Jovial. The Mr. Soave Bolla you all love.

"My only request is that you come to my funeral, but don't come to see me in my final days. You know what this disease does to people. Please allow me to go with dignity. As I said earlier, we have been through it all. Everything but death."

When Taylor finished his much-rehearsed speech there wasn't a dry eye amongst his filthy partners. That's right, cry you dumb, stinking, dirty bastards, he thought, I hope you and your money all rot in hell.

Chi Woods had phoned the WBB Car Service several times to speak with the manager about how Uncle Jim's car made its way back to the fleet the night he was murdered. She wanted to know why the car was never reported stolen when that was the story they initially gave the family and the police. Then she was told that the only person who could answer that was Rick Bray and he would be in his office on Thursday.

When Celeste finally got the car service's manager on the phone, Mr. Bray was totally uncooperative in answering her question.

"Well now let's see, Ms. Wood," Rick said, mispronouncing her name intentionally, I right never thought about that." He chuckled, "Alls I know is that my car was back in place here like it ought to have been. You know, just as if Jim himself drove it right back here."

"What day and what time of day did you notice the car back, sir?"

"Lady, who knows? I was probably stoned outta my mind by then," he said, snickering. "Likes I told ya, that car was right here wheres it belonged."

"Please forgive me, Rick, but is it your responsibility to ensure the safety of the cars?"

"That's right Ms., every damn one of 'em."

She desperately wished he would stop calling her Ms. "So what would your boss say to your not knowing what happened to Mr. Jim Toussaint's car on the night he was murdered?"

"Lady, we done had enough of talking to you press folk and police folk and Jim's family folk about what happened, and we're real sorry, OK? So I gotta run now."

"Rick," she said gently, "please don't go yet, you haven't answered the questions."

"Say lady. What paper did you say you were from again?"

"The *New York Stand,* sir."

"Say lady. What would your boss say if I told you my boss doesn't give a shit about your questions or your stinking second rate paper? So kiss off!" he said before hanging up on her. Rick danced around in the floor laughing hysterically before phoning ET in Chicago.

The briefing Rick gave on the reporters call, compounded with the information about Taylor's terminal illness, was no laughing matter to Ed Townsend.

Maurice shook hands with the director of programming at New World Television Syndication. He had walked into their office and landed a syndication deal for *Entertainment Review* on the strength of their first recorded session and the photos of Celeste and Dre.

The TV people know great ideas when they are presented, Maurice thought. And looking at the check he'd just received, Maurice knew his pair was a definite gold mine. He couldn't wait to see Celeste and Dre and share the wealth of information.

The ringing phone shook a hard-thinking Detective Hamilton away from his work. "Hey baby," purred the voice on the other end of the line.

"Hey baby to you," he said lovingly.

"Remember when you told me to save a seat for you at a Luther Vandross concert? Well tonight's your night."

"Tonight?" he responded, looking at his watch and monitoring the pile of work on his desk.

"Yes sir. Tonight, your presence is requested with me front and center, at Madison Square Garden. There will be a ticket waiting for you at the pick-up window. Eight o'clock and don't be late."

"Yes ma'am," he said as he thought about Luther's love songs to set just the tone he needed.

"Will you call in sick to you know where?" Celeste asked, unable to resist.

"Done baby. Mission complete."

"Oooh. Tell me, tell me, tell me," Celeste prodded.

"Later," he promised, "I need to get my desk cleared or I won't be meeting you anywhere."

"Great. See you at eight. And Kenny," she said, rushing her words out before hanging up.

"Yes."

"I love you."

The show was utterly spectacular. Luther and his dancers were elegantly dressed in velvet formal attire. Celeste wrote for her commentary that they "looked like shimmering, painted, porcelain royalty." She, Dre and Maurice clowned a while, dancing in the aisles, Kenny arrived with flowers just in time for the first slow jam. He, Dre and Maurice even loosened up with each other and ended up having a blast.

At Poppa's Place after the show, Celeste relaxed as the three men she loved dearly bantered about their impressions of Luther.

"I have not been so entertained since I can't tell you when," commented Dre.

"It was a pleasure to see ladies in a show who look like ladies," admired Kenny.

"Here, here," agreed Maurice, "Yes, they did give us fashion with that upswept hair, those high-heeled pumps, and those gowns with 10-inch trains."

"You should have gone into fashion," observed Kenny.

"I need to find out who staged this show," raved Celeste, "I just can't stop thinking about it. But I am really upset that Luther didn't introduce his band. I know his keyboard player Skip Anderson from spending some summers in Michigan."

"What!" said Dre rolling his eyes, "Did Skip go to Kenwood too?!"

"What's this Kenwood thing?" asked Kenny.

"This girl is a walking directory of her alma mater," replied Dre.

Maurice interrupted, "Our alma mater."

"We can't help it if our school had a hand in producing Chaka Khan," bragged Celeste.

"Jody Watley," added Maurice.

"Mikki Howard."

"Anita's guitarist Ray Fuller."

"The O'Jays' drummer Perry Wilson, who happened to have been my class president," Celeste boasted, "and so on and so on."

"Speaking of producing great things," announced Maurice, "I forgot to tell you all that *Entertainment Review* was submitted in time to be included for the annual Communication Excellence Awards."

They all clapped.

"Please forgive me, but what are the Communication Excellence Awards?" asked Kenny.

"These awards are the barometer by which you are rated by your peers in the journalism and broadcasting fields. Consider them as our Grammy Awards," explained Dre, "It is an honor to even be nominated. We're nominated in categories all over the place and not just for the show, but for our day jobs as well."

"I didn't know any of my stuff had been submitted," remarked Celeste, "Marcia didn't mention it."

"I hear she submitted a whole mess of your work, honey chile," reported Dre, "I even turned in some of the work done by Chi Woods."

"Interesting," said Celeste, "I wonder who would accept an award if Chi were to win?"

"I'll accept. I'll accept," said Dre excitedly. "And speaking of Chi, she had several phone calls come into *The Stand* from a Newt Pickney at *The Courier*," remembered Dre. "I finally returned the call to advise him that she was a freelancer on the road covering a piece and inquired about the nature of his business," he paused.

"Well?" they all said, not appreciating how Dre was dramatizing the moment.

"He said he was phoning at the request of Mr. Ed Townsend, who had requested a meeting with Ms. Woods to discuss possible employment."

They roared with laughter.

Kenny was not laughing, his mind was racing. Why was ET interested in meeting Chi and offering her a job? He drew squares on a napkin. Jane and Renee admitted to meeting him at the Show Time Lounge, which confirmed ET had an insatiable libido. So did hundreds of other men, or the Show Time would not be in business. According to Renee, his anger soared when the articles Chi wrote hit the press.

Muffin kept popping into his thoughts. His mental storage file kept pulling out their conversation about the powerful men at the helm of this murky activity. Kenny drew an arrow from ET to Chi to angry to Renee to Muffin to Show Time. In a box he wrote "they" and drew an arrow back to ET. Celeste saw him rip the napkin into shreds.

Maurice stood up to make his announcement, "I want you all to know that *Entertainment Review* debuted to rave reviews nationwide."

"But of course it did," said Dre triumphantly.

"And as a result," Maurice continued, "New World Television Syndication has agreed to air the television version of our program. We begin production at the end of the week for the pilot. And ... here is our first check," he said, tossing the check onto the center of the table, pleased with the business deal he had made.

Kenny was first to respond. "OK, when do I quit my job and come to work for you guys? Baby, now no one will say you're only dating me for my money," he said with a kiss.

Dre sighed, "Get real, Officer Friendly. Everybody knows that a policeman's pay is near poverty."

Celeste and Kenny looked at each other and were unable to control their laughter. This time, the joke was truly on Dre.

TWENTY-EIGHT

The television studio was sheer chaos. Dre and Celeste chose to share a dressing room so they could be near one another for support. They were still trying to get over the fact that all of these people were rushing around to make sure they would have a perfect show.

Annie Mae, Charles, Aunt June, Miss Diane, Miss Audrey, and the entire Hamilton clan came to view their first taping. Celeste was simply hoping that she was going to be able to talk straight in front of the cameras.

Dre looked dashing in his tailored suit but felt totally uncomfortable with the makeup. Celeste blotted the excess blush from his cheeks. She, too, felt just a tad overdone.

The Windy City Crew had a huge fight with the image consultants for the show, who wanted to insist that Celeste get a hair weave. Maurice had to throw around his 60 percent ownership of the show to get them to calm down with such an outrageous suggestion.

"I could see if she was bald," Maurice argued in the meeting, "but she has a head full of hair already. For God's sake, she's Celeste Toussaint - not Diana Ross," he had reasoned.

Kenny came to their room right before showtime, took one

look at Celeste with her ton of makeup, and demanded to know where was the woman he loved. "You look like a totally different person. You look good, don't get me wrong. Just different."

Celeste was almost in tears. "I know. I've worked so hard, now no one will recognize me."

"That ain't such a bad thing, baby," Kenny acknowledged with a raised eyebrow, referring to her assistance in his undercover work. He admitted to himself now that this television thing had him worried that her face would be splashed all over the place. He was happy about her success. The timing, though, was all wrong.

It wasn't fair to place his work on her mind before this special moment she was about to encounter. "Our families are getting along famously," he said, changing his tone.

"I knew they would."

"Especially your Dad and Jacqueline. She's already calling him Pops. Well, they all send their love and wish you both good luck," he said, shaking Dre's hand.

"I keep telling you, sweetie, that luck is for losers," Celeste said, "I'm a winner, so wish me blessings."

"OK winner. I am trying to figure out how I can kiss you without all of that lipstick coming off."

"Who cares about the lipstick. Just do it."

Dre excused himself, while Celeste and Kenny broke their promise not to kiss, and unmercifully swapped bodily fluids until the production assistant knocked, "You're on!"

They were both reeling from the intensity. "I love you," they said at the same time.

As Celeste took her seat in the high chair on the set, Dre was grateful for whatever Kenny did and/or said in the dressing room because she had just the spark the camera was going to be unable to resist.

The Communication Excellence Awards Dinner was the most anticipated black-tie event of the year for journalists. Everybody

Web of Deception

from Barbara Walters to Ed Bradley to Oprah Winfrey to Frankie Crocker was present. The Toussaint/Hamilton group took up two tables.

Ed Townsend couldn't resist talking to Celeste's guests.

"Hey y'all please allow me to introduce *el gran queso,* the publisher from the paper," she announced as she introduced each person as Aunt, Uncle or Cousin, even Kenny and Jacqueline.

ET went to Aunt June with sad eyes. "My deepest sympathy to you. *The Courier* would like to do an in-depth interview with you about how you are getting along now," he said, hoping to gain points with her.

Aunt June replied just as she had been briefed. "I'm sorry, Mr. Townsend, but our family has put that ordeal behind us. We are only looking toward the future," she stated. "Anyway, that Miss Woods did such a lovely story a while ago. We thank you. Don't we?" she said to the family.

Thank yous chimed from the family.

"Well, you people enjoy your evening," said ET.

The one thing that got Charles Toussaint's blood pressure rising was the "you people" phrase. "And YOU people enjoy your evening, because we certainly shall," he said as he raised his champagne glass to ET. Charles' statement was subtle but the eyes read "get lost!"

Red-faced and defeated, ET nodded and found his way back to his seat through the maze of tables and well-wishers.

The Hamilton/Toussaint clan were doing their very best to keep from falling out of their seats at the way June and Charles had handled ET.

"... And the winner for best entertainment reporting ... *The New York Daily Courier.* Celeste Toussaint."

She graciously accepted her award, "Thanks New York, but this one's for my Daddy," giving thumbs up to the crew.

"... And the winner for best homicide coverage ... *The New York Daily Courier.* Newt Pickney and T.J. Radcliffe."

"... And the winner for Best New Syndicated Radio program ... Windy City Productions. *Entertainment Review*." The audience went wild. Celeste let Dre and Maurice do all of the talking. The room was in stitches.

"... And the winner for the best investigative series ... *The New York Stand*. For the series 'The Times Square Massacre' by Chi Woods." The audience roared. Celeste clapped daintily and smiled. Dre stepped to the stage just as they had rehearsed.

"As Editor-In-Chief of *The New York Stand,*"- Celeste and Maurice shook their heads at Dre and his created title-of-the-moment, -"I accept this award on behalf of Chi tonight. She wanted to be here but she is out of town on assignment. Thank you for your continued support. And remember, no matter what the subject, for your right to be informed, we will continue to stand."

Celeste scanned the room for ET, seeking his reaction to Dre's speech. He was nowhere to be found.

The tenth floor at One Times Square Plaza was dark and empty; everyone else had attended the awards ceremony. They knew the layout of this floor well and moved through the darkness with ease. Using a master key to open Celeste's office, they crept in to access her Rolodex. In a matter of moments they found the home phone number and address of Chi Woods.

"I told you she would have what we needed," said Marcia Mason, taking the Rolodex card out of the spindle and handing it to ET.

"You're right so often," said ET amazed.

"I told you all of these guys run in the same circles. Sooner or later you're bound to meet every reporter in town."

"How come I keep doubting you?" asked ET.

"Hopefully after tonight you'll never doubt me again," said Marcia as she took off the sequinned blazer, exposing her breasts.

ET Townsend frantically kissed and finished undressing Marcia until they ended up on Celeste's office floor.

The Hamiltons had rented the penthouse of The Plaza Hotel for their visit to the city. The private floor had ten bedrooms, several sitting parlors, and a massive columned living room. They hosted an intimate reception in Celeste's honor with soul fixin's catered from Sylvia's in Harlem.

Kenny proposed a toast: "To the most talented, most beautiful, fast thinking, fast talking woman I know this side of the Mississippi."

"Here, here," agreed the crowd.

"You made us all real proud tonight," said Charles, clinging to his daughter's award.

"Thank you guys for believing in me. For staying out of my way when I needed you to stay out of my way, and for your love," said Celeste emotionally.

"Now Chi Woods would like to acknowledge the person without whose love, support, and endless knowledge, this would have never been possible," she said, presenting her award to Kenny. They stood hugging in the center of the room oblivious to anyone else.

The next few days the Toussaint and Hamilton bunch enjoyed New York City as if it were their first visit. The Hamiltons insisted that the Toussaints, Miss Diane, and Miss Audrey stay at The Plaza to be close to the action. Celeste fulfilled her promise and provided the best house seats she could find, "down front" as Uncle Zeke had requested, for three plays and two concerts.

Kenny was elated that their families were getting along so well. The ladies shopped till they dropped, even Aunt June. Somewhere along the way, with Celeste sharing those bonus checks with her Auntie and receiving her own insurance money from Uncle Jim's death, June lost that frugal spirit. Shopping sprees with her lady friends had suddenly become no problem.

Jacqueline spent every possible moment with Charles trying to convince him to come out of retirement and become legal counsel for Notlimah Realty.

"You see, Pops, although our attorney has been with us for six years, he is the only member of our organization who is not related or does not have some tie with us from way back when," Jacqueline explained while showing off Hamilton properties as Winston drove them around Manhattan. "And in my opinion, it is a major weak link."

"Don't get too excited, we ain't family yet. My princess still has to say yes, you know," reminded Charles.

Jacqueline sighed, "I wish she would hurry up and say yes. The whole family is on pins and needles waiting."

"They really are a good match," boasted Charles.

"Yeah, they are. That's why K-Trey said he's not worried about her saying yes, and we should stop sweating her."

Charles admired Jacqueline tremendously. This young perky woman possessed the same zeal about life as Celeste. She had the ability to bounce back and forth between talk of million-dollar property purchases to playing the dozens. He loved her business sense and her youthful approach to it. Jacqueline took over from where her father left off and led Notlimah Realty to even further success with her daring, risk-taking purchasing. Charles was most in awe of her lack of conceit.

Winston rolled up in front of one of their Park Avenue condominiums. "Well do we have a new legal beagle aboard?" questioned Jacqueline, anxious to solidify this deal.

"Yes Miss Jacqueline Hamilton," said Charles, reaching for her hand, "you do."

She shouted, slapped him a high five, and grabbed his neck. "Everybody is gonna be so happy! It's a wonderful thing, you wait and see. Come on, I want you to take a look at this building. It's one of our most beautiful projects."

"It really is," complimented Charles, admiring the outside.

"Winston, wait here, we'll only be a few minutes."

He opened the curbside door of the Lincoln limo and then

Winston saw Ed Townsend furiously pointing his finger in Rick's chest in the building's lobby. Jacqueline had one leg out of the door. "Get back in the car and roll up that window now!" Winston commanded.

"Don't be silly," Jacqueline said, still trying to get out of the car. Charles read Winston's eyes and snatched her back in just as he slammed and locked the door then peeled away from the curb.

Winston fumbled with his hand-held computer to access the home address of one Ed Townsend. "Bingo!" he shouted.

Taking advantage of a red light to chastise Jacqueline, Winston said, "Little girl, listen here. I have known you since before you were born and you have never tried to disobey me before today. Why did you have to try it then?"

She shrugged with tears in her eyes.

"Don't cry, Jackie. But next time I tell you to do something. DO IT! One second can cost you your life," Winston said, intending to scare her. "Now, who is the property manager for this building?"

"Uncle Lester manages all of Park Avenue."

Winston called Kenny's cellular phone. Since Kenny was with the only other person who had the number to his phone, he knew Winston had news, "What's up man?"

"Yo buddy, we need to get more involved in the family business."

"I know, it's much safer," replied Kenny jokingly.

"You are never going to believe who resides at a Notlimah property. Never in a million years ..."

Kenny and Celeste stole away from the perpetual party atmosphere at The Plaza to the Poconos for the night. Each one had reports as more circles and arrows were drawn. They found that at first the information Wayne initially sent them did not compute, but the more this little caper unfolded, his information fit in quite nicely.

Wayne's latest package, postmarked from Evanston, Illinois, contained the news about Taylor Reed's unexpected resignation. Celeste could not wait until this entire thing blew over so she could once again be in contact with Wayne.

They let Winston, the espionage expert, look over their plans drawn out on the easel paper. He closed the holes that were wide open, rearranged some of the order, and questioned why they were trying to do some things that should have been left for RICO.

"I'll tell you why," Celeste explained. "Because RICO is no kin to my Uncle Jim and RICO is no friend to Renee. And RICO certainly did not care about the welfare of Julie Ryan. And RICO will not care about the welfare of Jane or Muffin or the countless number of other women who are unknowingly in danger. But mostly RICO does not give one iota about the people's right to know. That is why I'm doing this more than anything. To inform the masses. Period."

Winston smiled approvingly at Kenny. "This woman is a pistol. Hey, either of you ever think about joining the CIA?" he joked.

"One case at a time, my friend," laughed Kenny.

"Overall though, this looks like a great plan," complimented Winston, "You two make a hot team."

"I can't take any credit for this, Kenny is the genius behind it all," acknowledged Celeste proudly.

"So, you have been paying attention to me all of these years," said Winston patting him on the back.

"You're pretty hard to ignore. OK, listen up you two," instructed Kenny, "let's get in at least two more meetings before we execute this thing. When we have something major to report, like Taylor Reed suddenly retiring due to cancer, or ET living in one of our properties, we'll call a meeting. Agreed?"

Celeste and Winston agreed.

"We need an emergency code. Something that says 'get your tails in position' so you can get the info," suggested Winston.

"Good idea," said Kenny happy that Winston was friend and

not foe. "Make up one."

"When my girlfriends and I at home used to call each other with gossip we called it a Dirt Alert," Celeste said seeking their approval. "How's that?"

"Honey, that's so cute," complimented Kenny.

"It works for me," said Winston.

Kenny kept thinking, that in two more weeks, max, he would place this dirt and dangerous lifestyle behind him. He looked at his Rolex and began his silent countdown.

TWENTY-NINE

aurice had canceled the taping of his show for the third
time in five days because Dre was not present. The
syndicators and the sponsors insisted Celeste do the
show alone. Maurice in return insisted she and Dre were a package deal.

It was highly unlikely for Dre to miss an opportunity to get
good pay. Why was he suddenly incognito? No one at *The Stand*
had heard from him in days and Maurice was beginning to take it
personally that his best friend was missing in action without so
much a peep as to his whereabouts.

Dre fell in love frequently with a variety of pretty-boy studs
who were less than desirable. He would pick them up in the gay
bars and would disappear for days at a time. Maurice did not want
to infringe on his privacy by marching over to his place just because he missed a couple of tapings. It was a pact that they had
between the two of them regarding their privacy.

However, Dre would never miss their recording sessions. He
loved the money too much. This is what had Maurice worried.

Maurice would joke that Dre was the type of man who could
lay up and do nothing but go to museums and to the theatre if he
had someone taking care of him. An accusation Dre never denied.

Neither Celeste nor Maurice wanted to verbally admit that they had a terrible feeling about Dre. They sat on the phone in silence waiting for the other to confirm it. Celeste knew she had dreamt about something awful happening to him. She did not want to deal with another episode. Emotionally she had already been wiped up and cleaned out.

"I can't take it anymore, Reese," said Celeste, breaking the silence they had held on the phone line for over ten minutes. "I'm going to ask Kenny to go over there."

"Well I called the super and he did say that he saw Dre two days ago. What if he's, you know?" implicated Maurice, "laying up with somebody? You need to know our good buddy is about as reliable as a diaphragm with a hole in it when he's in love. I don't want Kenny to walk in on that. We're getting along with him too well now."

"That's nice of you to care about what Kenny thinks. But I know one daggone thing. If Dre stood us up just to get his butt rubbed, we need to consider disowning him."

Maurice laughed and released some of his tension. "I hear ya. OK, call Officer Friendly and tell him to see what our friend is up to."

"Good. Hey Reese, I love you, OK?"

"Me too," Maurice hung up the phone and cried uncontrollably for reasons he could not explain.

Kenny advised his commanding officer that he was going off post to check on the well being of a friend, and took a few cops from Dre's precinct with him. When he arrived on Dre's floor one of the cops accompanying him commented, "This building smells horrible."

He carefully examined the door for signs of forced entry and heard the television blaring inside. Kenny drew his gun and ordered the super to open the door. The smell suffocated him.

"My God," said the super, reacting to the sight and smell.

"You, out!" Kenny barked pointing to the super.

There were fingers lined up on the couch and wads of blood on the walls, carpet, and furniture. In the bedroom Kenny found Dre tied to a chair with his throat slit and other body parts missing. He heard one of the cops scream Hail Mary's from the bathroom, where he found Dre's feet in the tub, his tongue nailed to the wall, and writing in blood which read: "You will never stand again."

Kenny phoned Winston. "Dirt Alert. Get Maurice too. Now," he said calmly, staring at the writing on the bathroom walls. "I'll be out there in a few hours."

The phone on Newt Pickney's desk rang six times before he decided to answer it. "Yeah, yeah, yeah. This better be good. I was trying ta think."

"Newt Pickney, I'm a big fan of yours, and I happen to be a cop. Listen carefully. I have an exclusive story for you and you only. Leave your buddy at the office and meet Detective Bradley at 2750 Broadway. Tell the policemen at the door he gave you clearance. Be there in 15 minutes."

Kenny leaned in the doorway of Dre's bedroom and looked at him tied to that chair with his fingers and feet cut off. The perps were obviously on a fishing expedition, and he knew why. It was Kenny's idea to create a false address for Chi Woods and put it on Celeste's Rolodex. But it was Dre who insisted that they use his address. He had said it would be his small way of helping out. Dre also said he didn't think anyone would go to any great lengths to find Chi, because he had published stories more explosive than "The Times Square Massacre."

Dre was wrong. Dead wrong.

Winston and Celeste gave Maurice all details from A to Z. They studied the outline of The Plan until it was committed to memory. Kenny arrived at the house in the Poconos four hours later and everyone waited for him to speak with great anticipation.

Without any preamble, Kenny said, "Dre has been murdered," tying to sound emotionless.

Maurice was beside himself. Celeste ran outside into the night of the woods.

"Celeste, come back!" Kenny shouted after her.

She ran until her legs could no longer carry her before collapsing into a fit of tears. Her grief was like none she had ever known. Celeste had not even overcome her Uncle's death and now this. She got on her knees and prayed she would make it through yet another ordeal. She rocked furiously back and forth, hoping her rapid motions would shake her grief.

In the darkness of the night, Kenny followed the sobs until he found Celeste rolled into a ball with her face pressed hard against the earth. It was plain for him to see she was totally consumed with sadness. If he did not try to snap her back to reality now, he probably never would.

Kenny's psychology training taught him that the first thing to do for someone dealing with tragedy is not to say anything. The wrong words could send them into hysterics.

Kenny knelt down beside Celeste and simply held her hand. The rugged terrain was very rocky and cold. Sounds of the night as well as the whimpering coming from the lady he loved echoed off of the mountains. She managed to lift her head and lay it in his lap while he stroked her hair in silence.

Eternally thankful for his understanding, Celeste was desperately trying to scrape together her emotions. She could feel herself reeling down a dark tunnel into a severe depression. It would be the first time in her life that she had actually come face to face with even the possibility of depression enveloping her. Permanently.

She managed to slip her arms under Kenny's shirt, partially for his warmth, primarily to be as close as possible. She pushed him to the ground and climbed on top of him taking full control, exploring his body with tender kisses.

Kenny was not prepared for such sensations at the moment, because her reactions were totally opposite from what the "books" had said happens to one in shock. Leave it to Celeste Toussaint to defy predictability, even in the midst of her grief.

Kenny did not know how to react when she started tearing at his clothes. The intense throbbing of his manhood was his physical response. Mentally he was totally stimulated by the cold of the fresh outdoors, the stillness of the night, and the possibility of being caught by Winston or Maurice. Kenny had his eyes closed and allowed himself to indulge in the moment.

He didn't know at what point she got undressed, but when he felt her soft naked body against his, he nearly screamed out loud from the pleasure of ended anticipation.

"What are we doing?" Kenny asked bewildered as to how they had gotten so far. "We are breaking a very serious promise to one another."

"We've been so busy, I forgot to tell you," she said, tickling his ear. "We are negative, my dear."

"How could you forget to tell me something so important?"

"Understand something about me now, sweetie," she explained, "when I'm in my work mode nothing else matters."

He smiled, "Well then, how in the world did you get my results?"

"I knew your number," she admitted, "and on occasions I can sound like a man," she mocked changing her voice to a deeper tone.

"You're a nut," he said, holding her face looking into her eyes. "I love you like I have never loved anyone before. And I promise that as long as I'm around no one will ever harm you."

Celeste cried as he kissed away all of her tears. She whispered into his ear, "Let's go get the bad guys, Detective. But right now I'm ready to make love to the love of my life, right here."

"Really," was all he could manage to say, thoroughly aware that he was being seduced.

"Yes, really. Remember, I told you when we got our negative results that I was going to tear your clothes off. Are you ready?" she said, allowing her leg to press against the hardness between his, "Oops, don't answer."

They rocked gently under the moon and starlit sky. Peeling away age-old emotions. Shedding all fears and doubts. Linking life and love to one another. Renewing their hearts and souls forever. Their orgasms were simultaneous and so intense that neither of them could control their screams of passion.

Kenny slowly dressed Celeste, promising her much more where that came from if he could escape the cold outdoors and enter into what he called "his turf ... the great indoors."

They chose to jog back to the house, both of them too charged up to merely walk. Entering the house breathless, they found the guys asleep on the couches in front of the fire. Kenny swept Celeste off of her feet and carried her up to the master suite.

Winston opened one eye as they ascended the stairway and exhaled, "Finally."

Kenny locked the bedroom door and proceeded to finish what she started outside.

THIRTY

F rom this day forward, Celeste declared to hate showbiz. She had heard the phrase, "The show must go on", but never did she imagine that she would be sitting in front of a camera alone doing *Entertainment Review* without Dre.

She and Maurice discussed walking away from the project totally, but the studio reminded them that's what contracts were for. So she sat in the high chair with an attitude, no smile, and blowing her lines all over the place.

"Cut. Cut. Cut," ordered Maurice from the floor. "Everybody take 30 minutes. You come with me, Miss Girl," he said, taking Celeste by the hand to her dressing room.

He threw her into a chair. "What were you doing out there? I thought we were not going to let them win. Neither of us wants to be here, OK but we are not going to dishonor Dre's memory by making a mess of this show. He would not want that."

Celeste knew he was right but she had not been able to bring herself totally around. For the past week she had been going about her daily duties dazed. Mechanical in everything; an android. She could not even sleep. She wouldn't cook, or clean up. She just vegetated, withdrawing into herself, hoping the Lord would give her strength.

She and Maurice would sit on the phone and sigh, as though he was her only link to the world they had all known. Dre was the completion of the chain-link fence. Celeste and Maurice were trying desperately to hold the fence up; although one of the original links was missing and would be forever.

Tears streamed down her face. She had been holding back her tears since they came from the mountains. Even at the memorial service she made it through with dry eyes. Celeste felt Dre's presence at the service that night, and as she boarded the elevator to leave, she felt him there, too.

In the lobby, when Kenny kissed her cheek hello she felt Dre kiss the other goodbye. She had turned around just as the elevator doors closed and Dre went back upstairs to join his friends in spirit at his memorial.

She cried now at those thoughts of Dre, of their not being able to share in the success he helped begin. Not caring about her makeup, she felt really good crying. Maurice joined in the tear shedding too, for he was only trying to remain strong for Celeste.

"Reese, I feel 100 percent better now. I really needed that one last cry," she admitted. "Thanks for being here."

He turned up the radio and whispered, "I'm glad because I was going to call Officer Friendly and tell him tonight was off."

"No way my brother. Celeste Toussaint is back."

The makeup artist had to start from scratch on her face. Always too much for her taste, Celeste didn't let the makeup bother her now, she concentrated on the show.

"Places everybody," commanded Maurice, "Five. Four. Three. Two and ..."

"Welcome to *Entertainment Review.* I'm Celeste Toussaint. Our program today is dedicated to the memory of Dre Tyson. A fine gentleman, journalist, and friend. We love you and we'll miss you."

A production assistant brought to Maurice's attention that Celeste's introduction was not in the script.

He shooed her away. "It's perfect," he confirmed, "It's a take." Celeste did the rest of the show like a pro. She was flawless.

Muffin helped "Monica" prepare for her first night at work as a waitress at The Show Time Lounge. Kenny had Muffin pay one of their regular waitresses to disappear for a week, which left Sal minus the much-needed help. Muffin told him about her friend, Monica, who would gladly take the post. Sal had hired Monica sight unseen.

Celeste found the perfect jet-black, waist-length, braided wig for her Monica honky-tonk-homegirl image. She also donned a gold tooth, red Lee Press-On nails, false eyelashes, piles of makeup, ruby red lipstick, and two pieces of tropical flavored Bubble-Yum, all the easier for her to smack and blow bubbles.

Her attire was equally tacky. Thigh-high leather, four-inch heeled boots, a micro-mini skirt, fishnet stockings, a halter top, rings on every finger, and strands of fake pearls. That, combined with her sho'-nuff-good-time-gal high-pitched dialect, Celeste was convinced her own mother would not recognize her concocted "Monica."

In undercover work, cops and all in conjunction with a bust were to wear a specified color somewhere visible. Kenny had advised the girls that the color of the day was green. Monica and Muffin both chose to tie green bandannas around their foreheads, Isis style.

"This is my friend Monica I told you about Sal," introduced Muffin.

"Well, well," eyed Sal approvingly, "you sure you ain't here ta dance baby?"

The list of players with their habitual descriptions given to Celeste by Muffin to study, proved helpful in her dialogue. "I ain't sayin' no an' I ain't sayin' yes," said Monica, cracking her Bubble Yum, in the spirit of Jane. "Let's see what kindsa tips I can make in this here trap and we'll see."

"Whoa, we gotsa hot one here," Sal admired while breathing down her cleavage.

"Looks like the only one hot here is you," Monica said, noting him holding his crotch, "Good ta meecha, Sal. Where's my station?"

"Right up front, baby. I want everybody ta see you."

"Great. That's exactly what I'm lookin' for, the up-front action."

"Good deal. Listen here. All the tips you get you keep. If anyone wants anything from you other than a drink," he said pinching his nose, "ring the buzzer under the register once and I'll accommodate them. If what they want is you, ring the buzzer twice and you and the Joe can take a walk upstairs. Your primary function is to monitor that credit card to make sure it doesn't run dry. Or if he's using cash make sure he has a roll."

"Got it."

"Also fill out your information on this sheet. The wages we's reports to the IRS is $2.50 an hour. You get a check every night for the hours you put in and any extras, is calculated at the end of the evening and given to you in cash along with the check."

"A check every night. Now there's a nice perk," Monica fished.

"It ain't no perk. It's a precaution," corrected Sal. "If you never come back, you owe us nothing. If we never want you back, we owe you nothing."

"Got it."

Monica completed the form with her left hand instead of her right, stating her address from Chicago but making the city Rosedale in Queens, her social security number was her bank account number, and the phone was Kenny's beeper number.

"Did you register all I just toldja, Monica?"

"I got it."

"Yes you do. And baby I'm gonna make you a star," said Sal giving his usual spiel.

Celeste thought, *This is going to be a long night.*

Members of the RICO team were waiting outside of Marcia Mason's apartment when she arrived from work. In the heat of her passionate evening with ET, they forgot to lock Celeste's office door and they left the Chi Woods Rolodex card petruding from the file. The police had lifted Marcia's and ET's fingerprints from the card in Celeste's office.

Marcia walked into the building lobby and was immediately surrounded by police.

"Marcia Mason," said an officer while cuffing her, "you are under arrest for aiding and abetting in the murder of Dre Tyson. You have the right to remain silent ..."

That damn ET, she thought, I'm going to kill him.

At One Times Square Plaza, the RICO team waited a full 30 minutes after the majority of the _New York Daily Courier_ staff had departed. They caught Jane placing orders to the car service for dancer pick-ups before she was cuffed and booked.

By 10:30, The Show Time Lounge was in full swing and Monica was a hit. She was getting five and six dollar tips a pop. She had to remain alert when processing the credit cards and when the dollars flashed. It was complicated keeping track of who had how much money, because there was plenty going around.

Monica counted eight men in plain sight wearing green. She wasn't sure if it was coincidental that they were wearing the color of the day or if they were indeed cops. Serving drinks, she felt her body tense at the thought of the danger in which she had placed herself, Muffin, and even Kenny throughout this ordeal.

Muffin worked with them like a real pro. She wanted out of this lifestyle very much, but she said that she wanted to have a seat front and center when the perps were cuffed and taken to jail. Then she was going to take the money she had earned and return to Macon, Georgia, to open a charm and acting school. "I do think I'm qualified," Muffin had said. "After four years in this joint, I have just graduated with honors."

Waiting for a Visa authorization number, Monica caught a glimpse in the mirror of a dashing young man in a baseball cap just seated by Muffin at her station. Her first response was to ask Kenny where he had been all night. It was after one o'clock in the morning.

"How you, good lookin'?" she asked swinging her pearls.

Kenny eyed her up and down, amused at her transformation, "Not as good as you. I'll be better once I get a seabreeze in me."

Monica poured the cranberry juice and replaced vodka with Seven-Up. He told her that the combination looked like a real alcoholic beverage. She placed his drink on the bar and tilted her head toward the door for him to note Ed Townsend making his grand entrance with three of his buddies.

ET knew practically everyone in the joint. He was escorted to a reserved section. Brandi, his usual waitress, fetched their drinks without being told. Sal began barking louder, moving faster, and commanding more order since the men made their entrances.

Monica watched ET moving around like he owned the joint from the corner of her eye and in the mirror while she served drinks and flirted endlessly with the fellas at the bar. Kenny summoned her with his index finger and requested a little something for his head. She nodded and rang the buzzer once.

"Whatta we got here, Monica?" asked Sal.

"The gennelman here wants a little something to help him get real nice," she vamped, nodding that he could well afford it.

Sal placed a small plastic bag in front of his drink and told Monica to charge the customer $50. The customer agreed and Monica rang the goods like it was a gift for Christmas.

Kenny excused himself before ordering another drink and was followed to the bathroom by another cop on the job. They went into a stall to accurately identify the substance and pretended to inhale the item he had just purchased.

ET and his pals were having a helluva good time. A select

group of women were table and lap dancing for his group, allowing them to put 100-dollar tips in their g-strings. They had many plastic bags delivered to their table and they tooted it right out in the open. Celeste was glad that she had a good view of them and that they could not see her.

Back at the bar Monica knew she had to make it look like things were getting steamy between she and this John, Kenny. It wasn't long before she was ringing her register buzzer twice. Sal bounced up to give the authorization for a 250-dollar transaction. He shook Kenny's hand, patted him on the back, and had another waitress relieve Monica for 30 minutes.

The upstairs looked like a flea bag hotel. What a contrast to the glitzy atmosphere in the show room! There were a total of ten creaky and pissy-smelling rooms, with mattresses so thin there may as well have been none at all. They opted to kiss one another and hug standing. Grunting and groaning as if more were taking place.

"I can't believe this place is so funky and dirty," Celeste observed quietly. "I mean I've seen the cash these guys have, and they could get a hotel room at the Ritz-Carlton if they wanted to. I. Don't. Get. It."

"The sleaze adds to the thrill baby. Of course they can afford the Ritz. But the Ritz is where they take the wife. Ya know what I mean?"

"Got it. I guess this environment is part of a voyeuristic experience the player wants to have when he comes to a place like this. So that is what Jane was talking about."

He nodded in between kisses and whispered, "Gal Friday, I'm darn proud of you. Two more hours and you're out of here. How are you doing, baby?"

"I guess I'm blessed, in spite of it all."

"There's no guessing to do in that department. I know you're blessed, I've seen you naked," confirmed Kenny.

Celeste laughed aloud at his humor, it helped her to play her role to the hilt. "Don't stop now," she moaned a bit frightened.

"More. More. More."

Kenny held her close hoping to ease her fear, thankful for the courage she had displayed thus far. For some reason the thought crossed his mind to jump out of the window, escape this whole mess, and go riding off into the wild blue yonder. He did not care about himself so much, but he had promised Charles Toussaint that his princess would be in good hands. Kenny knew their present environment was not at all what her Daddy had in mind.

Celeste felt herself getting too relaxed. It was time for Monica to get back to her station. She searched Kenny's eyes for reassurance that they were doing the right thing by even being there. Finding just the confirmation she needed, they held hands until they got downstairs. Before entering the main level, Kenny pointed to her eyes, her bandanna, and his green hat. Implying, keep your eyes on us.

Sal whistled when he saw them smiling happily. Kenny played the role and slapped her butt, Monica cut her eyes at Kenny and snatched his Visa. "Hey pal, that just cost you 50 bucks extra," she said flashing a gold tooth.

At four-thirty, the music had been turned off, the lights were on, and the only people left in the club were those who worked at The Show Time Lounge. In the back room a short man by the name of Rick stood in the center of employees calling names and handing out envelopes.

"Monica Wade," he belted.

"Right here," she squeaked and sashayed over to pick up her hard-earned pay.

Rick stared at Monica as she reached for her envelope.

"Monica, huh?" asked Rick scratching his head.

"Yeah, what's up babe?" she asked while wondering why Rick had singled her out.

"For a moment, woman, you vaguely reminded me of someone," he said.

Celeste knew he couldn't possibly recognize her, she looked completely different and towered over him at least a foot with those heels. "Yeah, babe? Who's that?" she quizzed.

"I can't put my finger on who."

She stood close enough so he could get himself a good look. He also got a good whiff of her cheap perfume and that bubble gum she was smacking and he shook off the resemblance he thought she had to Celeste Toussaint.

"It'll come to me, sweetart. It always does. Car number 12 is waiting outside for you," said Rick.

"Thanks," she said, snatching her envelope.

Monica said her goodnights to everyone and found Muffin in the lap of Ed Townsend. What were he and his friends still doing here? Sal interrupted her thoughts. "Monica, will I see ya tamorra night? You were a hit."

"Thanks, Sal. Yeah, dude, I'll be here," she said, kissing his forehead and leaving a blob of red lipstick. "Ya just keep it tight for mama."

"Did you meet my buddies here? Hey fellas, this is our new barmaid, Monica. And don't touch her, she's mine."

"That's right," she said, rubbing the lipstick off. "Hey y'all," she said addressing the men at the table. "Listen, it's been real. See y'all tomorra," she added running out of the door and jumping over one employee sweeping and one mopping, who both wore her colors.

"Hey y'all? See y'all?" repeated Ed Townsend, "I heard someone else say that recently. Who was it?"

Peeking into car number 12 praying the driver had on the color of the day, Monica said, "Hey," to the driver while leaning into the window to check out his attire.

Noticing he was not wearing any green, "I'm sorry ta bother ya. I need car number 21 not car number 12," she thought quickly.

A yellow taxi screeched to a halt at the red light and Monica sashayed to the vehicle thrilled, to see Winston behind the wheel. He weaved up and down the avenues before heading downtown on the West Side Highway. Kenny was hunched down on the floor in front.

Celeste tossed her envelope to him and he held a flashlight at her pay written on a WBB Enterprises check. She also had $250 in cash, her commission for selling her goods and theirs.

"Bingo," Kenny yelled into his walkie talkie. "No wonder ET moves around the joint like he owns it! He does. And I have the evidence. It's a bust! Now!"

Celeste was busy shedding her homegirl image. The gold tooth, false eyelashes, and bubble gum all went flying out of the window.

Kenny knelt in the front seat and leaned over for a long kiss. He playfully put on her wig.

Celeste was rolling with laughter, "You have got to take off that wig. You look a mess."

"Baby leave me and my wig alone. This is my moment."

"Yeah, a Kodak moment," she said. "Dag, now where's a photographer when you need one?"

"Baby, you are a genius! I swear I would have never thought of busting Ed Townsend by matching his signature on my check from the car service, and your checks from *The Courier* and Show Time."

"It was just a hunch," she commented, "a simple educated guess. I never knew that saving a pay check would be of so much help someday."

A major portion of the Midtown South precinct burst into The Show Time Lounge from every angle with guns drawn. One of the cops mopping the floor handcuffed Muffin and rode in the car with her to the precinct where she would be booked, just for show, and then shipped off to Georgia with an escort.

Winston zoomed the taxi down the West Side Highway with

Kenny and Celeste slapping high fives and were singing James Brown's "I Feel Good."

Kenny did feel good. This bust was great and his baby helped. He was kneeling over the front seat, kissing Celeste in back, and further examining those checks.

"Yep, it's a match for sure!" said Kenny still on a high. "Wee doggie!"

"Man, turn around and put your seatbelt on," warned Winston, while slowing down the taxi at a yellow light. Just then a car from out of nowhere plowed into them from behind. The impact sent Kenny crashing backward into the windshield head first, completely shattering the glass. The car had thrust them forward and Winston came to a screeching halt.

"Keeenny!" shrieked Celeste.

"Hold still," said Winston as he brushed the bits of glass from around Kenny's face and neck and helped him to sit. "Celeste, how are you back there?"

"Fine. Don't worry about me. How do you feel sweetie?"

"My neck and back are sore."

"Hey man, this is Winston you're talking to. How do you really feel."?

"OK," Kenny conceded, "its all really, really sore!"

"Man, you look retarded with that wig on," laughed Winston. "But I'm here to tell you it done saved yo' big head from being cut up."

"Shut up," Kenny moaned.

"I'm gonna check this other guy," Winston said leaving the car.

Celeste sat silently holding her man in the front seat thinking about the mess she had helped create. She was absolutely about to cry.

"The guy hit his head on the wheel," Winston reported of the driver in the other car, dialing 911 to come to the scene. "He's still alive, but unconscious and drunk."

"Kenny needs to get to a hospital," Celeste said worriedly.

"No, Kenny doesn't!" he yelled.

"Yes. You do!" Celeste yelled back. "Boy, don't you know your big head done cracked a windshield!"

"Let's just go!" Kenny yelled frantically. "We don't need to explain how we got a taxi, and why I'm riding in it. Just help me lay down in the back. Winston, call Doc."

"Gotcha," Winston acknowledged, placing the call.

"Come on baby, you're spending the night out on the Island tonight," informed Kenny. "Don't worry about explaining why you look like you do. Let me do the talking."

He laid across the back seat with his head in Celeste's lap. She stroked his head gently not touching his cuts, thinking of the scene similar to this one a couple of weeks ago. Only their positions were reversed. She looked down at him thinking how much they needed one another, and yet her heart ached because she still was not sure if she would say yes to his proposal. Ever since she met him, tragedy had followed her. Was this a sign? She was not sure.

So much had happened in a short period of time that Celeste did not know if her feelings were manufactured because Kenny had constantly come to her rescue, or if she was really in love. There was plenty to consider. She toyed with the idea of moving back to Chicago and starting a newspaper called *The Chicago Stand,* something she and Dre had spoken of often. More than anything she wanted out of that television contract and her Daddy was working on making it happen. Charles Toussaint's favorite motto was, "Contracts are made to be broken."

Celeste sighed and looked forward to that day.

Doc and his crew were waiting at the Hamilton home when they arrived. Mom had prepared a light meal and was relieved to see that her K-Trey was not seriously injured. She dared not ask any questions about Celeste reeking of cheap cologne and being dressed like a hooker. No one volunteered any information.

After a couple of hours of cleaning, prodding, and examining, Doc concluded, "Kenny only has a sprained neck and needs two stitches on his forehead."

"That's good news," sighed Mom.

"Good news?" repeated Doc. "Not many people get away so easily after crashing into glass. And Kenny, you say your head shattered the windshield, but you were turned backward, huh?

"Yeah, that's right." Kenny bragged of his survival.

"Listen here, young man," Doc lectured. "You're almost 30 and I'm almost 70. I'm not going to always be around to patch you up, you know. You've always been a klutz. Be more careful."

"I was careful, Doc." Kenny explained. "Tonight I had on some good head protection," he said twirling the wig in the air.

Kenny, Celeste and Winston fell out laughing.

Mom Hamilton scrutinized the wig and put her hand on her hip, "Oh, so the three of you think this is funny?"

They couldn't stop laughing.

"Doc," commanded Mom, "commit them all."

Doc gave his orders. "What he needs is bed rest for at least a week."

"A weeeek," wailed Kenny.

"Yes, a week, young man," stressed Doc, "and you need to wear a cervical collar until your neck sprain is well."

"Listen, Doc. I'll rest, but while I'm resting I ain't gonna look like no geek with that old ugly, chunky, plastic neck brace."

"For your information, young man, we now have designer neck braces for the fashion conscious, like yourself," quipped Doc.

"Now that sounds good," smiled Kenny.

"The question is where do you want to lay low?" asked Winston. "The timing could not be more perfect for you to do that, you know."

"Mmmm," mused Kenny. "Will you join me for a trip to Negril my dear?" Kenny asked Celeste. "It's time we paid the newlyweds Sammy and Renee a visit anyway."

"Maybe you can skip out of the country for a few days, but I have a contract to honor," Celeste reminded him, though not wanting to be reminded herself. "I have a better idea. How about you going to the Poconos, that way I can meet you there after the show. If Winston does not mind the drive."

"I never mind," Winston stated.

"It's settled. I will go up tomorrow, and begin to follow the doctors orders."

"I must mark this date that my K-Trey conceded to follow anyone's orders other than his own," said Mom Hamilton. "Celeste, dear, I see that you are exactly what the doctor ordered."

Kenny smiled, "Yes she is."

THIRTY-ONE

The front pages of *The New York Stand* and *The New York Daily Courier* shared the same headline:

The Times Square Massacre:

Its Final Chapter
by
Newt Pickney and Chi Woods

New York - November 14, 1988 - At the Show Time Lounge located on West 43rd Street and Eighth Avenue, the last strip tease was danced, the last song was played, the last "John" was laid, and the last bag of illicit substance was exchanged, after a major police bust last night that put an end to a wide-ranging criminal operation.

A team of police investigators, working with local newspaper reporters, was able to expose and arrest members of an organized crime ring known as The WBB, or the Wharton Business Boys. Four members of the WBB have been arrested and are awaiting trial. The fifth member of the organization appears to be missing, according to investigators.

The WBB is directly responsible for the last three murders in New York within the last three months, and may be linked to many more within the last year. The Racketeer Influenced and Corrupt Organizations (RICO) investigation unit has asked that the names of those victims be withheld until the completion of the investigation. In addition to murder charges, other racketeering activities for which the established business illegal, profit-making ventures. Informants close to the operation all revealed that the members took a blood vow to complete assignments "at all costs" and that any member who failed was subject to serious censure—even physical injury-from the others.

COPS INVESTIGATE NATIONAL TIES; ONE MEMBER STILL AT LARGE

Police have linked activity at The Show Time Lounge with The WBB; a further investigation will call in police from the other WBB stronghold cities to look into possible illegal links there.

Ed Townsend, publisher of *The New York Daily Courier* and the chairman of this corrupt organization, now awaits trail. Investigators have seized all his assets and it is expected that the paper will be sold at auction later this year.

In a mysterious development, member Taylor Reed of Chicago is still missing. This key member of the WBB recently resigned his post as publisher of *The Chicago Daily Courier* for health reasons, reportedly a diagnosis of a fatal cancer. *The New York Stand* has received confirmation that Reed paid top Chicago oncologists to fabricate a fatal cancerous condition through extensive false records. It is believed he used the diagnosis as a smoke screen to exit both his posts within The WBB and *The Chicago Daily Courier.*

The charges under which The WBB will be prosecuted include drug trafficking, prostitution, and the sale of pornographic materials.

The closing of The Show Time Lounge, which was owned and operated by WBB Enterprises, "is the beginning of a commitment to put an end to organized crime activity in this city," stated New York District Attorney James Ellerby.

COLLEGE PRANKSTERS TURN DEADLY

The WBB organization was formed in the early 1970's by five students at the Wharton School of Business in Pennsylvania. Initially the group's purpose was fun. School records indicate that the group was run by Ed Townsend, president, and Taylor Reed, vice president, whose campus antics kept them under threat of expulsion by the school's dean. The three other members charged are Dean Swindel of Dallas; Mitchell Cass of Los Angeles; and Samuel Pitt of Philadelphia.

"Whenever a test was passed around, sup-
plies stolen, or a building defaced, you could
bet a member of The WBB was responsible," said
a former classmate who requested anonymity.
"The problem was proving it."

After its wealthy members graduated, the
organization gained power by incorporating and
gaining business clout, primarily in the field
of newspaper publishing. Using the trust funds
of the members, The WBB bought and operated
the then failing chain of *Daily Courier* news-
papers in New York, Chicago, Los Angeles, Dallas
and Philadelphia. Each member took charge in
their home town and embarked on a number of
legitimate and illegitimate business dealings.

A nationwide search is underway for Reed,
now considered a fugitive from justice.

Ed Townsend ripped the paper that was once his into shreds
and tossed them onto the floor of his jail cell. How dare Newt join
forces with *that* woman? How dare they allow that woman to make
those allegations against his T?

Taylor would not *dare* break their oath. They had been friends
too long. ET could hear Taylor scorning him after each of the
WBB's dastardly deeds.

"ET, you should be more careful."

"I'm not always going to be here to fix your troubles and money
does not do it every time, ET."

"One day ET, your sloppy, dirty work is going to get you killed
or jailed."

"ET, stop relying on your money and put your brain to work
occasionally."

ET knew even when Taylor was saying these things to him

that he was right. Why, though, would he have to lie about his condition? Cancer was not a joke. He had read the reports himself, they looked legitimate.

The only rationale ET could deduce was that his good buddy personally knew, somehow, that this day was coming. Now he wondered if Taylor was in cahoots with the woman who had written the "Times Square Massacare."

"Damn!" ET seethed aloud, "While we've been busy chasing down a possible leak at the Show Time, and it must have been Taylor who was the leak all along."

That had to be it - ET thought. How else could this Chi woman have known so much? He knew the WBB had always been so careful ... so he thought. Now he realized there had to be a leak from the WBB. And that leak was Taylor.

ET sat with his head resting against the cold, hard bars, confused. He went over and over the turn of events from the night of the arrest. He was so zooted that night. The one thing that he could really remember was that new barmaid. She was some vixen. Now what did Sal say her name was?

Ed Townsend resigned himself to the fact that he was totally in a fog. But through it, he could hear that barmaid saying, "Hey y'all. See y'all." And he asked himself the same question again, "Who have I heard say that recently?"

While trying to find a comfortable spot on the lumpy cell bed, ET's eyes fell on the only section of the paper he had not ripped to pieces. There smiling directly at him was the face of Celeste Toussaint above her entertainment section.

He sat straight up saying in a voice like hers, "Hey y'all. See y'all." Shaking his head he whispered, "Well I'll be damned."

THIRTY - TWO

D riving from the Pocono estate in the 4 x 4 truck to get more provisions from town, Winston rubbed his blood shot eyes. He took a couple of swigs from the champagne bottle Celeste had left in the limousine.

Kenny was adamant about him driving her from the city to the mountains daily while he recovered. All of the running back and forth had left him exhausted. Winston hoped they would take that trip to Negril. He needed to see his feet in the bottom of some blue water soon — before he killed somebody.

Just as Winston was about to exit the estate's main gate, he sighted a van hiding in the woods. He left the Jeep at the edge of the road, out of plain view, behind a cluster of trees. Tipping toward the van, he saw the New York plate number WBB 883.

"Damn. I thought we got rid of those dirty bastards," Winston whispered to himself through clenched teeth. "These suckers are worse than city cockroaches."

Looking through the van window he spotted rope, gun ammunition, walkie talkies, and a tracking device machine. Wondering when these guys had an opportunity to place a homing pigeon on Celeste, Winston crouched behind the van to put the silencers on his guns and listen for any branches snapping or hushed conversations.

"I can't believe we got stuck out here laying on this cold ground," the thug complained, "I feel like a grunt in the Army."

"It's called paying our dues because one day we'll be inside and someone else will be out here on their bellies," the other thug replied peering through a pair of binoculars.

"I hope so. And I hope soon."

"Find what you're looking for?" commanded Winston with his gun to one thug's head and his combat booted foot on the others neck.

They were speechless.

"You," Winston barked, "Get up."

"If you get your foot off of my neck, maybe I can," the thug retorted.

Winston eased the pressure from his neck for a moment and thrust his face back into the dirt, "Sorry. I changed my mind."

"Man who the hell are you to come in here shouting orders at us. God?" the other said.

"OK, Bible scholar," Winston said jerking him face up, "what is the eleventh commandment?"

"Man you can't be serious. Everybody knows there are only ten commandments."

"Wrong answer," Winston laughed, placing the gun between his eyes. "Thou shall not trespass," he said and pulled the trigger.

Standing on the other's neck, Winston asked, "Are you a Bible scholar too?"

"Thou shall not trespass. Thou shall not trespass," he trembled.

"Sssh," advised Winston, "not so loud,"

The thug nodded desperately.

"Very good. Now, how many are trespassing in the house?"

"Two," he whispered.

"You wouldn't tell me a tale, would you?" Winston asked holding the gun to his temple.

He shook his head no furiously and wet his pants just before Winston snapped the neck of the thug with his booted foot.

He took the binoculars and scanned the perimeter of the house. No signs of any movement. There was a branch from a willow tree moving back and forth further behind the house nestled in the trees.

Winston focused the binoculars in on Kenny's body hanging from the rope.

"Jesus!" Winston screamed dropping the binoculars.

He ran to the stables, grabbed an axe and mounted Shadow bareback. Dashing toward the tree in one sweeping motion, Winston cut the rope and laid Kenny's body across the horse, carrying him to the stables for refuge.

Celeste was so blinded by her tears that she could barely see in front of her. Managing to feel her way to the table where the phone sat, her mind drifted in a thousand directions of "if only's." She was doomed. She could feel it.

All of these people had died because she could not let one little story go. Almost everybody close in her life was dead now. There was no one else left for them to kill but her.

She needed to face facts. Somewhere out there, the WBB was waiting for her. Even though Ed Townsend and his schoolboy cronies were behind bars, the enterprise they had begun was far from being dismantled.

She had so much floating in her mind, that she had not realized the phone she was holding had no dial tone. Pressing the button on the receiver a few times to be certain, she reached for her purse and clutched it tightly. Just as she stood with her antennae up, she heard the circuit breakers being flipped in the basement and the house went black. A very strong arm grabbed her around the neck.

At that moment her thoughts floated around the world and back again. Kenny's Mom would never be able to forgive Celeste for involving her son in an investigation which ended in his death. Never.

She was thinking, How do you call somebody's mama and tell them "Your son is dead?" No. Not just dead, but "he's been lynched?"

Then, as she heard a set of feet climbing the basement steps, Celeste figured it would not matter what his Mom thought, because soon she would be dead, too.

For a moment she thought of not going without a fight, and looked for ways to break free of the bruiser's hold, run out of the house, and find a place to hide in the woods. She was only going to go so far in silk pajamas and bare feet. Then again, she thought of how she should just surrender. She knew now that without Kenny in her life, there was no real reason for living.

The one thing she truly came to know in a short amount of time, was the art of human suffering. The emotional suffering she had come to endure strengthened her inside. Because after seeing Kenny on that tree, she knew she should have been rolling on the floor in a conniption fit.

But that was the old Celeste. The one who would have truly lost her mind then and there. The new woman on the inside had been delivered from the kind of pain in her heart that could kill her. She remembered the Reverend's sermon now:" You will find yourself growing in the only place of total surrender; in that place of your heart."

It was odd how the very spot that Kenny considered to be his place for respite, would actually be his final resting place. Winston thought of that irony now, lifting Kenny's body from the horse. He untied the noose from his neck, thinking those thugs could not even make a decent noose, while he cried, "I failed you. I am so sorry."

As Winston went looking for a blanket he heard a voice say, "Man, help me up from here."

With his gun drawn Winston dropped to one knee, looking in each direction for the sound he thought he heard.

"Psst," Kenny strained, "Down here. It's me man. I ain't dead yet."

Relieved, Winston hugged his best friend. "How the hell do you survive a lynchin'?"

Kenny rolled down his ultra-thick, wool knit turtleneck sweater to show off the designer padded neck brace. "I've gotta give it to Doc. I'm glad I protested wearing the geeky brace, this 'lil 'ol soft thang saved my life," he said of the neck brace.

"It damn sure did," Winston marveled slapping him a high five. Because the fool who strung you to that tree would have seen the geeky one."

"It was that knock on the head they gave me that could've killed me," he said rubbing his block.

"No way, man. That bean has already proved to be your most invincible body part."

"Right." Kenny asked looking around, "Where is Celeste?"

Winston had been so caught up in getting Kenny down from that tree that he'd momentarily forgotten about Celeste. "She's in the house, man."

Kenny punched a hole in the stable door, "No. No. No!"

There had been no conversation between her and the man holding her. Celeste's neck and brain had gone numb. Suddenly the phone ringing upstairs jolted her to the present. The cellular phone in her duffle bag rang once and stopped. That was the signal from Winston to stay put, he was near.

Totally relieved, she wondered why she had not thought of her cell phone before. There was the cue to throw on her survival cap now, and to grieve later. The last few months had taught her those tactics well.

The floor in the kitchen creaked, and a voice spoke. "Do as we tell you and you won't get hurt," it said just as the grip tightened.

"We simply want to talk to you. If you do what we say quietly, there will be no trouble."

No trouble? Celeste thought, *what more trouble could she have subjected herself to at this point?* She nodded and stared in the direction of the familiar voice in the shadows. A slight movement of the trees allowed the moonlight to expose the face of Taylor Reed, who walked slowly toward her.

"I know," Celeste said. "You came back to get me for printing that your cancer and resignation was all a show."

"Miss Toussaint, even in your most vulnerable state, you are correct."

"You're a coward, Taylor. You ran from your buddies because you knew all hell was going to fall on them and you did not want to be anywhere around when it did," she steamed. "So now you want to silence me because you know they will find you no matter where you plan to hide. They will kill you dead when they discover you've betrayed them and that stupid oath."

Taylor slapped Celeste in the face. "You see. That is precisely your problem. You are too damn smart. I knew from the very beginning that Chi Woods was you. My buddies are not as smart as we are, Celeste. In college ET and the rest of them cheated their way through while I studied and did their papers," Taylor ranted. "Once we had enough money, I wanted to move out of the dirty business dealings years ago. When you finally uncovered the scandal at the Board of education in Chicago, I knew that by sending you to New York, you would eventually discover what we did here also," he confessed, stroking her face sensually. "I only wanted your uncovering the truth to prove to them that I was right. That after all of these years, we should go legit. So do you think I care what happens to them?" he asked angrily.

"In school they taunted me with their trust funds while I struggled to buy new clothes. I hate those stupid motherfuckers and you are not going to ruin it for me now that they are behind bars. I have waited 22 years to see this day come to pass.

"You should know, however, I was against the order to kill your Uncle Jim. I suggested that we simply fire him. You have to admit, it was just an eerie coincidence that your family member was an employee of ours," he mused.

"We thought Wayne Stevens was going to be cooperative for a while there. Did you know he was extremely money hungry? I think he just got cold feet. Anyway, I only wanted to fire him too," he sighed, "But there again, the fellas thought we should kill him too."

Celeste thought, *Yeah, and your boys didn't finish the job.*

Taylor continued, "They knew how bright Wayne was too. Your friend Dre Tyson though, now he was a problem all around. With a platform like *The Stand* he remained a problem."

She coughed up mucous from down deep and spit it in his face. Taylor slapped her face so hard Celeste's knees buckled.

"If you touch her again, I will kill you," said Kenny from the doorway, pointing a shotgun at Taylor.

On her knees dazed, Celeste knew she was dreaming.

Kenny was hanging outside on that tree.

She was certain.

A vision like that was no figment of her imagination.

Taylor was also stunned. He knew his hired hands did not do the job sufficiently if Kenny Hamilton was standing here before him. He too was smart enough to figure that he did not get down from the tree alone. Taylor could estimate correctly that Kenny's secret weapon was definitely near.

As the thought crossed Taylor's mind the sound of a shotgun rang out and the bruiser fell forward on top of Celeste pinning her to the floor. She saw Kenny cock his gun to shoot Taylor Reed.

"No. don't! Please. I don't want you killing anyone else on my behalf," she begged from underneath the lug on top of her.

"You're a kind woman, Celeste. I'm sure we can work out a tremendous financial compensation package for both of you," pleaded Taylor nodding, his head toward Kenny also.

Still clutching her purse, she reached into it and said, "I only have one request of you, Taylor." Celeste slowly closed one eye.

"Simply ask me and I'll decide if it is reasonable," Taylor responded.

"Suffer," she said bitterly and unloaded her gun into his body.

Police cars screeched up the driveway.

Newt Pickney made sure he was the first person in the house. He looked around at the bloody mess and was pleased to find Celeste and Kenny still standing—unscathed.

"Listen baby girl," Newt explained, "Chi Woods may have covered the 'Times Square Massacre' well, but her personal life was in shambles," he smiled.

"I have been following you and these goons around for days now hoping I could help. But when they knocked your man here in the head and began to string him up on that tree, I figured I had better get the real po-lice."

"I know what you really want, Moe," Celeste chided him, "you've got your exclusive story."

"Yeeees!" said Newt happily.

Celeste held up her hand, "With two conditions. Number one, no photos of Kenny, Winston, or me."

"Got it."

"Number two, no cross references between Chi Woods and me. You've got it all because I quit."

"Celeste you can't leave me. It was bad enough that T.J. was wrapped up in that shit with ET. I tell you the truth. You never really know a person. I worked side by side with that son of a b. for over ten years and I never knew he was dirty," whined Newt.

"Hey, what are you possibly going to do with yourself if you quit?" he quizzed.

"Who, me?" asked Celeste.

"Yeah, you. You know you're the type of woman who needs to stay close to some action."

"Oh, I didn't tell you."

"Tell me what, baby girl?"

"I'm getting married," she said beaming at Kenny, "and I guarantee there is never gonna be one dull moment."

Kenny ran all through the house before tenderly embracing his lady love. "I'm so happy I could cry," he said.

"Speaking of crying," Celeste said seriously, "before I say 'I do" there is a condition for you too."

"Anything."

"Really?"

"Yes. Really."

"I would like for you to leave the police force. All of these hustles have proved just a little too dangerous for my taste."

"Oh, I haven't told you? I handed in my resignation with my final report on this investigation."

"When were you going to tell me, Detective?"

"I'm telling you now. I was going to surprise you tonight," he said, opening a velvet box.

She gasped at the three-carat, pear-shaped diamond. Its brilliance was captured by the flames from the fireplace. The near-death experience he had earlier still had her heart aflutter. She was never going to let so much time pass between them again, because from this day forth Celeste was going to wake up next to the only man she truly loved.

"Kenny, are you really sure that you no longer want a life in law enforcement?" she asked looking into his eyes as if the answer was printed on his eyeballs. "I mean, I do remember when you told me that busting up bad guys was like a high you've never known."

He noticed she didn't take the ring from the box. "I guarantee that life with you is all I will ever need," Kenny pledged, placing the ring on her finger and kissing her hand. "I promise. No more busting up hustles or participating in them. Especially if it will make you happy."

"I just want you safe" Celeste dreamed, "I want us to grow old together and to have a house full of children. Most of all I want you to be happy. What are you going to do without solving murders and living on the edge?"

"Who, me?" smiled Kenny. "I'm getting married."

Celeste hoped that she would be able to guarantee Kenny's happiness, but she knew that was an impossibility. Her only wish was that she could have helped to save Uncle Jim, Dre, Renee, Muffin, and Jane from a life that demanded the type of lifestyle that placed their lives in jeopardy.

Hugging the man she was going to marry as the police carried dead bodies from his living room, she thought of the paragraph she wrote in her journal the night Uncle Jim was murdered. It calculated her feelings precisely:

Dead in the middle of a hustle
you could wind up dead.
On the streets-
Fast streets-
Enmeshed in a
Web of Deception
that breeds in the streets of
That Place.

WEB OF DECEPTION... Celeste Toussaint is a reporter who uncovers a major scandal at the Board of Education. When it hits the front pages of the *Chicago Daily Courier* that several are being jailed due to her nose for news, some very itchy business men panic. Celeste is then transferred to the *Daily Courier* in New York City.

Harlem U.S.A. becomes Celeste's new home with her aunt, uncle and crazy cousin, who teaches her the art of a New York "hustle." While her dear uncle is murdered working on his "hustle", Celeste unofficially teams up with Detective Kenny Hamilton to solve the crime. Their snooping about leads them to love in the process of trying to find the perpetrators. Ultimately, Celeste cleverly exposes the very entity "they" were hoping she would not.

ADVANCE PRAISE FOR Web of Deception...

"LaJoyce Brookshire has woven a riveting tale of suspense and romance that is impossible to put down. The twists and turns keep you guessing. A great mystery novel."

Charisse Jones, National Writer, USA Today

LaJoyce Brookshire shines! With great expectation, she grabs you right from the beginning taking you on a non-stop roller coaster ride. Watch out...this book will have you up all night.

Lolita Files, Author,
Getting To The Good Part, Scenes From A Sistah

Web of Deception is a real page-turner. This book hooks into you from the very first chapter. LaJoyce proves that she has what it takes in the mystery writing genre.

E. Lynn Harris, Author,
If This World Were Mine, Invisible Life,
Just As I Am, And This Too Shall Pass